BIG

MAGIC

THE WITCHES OF HOLLOW COVE

BOOK FOURTEEN

KIM RICHARDSON

FABLEPRINT

This book is a work of fiction. Any references to historical events, real people, or real locales are used fictitiously. Other names, characters, places, and incidents are the product of the author's imagination, and any resemblance to actual events or locales or persons, living or dead, is entirely coincidental.

FablePrint

Big Magic, The Witches of Hollow Cove, Book Fourteen
Copyright © 2023 by Kim Richardson
All rights reserved, including the right of Reproduction in whole or in any form.
Cover by Kim Richardson
Printed in the United States of America

[1. Supernatural—Fiction. 2. Demonology—Fiction. 3. Magic—Fiction].

BOOKS BY KIM RICHARDSON

THE WITCHES OF HOLLOW COVE
Shadow Witch
Midnight Spells
Charmed Nights
Magical Mojo
Practical Hexes
Wicked Ways
Witching Whispers
Mystic Madness
Rebel Magic
Cosmic Jinx
Brewing Crazy

THE DARK FILES
Spells & Ashes
Charms & Demons
Hexes & Flames
Curses & Blood

SHADOW AND LIGHT
Dark Hunt
Dark Bound
Dark Rise
Dark Gift
Dark Curse
Dark Angel
Dark Strike

BIG

MAGIC

THE WITCHES OF HOLLOW COVE

BOOK FOURTEEN

KIM RICHARDSON

CHAPTER

1

I stood before the mirror, licked my lips, and started again.

"*Husband*. This is my husband, Marcus. Hussssbbbbaaand. Huzzzbennd. Huuuussbaaand. Husband. Husband. Husband."

Yep. It was official. I—was a crazy person.

In my defense, it's not every day you get to say the word *husband*. I really never had to in my daily life. But now I was a married woman—witch—and I had to get used to saying it without my tongue getting stuck between my palate and teeth.

Two weeks had passed since the big day, and I couldn't be happier. I was married to the hottest town chief that ever was, I had a job I loved,

1

and I lived in my own home—Davenport Cottage, which was a miniature, charming version of Davenport House. Its white wood siding and wraparound porch gave it a lovely farmhouse vibe. House had given us this home so Marcus and I could start our life together with some privacy—with the added bonus of being close to the big house and my aunts.

What more could a witch ask for?

Orgasms. Can't get enough of orgasms. Especially when they were initiated by my sexy, wereape *husband*.

All kidding aside, it was the best outcome I could have hoped for. When I showed up here more than twelve months ago, life had punched me in the gut and left me miserable. I'd been poor, single, and unhappy. Now, I was as happy as a dog with two tails.

Still, I *could* be happier with coffee. And right now, I needed coffee like I needed air.

I walked out of the bathroom and halted on my way to the kitchen. The coffee machine was not on, and Marcus hadn't left me a fresh pot on his way out. He did some days, but when he was in a rush, he didn't, which was totally fine. Making coffee wasn't a big deal. But when I lived so close to my aunts' home, who most probably had a fresh pot brewing this very instant, why waste time making one here when I could just pop out, walk a few steps, and have my hands around a fresh cup in a matter of fifteen seconds?

Sounds like a plan.

With an added hop to my step, I shut the cottage's door and crossed the backyard. The cool morning grass tickled my toes as I climbed the back porch to Davenport House and pushed open the back door.

Immediately, my nose was assaulted by the wonderful aroma of roasted coffee beans. The air smelled of toast and something sweet like vanilla. I made a beeline for the coffee machine. Grabbing a mug from the cabinet, I poured myself some brown liquid heaven.

"You know, it's considered good manners to say good morning before you *steal* coffee from your neighbor's house."

I turned around, the mug to my lips as I took a sip. Dolores eyed me from the kitchen table. Her deep brown eyes sparkled with intelligence, her professor-like demeanor lending her an aura of authority. She lowered the newspaper she'd been holding and swung a long gray braid over her shoulder.

"In fact, some would construe stealing as rude."

"You're not my neighbors. You're family. It's different. What's yours is mine, and what's mine is yours. Right?" I smiled and took another sip of glorious coffee.

"Why would I want anything of yours?" Dolores pushed her reading glasses up her nose and flipped open the newspaper pages.

"Ignore her." Ruth turned from the stove, her white, cloud-like hair wild. She had attempted to keep it tamed by stabbing it with what looked like a pencil. She leaned over, widened her eyes, and whispered, "She got stood up last night."

"What?" Now, this was nice juicy gossip to mix in with my morning coffee.

"I *didn't* get stood up," growled Dolores over her newspaper.

I blinked. "You had a date with a man?"

"No. With the mailbox." Dolores's left eye twitched.

Ruth let out a little giggle. "Mailboxes are cute."

Dolores sighed and pressed her hand on her newspaper. "Daniel had to cancel because he wasn't feeling well. People get ill. It happens."

Ruth snorted. "Like we haven't heard *that* onc before."

"I swear, Ruth," snapped Dolores. She pointed a finger at her sister. "One more word, just one more, and you'll be experiencing intestinal failure for a week."

Ruth clamped her mouth shut, but it did nothing to hide the laughter in her eyes. She looked at me. "You hungry, Tessa? I'm making French toast."

4

"French toast sounds divine," I told her as I made my way to the kitchen table and pulled out the chair next to Dolores. I looked around. Something was missing. "Where's Tinkerbell?" Now that I noticed that the tiny fairy was missing, so was Hildo.

Ruth glanced over her shoulder while whisking the batter into a large ceramic bowl. "She and Hildo went out to hunt fireflies last night," she said. A few droplets of batter splattered her face, but she didn't seem to notice. "Came in early this morning. They're both still sleeping. Must have been quite the hunt."

"Yeah, I'm sure it was." Funny how Hildo and Tinky were now besties when the cat familiar hated the fairy when she first traveled to our world. I suspected he'd felt he might get replaced. That would never happen, of course. Ruth loved them both equally like she loved everything and every creature. Guess Hildo had come to his senses.

"Has Marcus left for work?" Dolores spied me over her reading glasses.

"He did. Left early this morning. Something about Gilbert harassing one of his neighbors because of the height of their hedges."

"That damn owl," commented Dolores. "Always sticking his beak in everyone else's business. One of these days, he's going to end up as the centerpiece for Thanksgiving dinner."

I smiled. "That's a great visual."

The backdoor swung open, and a slender figure waltzed into the kitchen. The petite witch was dressed smartly in dark jeans and a crisp white blouse, her tanned skin complementing her shoulder-length blonde hair. Her kitten heels tapped lightly on the floor as she placed five large shopping bags onto the kitchen island.

"Good morning, girls," said Beverly, her green eyes sparkling. "Great day to do some early shopping."

Dolores pulled off her glasses and leaned back in her chair. "It's barely nine in the morning. What idiot opens their store at this hour?"

"Maddalena was nice enough to open her boutique early for me before the ten o'clock rush," said Beverly. "Before the vultures could snatch up *my* dress."

"What dress?" asked Dolores, looking at her sister like she'd grown a third eye.

"No man can take his eyes off me in this." Beverly reached into one of the bags and pulled out a red mermaid sequin with a high split-thigh gown. "Every warm-blooded man in a five-mile radius will throw himself at my feet," she added with a dramatic flair.

I took another sip of my delicious coffee. "I don't doubt it." The fact was, my Aunt Beverly was a knock-out. She could be wearing pajamas and still turn heads. In that dress, she'd hypnotize the entire male population.

Beverly flashed a smile my way. "Thank you, darling." Her eyes traveled over my face, and her smile changed to a knowing one. "Married life suits you."

I blinked. "Really. Why do you say that?"

"Because you've got that newlywed sex glow." She giggled and said, "The sex all day and all night glow."

Ruth snorted, and I felt the blood gush to my face.

I wanted to disappear. Maybe I should have stayed in my cottage.

"Totally normal." Beverly waved a red-manicured hand at me. "All newlyweds should be having as much sex as they can. It's all about exploring each other's bodies and seeing what pleasures you. What positions you like, what positions you don't like." She paused and added, "Don't try the reverse cowgirl. That's only for the circus."

I blinked. "I have no idea what you just said."

Beverly tapped a finger to her lips. "You know… I have an excellent illustrated version of the Kama Sutra." She wiggled her eyebrows. "The X-rated version."

I raised my hand. "Okay. Stop. I think I get it." It was way too early to be talking about sex with my aunts. Though she wasn't wrong, Marcus and I *had* been exploring each other's bodies whenever we could. "So, why do you need a new dress?" I asked and took another gulp of coffee in an attempt to hide my discomfort and change the subject.

"Yes. I'd like to know that, too," said Dolores. She reached out and grabbed her coffee mug. "Why *do* you need a new gown? The Halloween Ball isn't for another two months."

Beverly pressed her dress against her body, eyeing it lovingly. "It's for the Miss Hollow Cove pageant."

Coffee spewed from Dolores's lips like a jet blast. "I'm sorry? Did you just say the *Miss Hollow Cove pageant*?"

Beverly sighed. "Really, Dolores. You might want to get your hearing checked. That's what happens when you've been around for centuries. Your hearing starts to go."

I perked up, curious. "There's a Miss Hollow Cove pageant? I didn't know this." Though I'm not sure why that would surprise me. Something was always going on in Hollow Cove, always a reason for a celebration or a festival. It was one of the reasons I loved it here.

Dolores wiped her mouth, her eyes on her sister. "You? Competing in a beauty pageant with women half—no, wait—*a third* of your age? You can't be serious?" snorted Dolores.

Beverly stuck out her chest and cocked an eyebrow. "I have the breasts of a twenty-year-old."

"More like a fifty-year-old," muttered Ruth.

Beverly shot daggers at her sisters. "There's no reason why I shouldn't participate."

"Being old enough to be the contestants' mother is one," Dolores shot back.

A frown creased Beverly's perfect forehead. "You're just jealous because the only beauty pageant that ever accepted you was the Sasquatch Female of the Year."

It was my turn to spit out coffee.

Damn. I should text Iris to get her butt over here. This was way better than reality TV. I didn't know if Beverly had just made that up, but judging from the large vein that pulsed on Dolores's forehead, it was true.

"That's true." Ruth giggled as she dipped a slice of bread in the batter and then tossed it in a sizzling hot pan. "But it was really hard to tell the females from the males. They were all covered in hair."

Beverly folded her gown and placed it back delicately into her bag. "I don't know why you're being so negative. I've got the pageant crown under my belt already. I've won Miss Hollow Cove before."

"You did?" I asked, though I wasn't surprised. If anyone could win a beauty pageant, it was my Aunt Beverly.

Ruth turned around, sending batter all over the kitchen floor. "Yeah. In nineteen seventy-two."

Beverly's face flushed. "I've got the best ass in town. Ask any man, and he'll tell you."

"It's not just about looks," commented Dolores. "It's about personality, intelligence, talent, and character. If this were a pageant about how many men you slept with, then yes, you'd definitely be crowned the victor."

"That's true, too." Ruth shrugged, whisking away at her batter. "Everyone knows you're a slut."

I thought Beverly would be mad at that comment, but she cocked her hip and declared proudly, "Yes. Yes, I would."

Dolores leaned forward and waved a hand at Beverly. "The pageant is about demonstrating a range of skills, leadership, poise, and artistic talent. I don't remember you having any kind of artistic talent."

Beverly raised her chin. "Well, just last night, I painted my glorious body in whipped cream for Jack Spencer. It was a true work of art."

Damn. I didn't want to, but I'd already formed a visual.

Dolores rolled her eyes. "Not that kind of talent. And you know this. For example, what are your skills? What have you given back? What did you do in town lately?"

Beverly beamed. "Jack, Tom, Franco, Morris, Vaughn, to name a few."

I barked out a laugh. "You're killing me."

"Face it," said Dolores, her face turning serious, "you're too old. No one will take you seriously. When those twenty-something women strut their bikini bodies on stage… you'll be the laughing stock of Hollow Cove."

Beverly's face flushed further, and I was surprised she didn't comment. Maybe she'd been thinking that. Or she didn't want to admit that perhaps her sister was right?

Hmmm. Not sure I liked that comment. "I don't see why Beverly wouldn't win. I mean… look at her. She doesn't look her age, and she's hotter than most twenty-year-olds."

"Thank you, darling," Beverly said, winking at me. "At least my niece believes in me."

"It's not that we don't believe in you," said Ruth. "It's just that we don't think you'll win."

Dolores rubbed her eyes with the heels of her palms. She looked up and said, "We just don't want you to get hurt. The younger women in these pageants can be cruel. Ruthless."

Beverly straightened her posture, and a look of defiance came upon her face. "I can be ruthless, too. I've lots more to offer than they do. I'm wiser and much better at pretending to know what I'm doing."

"Hear, hear," I said, lifting my cup in solidarity.

"I'm *going* to compete," continued Beverly, "and nothing you can say will change my mind.

And I'll tell you something else… I'm going to *win* this."

"How can you be so sure?" asked Ruth.

Beverly flashed us one of her million-dollar smiles. "Because. All the judges are male."

Okay then.

Dolores coughed out a laugh. "You're going to sleep your way to the top? I'm sure that's against the rules."

"I don't care." Beverly looked at me and smiled like she thought I'd agree with her on that. I didn't. "Don't think the others won't try it. They will. But I'll win that round. Trust me. I've got years of experience in the sack. I was already in my sexual prime when they were still in diapers."

"True," I agreed.

"Fine," said Dolores. "But don't come crying when you don't win."

"I don't cry," said Beverly. "Only ugly women cry. Beautiful women know that crying ruins your makeup."

Ok-a-a-a-ay. "So when's this pageant?"

Beverly looked over at me. "This Friday." She studied my face for a moment. "Are you thinking about competing?"

"God no," I said. "No one wants to see me in a bikini. Trust me." Well, only Marcus.

Beverly grabbed her bags. "Well, I am. And I'm going to represent the Davenport witches."

A sound pulled my attention away from Beverly. The toaster made a popping noise, and a small, white card, much like an index card, shot out into the air. Without thinking, I stuck my arm out and snatched it mid-flight.

"A new job?" asked Ruth, coming closer to the table, her spatula dripping batter all over the floor.

"Maybe." I drew the card closer for a better look. Written in elegant gold script:

The honor of your presence is requested for dinner and cocktails at seven-thirty this evening at 4 Gallows Hill

"And?" Ruth bumped into my shoulder as she leaned closer, causing batter to plop onto my arm.

"It's not a job," I said, re-reading the note and getting a familiar vibe from the address. "It's an invitation to dinner and cocktails."

"What?" Dolores snatched the card from me. "How odd. It doesn't say who it's from, just that the dinner is tonight. And at the Crane family manor."

Tension rolled up my spine at the mention of that old mansion. Samael had created another portal to Storybook inside, where he planned to keep me forever. I didn't want to think about that right now.

"Must be that new guy Martha was telling me about," said Ruth, walking back to the stove and plopping a fresh French toast onto a plate.

"What new guy?" asked Beverly. "And why haven't I been told there's a new guy in town?"

"I don't know," said Ruth. "He's new."

Dolores made a sound in her throat. "Martha. Of course. Why am I not surprised she would know before us Merlins? What did she tell you about him?"

Ruth shrugged. "Not much. Just that he was new in town… Oh. And that he bought the Crane family manor."

I stared at Ruth. "He bought *that* house?" The manor was abandoned. It needed lots of TLC and money to make it livable. Not to mention, it already had a few tenants—ghostly ones.

"He did," answered Ruth.

"And?" pressed Dolores. "What else?"

"Is he single?" Beverly grabbed the card from Dolores and inspected it as though the card would disclose the stranger's status. "He must have a lot of money to buy that size of property."

Ruth shook her head. "I don't know. That's all Martha told me. Oh—and she thinks it's suspicious."

"Why is buying a house suspicious?" asked Dolores.

Ruth looked at her sister and said, "He moved in at night. Why would he do that?"

"Okay, I'll admit that was weird." Very weird.

"Well, looks like we're going to find out who he is tonight," said Dolores. "As Merlins, it's our job to know about new people in our town. Assuming we're all going."

Beverly flashed a dazzling smile. "Of course we are. This is going to be so much fun. I've got the perfect mini to go with my new heels." Grabbing her bags, she sashayed her way out of the kitchen.

I didn't like that a new guy was in town, and no one seemed to know who he was or much else about him. I wasn't about to wait until tonight. I wanted answers now.

And I was going to get them.

CHAPTER

2

I stood on the sidewalk of Gallows Hill. At the end of a long gravel driveway stood a century-old stone mansion, a three-story brick structure with a mansard roof and tower in the revival-style architecture. The Crane family manor.

But it looked nothing like it did the last time I was here. Instead of the dilapidated house with a moss-covered roof, stained brick façade, and knee-high grass that covered a stone path that had seen better days stood a gleaming red-brick estate with white moldings and elaborate white cornices.

Samael had pretended to be Dolores and had lured us here on one of his many mind games.

If Lilith hadn't transformed him back into a wee little babe, I would have kicked his ass. Or died trying.

I sighed and rolled my shoulders, shaking the feeling of trepidation. This didn't look like the same house.

Manicured lawns surrounded the manor with trim boxwood hedges lining the red and white rose bushes. Even the large oak tree that stood on the manor's left side had been trimmed, the dead branches cut and giving more sunlight for the roses below.

If not for the landscaping company truck parked out front and the four paranormal men, badger shifters from the energies that emanated from them, I would have said that magic was used to refurbish this house. Even then, with a home this size, it would take a great deal of magic and a skilled witch or wizard to pull this off in two weeks. The house looked newly built. It reminded me of Davenport House, always looking freshly painted. But that was because House was a magical entity. I knew for a fact that this manor wasn't.

Maybe the new owner was a magical practitioner? That was the most logical explanation. Or he could have paid a witch a large sum of money to do it for him. But why the secrecy? Why move in at night? Either the new owner was hiding something, or he was a serious introvert. But if he was an introvert, no way in hell would he be hosting a party tonight. None of this made sense.

I rolled my eyes over the manor. It was no longer part of the town's annual haunted house tour. It was a showstopper now. It belonged on the front cover of Architectural Digest. "Okay. Definitely an improvement."

"Talking to yourself again?"

I spun around and spotted a pretty, petite witch with dark, chin-length hair and smiling dark eyes. In her all-black ensemble, she looked like a gothic doll—pigtails, black lipstick, and smoky eyeshadow.

"It's hard to shut off all my imaginary friends."

The Dark witch laughed. "You're crazier than me. And I'm all about the crazy."

I smiled at her, seeing her large tote bag wrapped around her shoulder, which I suspected held her faithful paranormal DNA album, Dana. I'd texted Iris while I returned to my cottage and changed, bringing her up to speed on this mysterious individual.

On my way there, I'd checked the cottage's mailbox. Sure enough, I'd pulled out a white envelope addressed to me and Marcus with the same invitation as the one I'd seen on the card at Davenport House.

Iris looked over to the manor, concern showing on her pixie-like face. "You're right. That *is* an improvement. When did you say he moved in?"

"Last night."

"Hmmm. There's no way a crew of the best contractors could have restored this place in a few hours. And at night. Magic was involved. I'm sure of it."

"That's what I'm thinking." And that was high-level magic. I was sure of it.

"And no one knows anything about this guy? His name? Where's he from?"

"Not as far as I know." I looked at Iris, seeing her pretty face scrunched up in thought. "Did Ronin get an invite?" I wanted to know how many people were invited, who was invited, and if it was only us witches. The more I learned about this dinner party's host, the better prepared I'd be.

"Yes. He did." She reached inside her tote bag and pulled out a similar white card. "It appeared in the mailbox this morning." Knowing that Iris spent most nights at Ronin's didn't surprise me. She still had her room at Davenport House, but I had a feeling that, as things got more serious between them, she'd be moving in with Ronin soon.

"So it's not just us witches," I said, which only added to my confusion. If he'd only invited witches, I'd have more to go on, like wizards and mages like to make a show of the extent of their magical powers. Some also wanted to be surrounded only by other magical practitioners. I didn't like that.

"No." Iris's eyes widened. "Ronin is pissed."

"Really? Why? He's clearly invited."

Iris shook her head. "Not that. Because he wanted to buy this house. He's been trying to get it for years. I don't know. I think it's more of an obsession."

"Because it's haunted." I remembered him mentioning it, though I wasn't sure it was haunted anymore. At least it didn't look the part. But that didn't mean the creepy ghosts and poltergeists weren't still in there.

"Something like that. He was shouting at Pauline—that's the real estate agent—before I left. I mean, Ronin's got money. I'm sure he offered a fair price for the property."

"But this guy offered more." Which only raised all those red flags. We had a stranger moving here in the middle of the night. Who would do that? I had no idea.

But there was a reason. And I was going to find out what that was.

"And he fixed up the house and invited us to a dinner party?" Iris shook her head. "That's weird. Even for Hollow Cove."

She wasn't wrong. I nodded, my mind racing. Why would this stranger fix up a haunted house and then invite a group of witches and a vampire, as far as we knew, to a dinner party the very next day? It just didn't add up. Then again, it was Hollow Cove—a place infamous for its peculiar occurrences.

Still, I couldn't shake the feeling of unease that wrapped itself around my middle. Something was definitely off.

I let out a sigh. "I wonder who else is invited. If we knew, we might get a better sense of who we're dealing with. Because right now, we don't know much, apart from that he has loads of money and possibly magic."

"We could ask around." Iris slipped the card back into her bag. "We could pop by Martha's. I'm sure she'll know more about him than any of us. Knowing her, she's probably met him already."

"True. But we're here now."

Iris shot me a look. "What are you thinking?"

"I'm thinking I'm going to walk up on that porch and knock to find out for myself."

Iris flashed me a smile. "I like the way you think."

"Me too."

Together, we walked up the flagstone walkway that looked like it had been laid recently, past a few landscape workers, and made it up the porch.

A faint magical pulse tinged my senses. Definitely, magic was used to fix up the house and was still lingering. Or it could be a ward.

With my heart beating against my chest and my nerves spiraling, I reached out and knocked on the door. I hated how nervous I felt. Nothing I could do about that. This stranger might not appreciate visitors so early in the morning. Too late. I'd just knocked. Hard.

Just as I'd finished knocking, I realized that Marcus probably wouldn't approve of me going alone with Iris. He would argue that he wanted to be here. We knew nothing about this stranger other than he'd bought this manor and had invited some paranormals to his dinner party. But we were here, and I was a curious beast. I wanted to put a face to this guy. I needed something.

"What do we do if he's all angry," whispered Iris.

I thought about it. "We run."

Iris let out a nervous giggle. "What if he opens the door and he's naked?"

"We definitely run."

We waited for what felt like a whole two minutes, but no one came to the door.

I met Iris's disappointed gaze. "Looks like no one's home, or he just doesn't want to see anyone." I looked over my shoulder and called out to the workers. "Hey. Do you know if anyone's home?"

One of them, the youngest male with deep-set eyes and a large nose, looked up at us. "No idea." And then he went back to edging the flowerbeds.

"Good talk." I sighed. "I'd push in, but I have a feeling it's warded."

"It is." Iris raised her palms to the door. "Heavily. This guy definitely knows magic."

A flutter of wings caught my attention as I noticed movement out of the corner of my eye. A small human woman, about the size of my hand, flew around the porch. Her delicate, clear wings were reminiscent of a butterfly's as she moved closer. Her strapless green dress was striking as it contrasted with her fair skin, the same color as her flat shoes. She had pulled her blonde hair up in a bun, showing off her delicate elf-like ears.

"Hi, Tinky."

"Ruth told me I might find you here," said the fairy in her familiar, bell-sounding voice as she hovered around the door. "I know all about the invite and the new guy."

I opened my mouth to ask her about her firefly hunt with Hildo last night, but instead, I asked, "Tinky. Can you do me a favor?"

"Shoot." The fairy's wings fanned my face as she hovered at my eye level.

I pointed to the façade of the manor. "You think you can fly around and see if there's a window open?"

The fairy grinned. "You want me to spy for you? Give you the scoop on Mr. Stranger? See what he's hiding in there?"

"Yeah."

"I'm on it."

I blinked, and the tiny fairy was gone, leaving a golden splash of glimmer in her wake.

I loved Tinky, and I was happy she was living here with us now. "I wish I could fly."

"I wish I could get one of her wings for my collection," said Iris, tapping on her bag. I loved Iris too, but she was a strange one sometimes.

Iris and I leaned back and watched as the fairy zoomed past and disappeared around the right corner of the manor. Next, I spotted her on the second floor, going from window to window. She did another round on the third floor and then came flying back.

"Sorry," she said, slightly out of breath. "All the windows are locked. I tried opening them, but I couldn't. And I felt magic, too. Like a protection or something."

"Wards," Iris and I said at the same time.

Tinky shook her head, looking disappointed. "I can't get in."

"Don't worry about it," I told her as I climbed down the porch with Iris behind me. Even though Tinky couldn't get in, it still gave me valuable information. The fact that the house was so heavily warded meant something was inside that this stranger didn't want anyone to know about.

A buzzing sounded from Iris's bag, and she yanked out her phone. "It's Ronin. He's freaking out. I'll have to leave soon and calm him down before he does something stupid. I know just how to do that." She flashed me a smile.

I laughed. "I guess he's not used to not getting what he wants."

The Dark witch nodded. "Especially when he's been trying for so long."

"Go," I told her, watching Tinky glaring at the manor, clearly upset that even her fairy magic couldn't get her in.

Iris adjusted the strap of her bag on her shoulder. "What are you going to do?"

"I'm going to go see Marcus," I said. "He probably knows the name of the new owner by now. Then, with his name, I can check the Merlin database and see if anything turns up."

I'd take any excuse to feast my eyes on my *husband*. I still couldn't stop fantasizing about him in the Beast costume. He rocked that look. Hell, he rocked any look. But that one topped all of them.

We hadn't been married long, and we were definitely still in that honeymoon stage, as Beverly had pointed out. I would savor every moment, which meant taking advantage of my hot wereape husband any chance I got—including multiple times a day. Thank you very much.

"Good plan," agreed Iris. "You think he'll tell you?"

"He better. If not, I've got my ways to make him tell me."

Iris laughed. "Men. We love them. But they're so easily manipulated."

We both laughed, and then Iris got serious. "What if there's nothing on the guy? What if he's a ghost? If he took this much care at hiding and refurbishing this place without anyone in town knowing, I have a feeling you won't find much about him in the files."

"Hmmm." She could be right about that. These powerful types didn't want people to know their business. If I couldn't find anything in the Merlin database, there was just one other place I could search. "I've got an idea."

Iris searched my face. "Why do I get the feeling I'm not going to like this idea?"

Tinky came flying back and settled on my shoulder. "What's the idea?"

"We need to find out more about this guy. Right?" I said, determination in my voice. "And his intentions. Because I'm not really feeling the love. And I'm sure he's hiding something."

I wasn't sure, but I remembered Dolores mentioning when I first moved back that you had to follow a process if you wanted to live in this town—a screening of sorts. First, you had to be a paranormal so no humans accidentally bought a property here. And second, they wanted to make sure no shady types would move here. I'm not talking about Dark witches, wizards, rogue vampires, or werewolves. I'm talking about murderous types with evil in their veins. Those types. Hollow Cove was a peaceful paranormal community, and we wanted to keep it that way.

Another good reason why I needed to speak to Marcus.

"I'm with you," said Iris, her eyes gleaming with the excitement of a new mystery to solve.

"Me too," agreed Tinky.

"But how do we do that?" asked Iris. "We can't get in."

"Not now, we can't. But we *can* later," I said with a grin. "We'll have plenty of time to commit a few faux pas."

Iris tilted her head and then offered a sly smirk. "You've got a few screws loose up there in that noggin. It's nice to know I'm not alone."

Tinky bounced on my shoulder. "Ooooh! This is going to be so much fun. Can Hildo come?"

I shrugged. "I don't see why not. Of course, he can come." Plus, having Tinky and Hildo being so small, they could get into places we big mortals couldn't. It was perfect.

I turned back and looked at the manor, my pulse hammering with excitement. "Get ready, ladies. Looks like we're going to party tonight."

CHAPTER

3

I walked along Stardust Drive, breathing in the fresh morning air, my thoughts still on the manor and the mysterious new owner. I didn't like the fact that a new guy had moved into our quaint little town without anyone knowing or that he'd bought that manor out from under Ronin. Poor bastard. He sounded really angry.

Having a wild imagination like mine, I was thinking up all kinds of different scenarios. One: A Dark mage or wizard trying to infiltrate us so he could take over the town. Two: A wealthy vampire businessman searching for a quiet place to retire and escape the stresses of the city.

Three: A demon lord seeking to expand his influence over the mortal world.

The possibilities were endless.

Yet the demon aspect would explain why he moved during the night. And why he was unavailable during the day. The more I thought about it, the more I was leaning toward a demon. Not that I believed all demons were mortal-soul-sucking scum. Hell, I was part demon, and I thought my father was the embodiment of sophistication.

But just like mortals, not all demons were created equally. And if I was right, and this stranger was, in fact, a demon, I didn't think his settling in our town was because he was looking for a quiet place to retire. No. This guy was bad news.

Still, I could be wrong. And there was just one way to find out. I had to speak to Marcus.

Crossing Shifter Lane at a stroll, I hit the sidewalk and made a beeline to the Hollow Cove Security Agency building. I made my way inside, blinking into the harsh white lights. I navigated through the lobby, and a delightful scent of freshly brewed coffee filled my nose.

A desk rested at the end of the lobby, where it opened up into a larger space. Usually, a tiny woman with short white hair and a pointed look, making the wrinkles around her face sharper, sat behind it. But now it stood empty.

I glanced down the hall and noticed a few other doors that led to separate rooms and four desks. I walked up to the door marked MAR-CUS DURAND with CHIEF OFFICER printed underneath in bold print. A particular voice rose behind the closed door, its shrillness so distinct that I would've recognized it anywhere.

"… he never got the permits to do that kind of work on the manor!" the piercing voice screeched. "We have protocols to follow. Rules and regulations. If I give him a free pass, I have to give one to everyone! Can you imagine the chaos!"

Yup. The little shifter owl was having a meltdown.

The door was shut, but I figured I should be there since the stranger was the subject of this heated discussion. You know, because I was a Merlin and I was investigating the new owner of said refurbished manor.

Trying to keep my face neutral, I knocked once and pushed in.

Marcus's office looked exactly like it always did. On one side of the door stood a row of filing cabinets and next to his desk were stacks of books on shelves. His desk was inundated with documents, and a laptop was positioned in front of the only window in the area.

A tall, broad-shouldered figure seated behind the desk commanded my attention with his tousled black hair, chiseled jaw, and straight nose. His black T-shirt clung to him, revealing the broadness of his chest and the tightness of his stomach. His smoky gray eyes met mine, and I felt a flurry of butterflies in my stomach. That never got old.

Bonus? I was *married* to that. Yay me!

I stood in the middle of the office, my hands on my hips, and said, "So. Do we have a name to go with the new owner of the Crane family manor?"

"Pushing in on private conversations is considered rude," said a short, pudgy man with gray hair wearing a bow tie, his face creasing with disapproval. "This doesn't concern you. Out. Now. Witch." He lifted his arm and pointed dramatically towards the door behind me as if he owned the room.

I grinned. "Now, now, Gilbert. Look who's being rude now. By the way, new guys in town are my business. You know, background check, that sort of thing. You don't want to let in the wrong types. Do you, Gilbert?"

Gilbert squeezed his face into a sour expression. "You're the worst Merlin I've ever had to deal with. I'm astounded you still hold a license. If it were me, I'd have fired you by now."

I sighed, shaking my head. "Yeah, well, we don't always get what we want." No. Because if we did, he wouldn't be mayor of this town.

Gilbert's face darkened two shades of red. He looked at me, his eyes hard and full of contempt.

"If you're such a skilled and knowledgeable Merlin, you tell me who he is." He crossed his short arms over his chest.

I shrugged. "Hell, if I know. It's why I came here to see if Marcus knew."

"Ha!" Gilbert jumped in the air and pointed at me. "See? See? You're a terrible Merlin. An experienced, *competent* Merlin would have already figured out who this imposter was. But you haven't. See my point?"

I looked at Marcus, who raised a brow in warning at me. I reeled in my anger before I did something stupid like fry his annoying owl ass. Unfortunately, he was the town mayor, and the council did pay me a salary. I needed that money.

Marcus looked quite stoic and commanding as he sat with his fingers entwined on the desk. I remembered the feel of those large man-hands holding me close last night, and warmth spread throughout my body.

The faintest trace of relief showed in the chief's eyes—at my not frying the mayor—before he gave me that smile, and I very nearly tossed the little shifter right out of the window so I could be alone with the chief.

I gritted my teeth, pushing down my irritation as best I could. "And a good mayor wouldn't have let some stranger renovate what I'm assuming was a heritage house without the proper permits. Those kinds of restorations have to go through special councils. Am I right?"

Gilbert's mouth twisted like he'd bitten into a lemon. "It just happened. In the middle of the night. I wasn't aware of any work being done to the manor. I would have put a stop to it if I'd known. You can't pin that on me. This is not my fault."

"Just like it's not my fault or my aunts'."

The mayor watched me for a second, seemingly deciding I wasn't his number one enemy right now. The shifter glared at Marcus like he was responsible for all of this.

"The town is going to issue him a fine for unauthorized work. A very *big* fine." A tiny smile materialized on his face like the prospect of getting some money out of this made him happy.

"I doubt that'll make a big difference," I said.

Marcus looked up at me. "What makes you say that?"

I pursed my lips. "Just a thought." I didn't want to divulge all of my theories to Gilbert. Knowing him, if I said anything about my belief that the stranger was a demon, he would have a stroke. Then he would spread this little bit of information throughout the town before I had my second cup of coffee.

"Well, like I told Gilbert, there's not much I can give you apart from his name," said the chief, his voice deep and rumbling with a hint of authority behind it. "This is the deed of sale." He handed me a piece of paper.

I moved closer to his desk and took the paper, scanning it quickly. "*Benjamin Morgan*," I read. "Doesn't give a previous address. Just a PO box. Suspicious?"

Marcus nodded. "Very."

"Do you know any Benjamin Morgans?"

The chief shook his head. "I've been going through all the files since this morning. There's nothing on him. He's a ghost."

I stared at the paper, unease spreading through me. "I bet that's not his real name."

"What?" Gilbert's voice rose. Damn, I'd forgotten he was there. "Why would you say that? Is he a killer? An assassin! Kill us while we sleep in our beds!"

Killer and assassin were basically the same thing, but I wasn't about to interrupt another of his freakouts. "I didn't say that."

The shifter's eyes were round. "No. But that's what you're thinking."

"That's *not* what I'm thinking. I'm not thinking anything, really." Nothing that I would share with Gilbert. I looked at Marcus. "That's it. Nothing else?"

"He paid cash for the manor," said the chief.

I cursed. "Damn. That must have been a large amount."

"It was."

My eyes scanned the deed again, and they widened at the high six-figure digits.

"I refuse to go to that inappropriate dinner party," Gilbert was saying. "That'll show him. The mayor won't attend. There. Ha! Take that, you imposter."

I stared at Gilbert, both surprised and confused. "You got an invitation too?" It proved to me that the party was not just for witches or vampires. Our mystery man had a list of people he wanted at his dinner party. Not sure how I felt about that.

Gilbert gave me a pointed look. "Of course I did. *I'm* the mayor."

"Right. How could I forget."

"What invitation?" Marcus watched me, a touch of agitation in his tone.

Ah. He didn't know. I waved the paper. "This Benjamin Morgan sent out invitations to a dinner party tonight. My aunts got one. We got one. So did Ronin. And with Gilbert now, there are probably a lot more of us invited to this shindig tonight."

"Well. I'm *not* going," said Gilbert, and I swear I saw him stomp his foot.

"Your choice," said Marcus. "But if you want to know more about this guy, the best thing for you would be to show up. Get a feel for things. See what he's all about."

The mayor glanced briefly at the paper in my grip before focusing on Marcus again. "Maybe you're right. I'll have the fine drafted up, and I'll serve it as dessert!" He beamed at his cleverness before setting off from the chief's office as if he were preparing for battle.

"You know," I said, turning around. "I really don't like him."

Marcus laughed. "Not many do." His gray eyes fixed on me. "What are you not telling me?"

Damn, that wereape was perceptive. I knew I'd have to tell him about visiting the manor sooner or later. "I think he's a demon."

The chief's face went hard. "A demon friend like your father or the *other* kind?"

"I'm thinking the latter."

Marcus clenched his jaw, and I could see storms brewing behind those damn fine eyes of his. "And this is your witch instincts telling you?"

"The fact that he moved in during the night says so," I said. "And those extensive renovations were most probably done with magic. The house is heavily warded. No one can get in." Marcus's brows flicked, and I quickly added, "I popped by the manor before I came here. Thought I could use the walk. You know… got to squeeze in as much cardio as I can." I flashed him a smile.

He didn't return it. Marcus's brows pulled down in a frown. "You went there alone?"

Uh-oh. "Iris was with me. And Tinky. The point is he wasn't there. Surprise, surprise. And his house or lair is protected. Demons can't roam around this world during the daytime. He also restored the manor at night, probably with massive demon mojo. This all points to the fact that he's a demon. I'm almost positive."

I laid the paper back on his desk. "The fact that he's nowhere in your system is also a huge red flag. You told me all paranormals have files, records. He doesn't."

Marcus grazed the paper. "Not always. Some are not in the system. Some packs of were-wolves live off the grid. Many families and they don't have records."

I didn't know that. "Well. He's not off the grid. Is he? He's here. He's wealthy. But he's keeping his identity secret."

"If you're right, what does he want with this town?"

"Who knows," I said. "But I don't think he's here for our clean air. He did do a good job on that horrid manor, though. I could almost say it's pretty."

"Not as pretty as you."

"Damn straight."

Marcus chuckled, and his broad shoulders rocked with laughter as he scooted back from the desk and closed the gap between us. My breath caught in my throat at the sight of him, clad in his faded denim jeans and a plain black T-shirt. He was gorgeous.

He pulled me to him, one arm around my waist and the other cupping my butt. His large frame against mine created a warmth that poured over me like hot lava.

"Hi, husband," I purred, searching his face. "Miss me, *husband*?"

His gray eyes stared into mine, reflecting lust and possessiveness.

"*Wife*," he growled.

It was just one word, but it had my pulse rocketing and all the hair on my body standing at attention. And my nipples.

Damn. It sounded like a command. And I was both terrified and excited at the same time.

Marcus made a grunting sound in his throat that could have been some wereape language. I had no idea. But it did have my Lady V throbbing in glee.

He flashed a wild, crazed grin and shoved me towards the door. It suddenly slammed shut behind me with an echoing thud followed by a loud click as Marcus locked it.

"Is this a forced lockdown?" I teased. "Am I under arrest?"

The wereape's lips parted in a grin. "Something like that."

He pulled me closer. His warmth radiated through my body, and his breath on my face sent a delightful shiver down to my core. He kissed my neck, sending a wave of pleasure through me.

"What if someone hears us?" I asked, not that I cared, really.

"Grace is off sick. No one is here but us," he replied, his hot breath caressing my skin.

"Until someone decides to show up." But apart from Gilbert, I didn't see anyone else barging into the chief's office this early in the morning.

"You talk too much, *wife*."

There was that word again. Damn. My knees wobbled, and my head spun like I'd just drunk a bottle of wine in under ten minutes. Did wereapes have compulsion magic that I wasn't aware of? Or maybe it was just my raging hormones responding to him. He did smell amazing.

I gazed into his eyes. "What are you going to do to me, *husband*." Yeah, I was getting used to saying that word.

"All the things that husbands should do to their wives. And then again."

Yay! "Is that a promise?"

In a blur, the wereape pulled off his T-shirt, jeans, and underwear to stand in his naked glory, his long, perfect manhood pointing at me.

I stared at it. "Hello...*friend*."

Marcus laughed, but it was cut short when a savage growl released from his throat. "Clothes off," he commanded.

39

I yanked off my T-shirt and jeans, wiggling out of my underwear and bra as fast as I could. I'd barely finished before the wereape leaped at me.

I clung to him, feeling the power of his lean muscles and the warmth emanating from him. Our lips met in a passionate kiss that stole away my breath. I never wanted it to end. His intoxicating scent and heat stirred desires within me that threatened to send my hormones into overdrive.

Marcus swung me around and lowered me onto his desk. With a sweep of his arms, he tossed books, mugs, folders, and everything within reach to the floor, leaving a polished runway for our monkey business.

"It's happening. Isn't it?" I grinned.

"You bet your witch ass it is."

He lowered his massive frame on top of me, planting kisses along my jawline, neck, and collarbone. This wereape had skills!

A moan escaped him, sending a jolt of excitement right through me. My breath came in short gasps as he slipped his tongue into my eager mouth. He tasted like coffee and pastries. Could this be any more perfect? Nope. The passion between us throbbed through my entire body, leaving me in a state of pure ecstasy.

Okay, so we had an uninvited demon guest in our town. Things were ominous. But that would have to wait. Because right now, I was getting my groove on with my husband.

CHAPTER

4

"You think he's a demon?" Dolores had stopped mid-sip with her coffee mug still grazing her lips. Her left eye was twitching like a signal that, at any moment, it would blow out of its socket.

I pulled out a chair and sat. "I do. It makes sense."

"It does?" Dolores leaned on the kitchen counter and looked at me with her signature stern expression. "This Benjamin Moor character?"

"Morgan. And yes." I shifted in my chair until I got comfortable. "He moved in at night, he's reclusive, and he used high-level magic to re-store that old manor."

"And it's protected with magic, too." Tinky flew into the kitchen, a black cat trailing behind her with his tail in the air.

"With wards," I said as Hildo leaped onto my lap and stretched out comfortably. "Powerful wards." I scratched under Hildo's chin. "Tinky couldn't get in any of the windows. You should see this place. It looks newly built. Restored with magic."

"That just tells me he's a powerful witch or mage." Dolores gave me a skeptical arch of her brow. "Not necessarily a demon."

True. But my money was on a demon. Speaking of money. "He also paid for the manor in cash. Who do you know who can pay for a house these days in cash? Not many. That's for sure."

Tinky settled beside Ruth on the counter next to the stove. She stuck her finger in a large stain-less-steel bowl and then in her mouth. "Yum. What is that?"

Ruth beamed. "It's my famous potato salad. I'm taking some to the dinner party. We can't show up empty-handed. It's rude. Once Benny tastes it, he'll going to love us forever."

Dolores tsked. "Who cares what this Benny Hill character thinks of us."

I smiled at Dolores. "Careful. You're showing your age."

43

My aunt just glowered at me but said nothing.

I didn't like that Ruth had already given this stranger the nickname Benny like they were old pals. There was still a small chance I was wrong, and this guy was just a rich, reclusive paranormal who just wanted to get to know the town. But my gut said otherwise.

Dolores was shaking her head. "Buying the manor with cash just means he's rich. Doesn't necessarily mean he's a demon. There are rich paranormal families. Very wealthy, powerful old families."

"Yeah, like the Stansteads." Ruth stabbed her spatula into her bowl as though she was imagining decapitating one of those Stansteads. I wondered what that was about. A story for another time.

I flicked my gaze back to Dolores. "But you know *of* them. You know their names, their relatives. You have records of these paranormal families. This guy's not in the books. He's not in any system."

"But he could be a nice demon." Ruth turned around. Dijon mustard dripped from the spoon she was holding, spilling the yellow-brown condiment all over her bare feet. Her smiling face was speckled with mustard and what looked like mayonnaise. "He could be a good demon," she said again like she was talking about some cute Labrador retriever puppy. "You know, like your dad. He's a very good demon."

"Demons aren't puppies, Ruth," snapped Dolores, pulling that thought right out of my head. "Most demons are not to be trusted. They're unpleasant. Corrupted." She walked over to the table and sat. Her eyes met mine as she added, "Obiryn is an exception."

I nodded because what was I supposed to say? I believed there were decent demons, but they just weren't interested in us mortals.

"Jack was nice too," offered Ruth, and I recalled my adventures with the demon soul collector. I'd barely come out alive, but seeing my gran again was really nice.

Dolores spun around in her seat. "He was a soul-sucking demon. Not Santa Claus."

Ruth made a face. "I'm just saying that you might be wrong. He could be a nice demon who wants to live here with us. Because we're nice too."

"But he won't. Will he? He can't mingle with us during the day. Only at night. And most of us will be asleep or getting ready for bed when he's ready to venture out."

"What does Marcus think?" asked Ruth.

"I know he's not happy that he can't find anything on this guy," I told them. The memories of the chief's big, rough hands exploring my body sent warmth pooling in my middle, still very fresh. Like minutes fresh. "And there's nothing. It's like he doesn't exist. Which is why my demon theory works. But Marcus did say that not all paranormals are in the system. Could be someone who never was recorded."

I didn't like the sound of labeling any person, like keeping track of cattle, but even the human population had a census. It made sense that we had one as well.

"Hmm." Dolores tapped her mug with her fingers. "That's true. Not all paranormals agree with our rules and regulations, and some prefer to live out in the wild," she said, her eyes wide like she was describing something ill-omened.

Ruth whirled around, excitement lighting her expression. "Like Paddy and Timmy Gooberdapple. They live in a cave somewhere in California. Rumor is they don't come out until springtime. It's like they hibernate, just like chipmunks!"

"*Bears* hibernate in caves, you nitwit," snapped Dolores.

"Chipmunks too," Ruth shot back, her mouth a thin line.

Okay. "Well, whether he's a demon or a paranormal, I still think this guy is bad news. And what's this dinner party about? It's about getting to know the real players in this town."

Dolores narrowed her eyes at me. "What are you getting at?"

My eyes fell on the invitation card next to the wicker basket, and I snatched it up. Staring at the gold lettering, I said, "You got an invite. So did Marcus and me. Ronin. Gilbert. Martha. And according to her," I continued, having stopped by her shop before returning to Davenport House, "Joe Whitemane, Nancy Farleap, Brian Halfclaw, and Percival Kingsley were also invited. And more. All the pack leaders and heavy magical hitters. Doesn't that seem strange to you? Why single them out?"

Dolores stared at the tabletop, her eyebrows rising as she put the pieces together. "Like he chose *specifically* who he wants to attend."

"Exactly. The strongest in our community." I stared at my aunts, and I could tell they were bothered by that news. It was just a theory, but the more I thought about it, the more it started to make sense, and the more the pieces started to fit together.

"He wants to feel us out," I continued, the realization hitting me. "Get a sense for who we are and what kind of threat we pose to him." The fact that he knew who the heads of houses and pack leaders were didn't settle well with me. It seemed this mysterious stranger had already done his homework. He'd already scouted the town and picked out its leaders, its strongest. Had he been here for days? Weeks? Learning about our habits and skills with us having no idea he was studying us? Worse, we knew next to nothing about him.

But this guy was bad news. I felt it in my witchy bones.

"Why?" asked Ruth, her face scrunched up in bewilderment. "Why would he do that?"

I shrugged. "Because he's planning something." There was no other reasonable explanation.

"What?" asked Ruth and Dolores at the same time.

"Don't know yet." I searched their anxious faces. "But tonight, at this dinner party, is the best opportunity to find that out." If I was right, and he was a demon, he'd be using a glamour to hide his true nature. Just meeting him face to face wouldn't suffice.

I needed something else.

"Girls! How do I look?"

We all turned our attention as Beverly sashayed into the kitchen, swinging her hips like she was dancing a salsa. A red, sequin mermaid gown hugged her curves like it was painted on. The beading shimmered in the light. The dress was exquisite and moved like liquid wine around her as she halted in the middle of the kitchen, stood with one hand on her hip, and traced the curves of her lowcut dress with the other. Her blonde hair was up in a sophisticated bun, and red jewels that matched her dress hung from her ears. She looked amazing. Better than amazing. She was drop-dead gorgeous.

"Wow." I leaned forward. "Those twenty-year-olds have nothing on you in that dress. You look stunning."

Beverly beamed at me and gave her breasts a little lift. "I know. Many women would kill to have the body of a goddess like mine."

Dolores rolled her eyes. "Here we go again."

"But is it me?" asked Beverly.

Dolores shook her head. "It's way too tight. Shows too much cleavage for a witch your age. You look like a slut in a cheap show dress. Yes, it's totally you."

Beverly smiled at her sister and cocked her hip. "Thank you, darling. The judges won't be able to take their eyes off of me. They'll be too busy wondering how fast they can tear my dress off to appreciate the true glory of what lies beneath," she purred, running her hands over her body seductively.

Dolores scoffed. "They don't need to. We can *see* everything."

Beverly's smile turned victorious. "That's what I was going for. A sneak peek." She looked at me and winked. "And I'm *not* wearing any underwear."

Okay, this conversation was getting a little weird.

Ruth gave a throaty chuckle. "You can dress a woman in her Sunday best, but she's still a slut."

Beverly tucked a loose strand of blonde hair into her bun. "So. What are you girls wearing tonight for that dinner? Do we know anything about him?"

"His name is Benjamin Morgan," I told her. "We don't know if he's a demon or a paranormal. We have nothing on him. No previous address. Nothing."

Beverly's eyes lit up. "And?"

"And…"

Beverly let out a puff of air. "Is he *single*? Really, Tessa. That was the most important bit of information I was looking for. A rich, handsome bachelor coming to Hollow Cove to swoop me off my feet is one of my many fantasies."

Right. "I don't know. Possibly. Like I said, no one has anything on the guy. It's all very secretive." I scratched Hildo's head. "And that's where you guys come in."

The black cat looked up at me, his yellow eyes sparkling. "We do?"

"Yes!" Tinky flew over to the table and landed expertly like a gymnast finishing a jump. She looked at the cat on my lap. "I told you we were going tonight." Her eyes met mine, and she flashed me a smile. "We're going to spy on him. Aren't we, Tessa?"

"Yes," I agreed, "but more like snooping around in bedrooms and offices while we're all busy introducing ourselves. You're tiny and can get into spaces we can't. While the host is occupied, I need you to look for anything to help us figure out who he is. Is he a demon or not?"

"I can tell you that." Beverly pulled the slit of her gown higher. "All I need is five minutes with him, and I'll know if he's warm-blooded or not."

I opened my mouth to tell her that she'd been fooled in the past by an incubus demon—Derrick, the douche—but I didn't want to bring up bad memories, so I kept my mouth shut.

Dolores chuckled darkly. "How are you going to do that, oh wise one? Demons look just like us. You can't tell them apart. Even if he's naked. And he'll be using a glamour. You won't be able to sense his demon energies."

Beverly waved a dismissive hand at her sister. "I'll use the demon reveal potion, silly. The one Ruth made a while back."

I frowned. "The what potion?"

"The demon reveal," said Ruth turning around. "He needs to ingest a few drops. The potion will give off a rotten egg smell. That's when we'll know if he's a demon or not.

Holy crap. "Ruth, you're a genius."

"Oh, you." Pink spotted my aunt's cheeks, and she stared at the floor.

I perked up. "Do you have any around? Ready for tonight?" I leaned over and looked at her potions room. Though I couldn't see the inside from where I sat, I could imagine all the potions and vials of magical ointments she carried in there.

Ruth nodded. "Yes. I have a full jar. But you only need a little bit. I can give you a vial."

Dolores sipped her coffee and set the mug on the table. "This sounds all very helpful. But how do you plan on making him eat or drink it without him knowing? I don't take this stranger as being stupid. He'll know we don't trust him. He might be expecting it."

She was right. "I don't know yet, but I'll think of something. A distraction while I dump the contents? That could work." But that was going to be tough. Still, with Tinky and Hildo doing their own searching, I might not have to. It was good that we had options, though.

"Don't worry, Tessa darling, I can help you with the distraction," said Beverly, a wide smile forming on her full, red lips. "I have the perfect outfit that'll catch the attention of any male. Cold-blooded or not. Married or not."

"Spoken like a true slut," murmured Dolores, a tiny smile on her face.

"I'll have him eating out of the palm of my hand by the time they serve dessert," said Beverly, a sensual air to her voice as though her sister hadn't just called her a whore.

I didn't doubt her or her abilities to get men to do exactly what she wanted. She had talents that none of us could match in that area.

I thought of something. "You know, that's not a bad idea."

Beverly shrugged. "It's not an idea, darling. It's a *promise*."

I laughed. I admired her confidence. I really did. I needed some of that. "Okay, so while he's distracted by you…"

"While I've got him on his knees, begging me to do the things to him I whispered in his ear," purred Beverly.

"…I'll dump some of that potion into his food or drink. How soon will it work?"

"About a minute or so," answered Ruth. "The potion needs time to counteract with his blood. If it's demon blood, you'll smell him."

That sounded weird. "Good to know. Thanks."

I leaned back in my chair, running my fingers through Hildo's silky black fur and feeling much better now that we had a decent plan. We weren't going in without ammunition.

This Benjamin had investigated us. It was only fair that we return the favor.

And it was on tonight.

53

CHAPTER

5

I sat in the passenger seat in Marcus's burgundy Jeep Cherokee, holding on to the vial of demon reveal potion Ruth had given me before we all clambered into the chief's Jeep.

I lifted the vial closer and cursed on the inside. Unfortunately, its contents were bright green. That was going to be a problem. A transparent liquid would have been nearly impossible to detect poured over some food or dumped in a drink.

But this green stuff? It was an added complication. Not to mention that it looked... thick. Like almost pasty. Double damn.

I looked up and met Tinky's gaze. She sat on the dashboard, swinging her legs. I could tell from the apprehensive look on her face she was thinking the same thing. The green potion was going to be trouble.

"I'm glad you're wearing that black mini I bought you last week," said Beverly. "When I saw it on the rack, I knew it would look great on you."

I looked down at myself as Marcus slowed the Jeep at the next stop. "Thank you." Was it weird that my aunt bought me a dress? Maybe. But I hadn't had time to go shopping, and the witch lived and breathed shopping. Who was I to deny her?

"But those shoes look terrible."

I turned around to look at her and heard the contempt in her voice. "They're two-hundred-dollar shoes," I told her. "Cole Haan." Not that I was into expensive shoes or brands, but Marcus had bought them for me as a gift.

Beverly's face twisted like I'd just told her that her lipstick didn't match her dress. "They look like something Dolores would wear."

Ruth snorted, stroking Hildo on her lap a little too forcefully. But Dolores glared at her younger sister seated next to her.

"Nothing's wrong with my shoes," I told her, slightly annoyed.

"They're flat," Beverly told me, ignoring her sister's scowl. "You can't wear flats to a dinner party. And not with that dress."

I could. "I can't run in heels."

Beverly shook her head at me, disappointment ruining that perfect visage. "And why would you need to run? It's a dinner. Not a marathon. We don't run to get fed."

"My shoes are really comfortable, stylish, and pretty. What more do you want?"

"That dress needs to be respected." Beverly flicked a finger at me. "And wearing those flip-flops is an insult."

I scowled. "They're sandals. Not flip-flops."

"Same difference," she continued, speaking to me like a simpleton when it came to fashion. I guess I was. "The point is, you should have worn a pair of heels. Now you look like you're going to a barbecue. Not a sophisticated dinner."

"We don't know what to expect. Do we?" I countered, not really bothered by the fact that she hated my shoes. I loved them, which was all that mattered.

Beverly tsked. "No one sends out fancy invitations to a barbecue. You get a text message."

"I have to agree with her on that," said Dolores, though she still wore a frown.

"Of course you do," said Beverly, her eyes on me. "Dolores is wearing flats, but at least she had the decency to cover her disastrous sasquatch toes. No one alive should be subjected to those. They look like they could bite."

Dolores's face darkened, but she pressed her lips tightly, the corners moving like she was doing her best not to curse her sister.

I sighed. "Well, we're not turning around so I can change my footwear. Too late for that. We're almost there. Right?"

I looked over to Marcus and saw a shadow of a smirk on his lips. He looked fantastic in a dark jacket over a black shirt and black dress pants. And that musky scent from his cologne was doing all kinds of things to my body. It was all I could do not to leap over and straddle him in his seat, which would be weird in front of my aunts.

I was still on that honeymoon high, and it didn't look like it was going to fade anytime soon.

"We'll be there soon," answered the chief. "Are Iris and Ronin meeting us there?"

"Yeah. She texted me two minutes ago. They just left, so we'll probably get to the manor at the same time."

I stared down at the vial again, feeling nervous suddenly. What if my master plan didn't work? What if I got caught? I didn't want this Benjamin to know we were onto him. Not yet. He would eventually figure it out because I knew this guy wasn't stupid. I just needed time first to figure out who he was.

And most importantly, why he came to Hollow Cove. What did he want?

"It's strange that we were all invited but not Amelia," commented Ruth. "She must be very upset."

I stared out the window at the passing houses. "She was. She is."

I'd popped by her place after I'd left my aunts' house earlier to see if she'd gotten an invitation as well. My insides twisted as I recalled our conversation and how her face fell when she'd hurried to her mailbox only to find it empty.

"Are you sure it's supposed to be here?" My mother searched the mailbox again, three times.

"Everyone else got theirs in their mailbox," I'd told her, standing on the porch. Except for my aunts, who got theirs through their toaster, their usual method of communication.

"But where's mine?" My mother turned from her mounted mailbox next to her front door, looking both hurt and angry.

Shit damn. "I guess you didn't get one." I felt bad for my mother, but now I knew my theory was sound. It was no secret that my mother didn't have much magic. Her magical abilities were limited. And if I was right, and this Benjamin character had scouted the town, he would have discovered that Amelia Davenport was not like her sisters in terms of magical skill. It meant that Benjamin had only invited the strongest and the most influential.

"Whatever." My mother banged the metal front of her mailbox shut, her face flushed. "I couldn't go anyway. I'm busy. I don't have time for a stupid party."

"Oh. Well, okay then. I'll call you—"

She slammed the front door in my face. "Good talk, *Mother*."

I knew she was upset. Her sisters were powerful witches, and she was practically a dud. She was being overshadowed by her sisters again. Still, I felt strangely relieved that she *wasn't* invited. Until we knew more about this stranger, she was better off at home, safely.

"Amelia's a dud," said Beverly, echoing my sentiments. "It's no secret. Clearly, Benjamin only wants the more *desirable* persons at his party."

"Hmmm." My mother was close to matching Beverly in terms of beauty, so I knew her comment about desirable was off. Nope. It came down to power and influence. I was sure of it.

"Are you nervous?" Tinky swung her legs back and forth.

"Not nervous," I told her. "But I am anxious to get a feel for this guy. I want to know what he's up to."

"Well, here's your chance," said Marcus. "We're here."

As a unit, my aunts and I glanced out the window to feast our eyes on the manor. I'd already seen it completely restored, but now, with the fading light of dusk and all the exterior lights shining like tiny stars, it looked far more opulent and grander.

Marcus pulled over to the curb and killed the engine. I watched his face as he inspected the newly furbished manor, but he kept his features blank, and I couldn't tell what he was thinking.

"Would you look at that?" Dolores's nose was pressed against her window. "To think that just yesterday it looked like it needed a bull-dozer."

"It's beautiful." Ruth clapped her hands to-gether. "It's like one of those houses in those house magazines."

"Very eloquent, Ruth," hissed Dolores. "This is an architectural marvel in the revival-style de-sign. I was always interested in architecture. In another life, I would have been an architect. And a very proficient one at that."

"You can start by engineering what you call eyebrows," said Beverly, flicking a finger at her sister's forehead. "And then build from there."

Ignoring her sister, Dolores popped her door open and stepped out. Following her example, Marcus and my aunts clambered out and pooled around on the sidewalk, except for Ruth who stepped around the Jeep and grabbed a bowl with her potato salad from the trunk.

I stuffed the vial into my bra and followed them out.

Beverly wasn't kidding about wearing something no mortal male could keep his eyes off. She wore a figure-hugging green dress that matched her eyes with thin straps, and a deep neckline that plunged to the center of her chest with a high slit on the thigh. It was more than enough to show a generous amount of cleavage while still being tasteful. It was like a second skin drawn over every curve, accentuating them, and her face was a masterpiece. Perfect makeup like that had to be magicked.

Yup. Even if Benjamin was a demon, he wouldn't be able to keep his eyes off of Beverly.

Thank you, Beverly.

Ruth and Dolores both looked fantastic in their dresses. Ruth wore a dark purple dress with an A-line skirt and Hildo wrapped around her neck like a black scarf. Even though Dolores wore flats, she still looked statuesque and sophisticated in her long, black dress with tulip sleeves.

We were all put together nicely.

That's when I noticed all the other paranormals crowded around the manor's front walkway. My gaze traveled over the group. I spotted a familiar, plump witch in her early sixties. Martha looked sophisticated in a long, floral pattern dress in a mix of red and pink with a matching hat.

And there was Gilbert next to her. I recognized Nancy Farleap standing with Joe Whitemane, both pack leaders. There was also the large and imposing Ray Blackfoot, a massive werebear, Percival Kingsley, and Brian Halfclaw, the names Martha had given me.

A man stood next to them. His dark brown hair was held away from his eyes with a leather cord, revealing the tribal tattoo that covered half of his face. Boris Bravebird, an eagle shifter, and the largest of his kind.

As I kept scanning, I counted about twenty-five of us, including my aunts, Marcus and me, and Ronin and Iris. And as I'd suspected, these were all the most powerful and influential paranormals of Hollow Cove.

I narrowed my eyes. "Why are they all just standing there?" I said to no one in particular.

"Tessa!"

I turned to see Iris and Ronin walking up the sidewalk, both in their Sunday best. Ronin wore an exquisite dark gray suit that shimmered as he moved—as if it had been made just for him or tailored by magic. With his hair styled in a modern fashion and his chiseled good looks, Ronin made heads turn wherever he went—both female and male.

Iris was a vision in an off-the-shoulder gold and black dress. Her dark hair was up, showing off her heart-shaped face and pixie-like features.

It was no wonder Ronin had fallen for her. She was beautiful.

"See?" Beverly pointed at Iris's shoes. "At least Iris had the decency to wear heels."

I rolled my eyes. "Yes. I'm a fashion failure."

Ronin laughed as he reached us. "A what?"

"Never mind." I turned back to the group of guests. "Why are they just standing there?" We'd been here for a few minutes, and still, I hadn't seen anyone go up to the porch. "We're not that early. Are we?"

Marcus checked his watch. "We're two minutes late."

"So what then?" I cast my gaze around again. From the nervous shifting and the way the paranormals kept stealing glances at the house but never looking for very long, I understood. "They're scared to go in."

Tinky hovered next to me, her wings humming in my ears. "Oooh. You're right. They're terrified of the house."

"You think?" Dolores propped her hands on her hips. "Well. The house is intimidating. It does have the reputation of being haunted. Perhaps they're afraid of ghosts."

"Ghosts are fun," chimed Ruth. "When I was seven, my best friend was a specter."

Dolores gave her sister an odd expression. "Isn't that the same thing as your make-believe friend?"

Ruth nodded. "My imaginary friends are all ghosts—which is why I called her Susie, my Spectral Companion."

My eyes found Martha, and I started for her. "Martha," I said as I joined the witch. "What are you all doing outside? Are you waiting for something?"

Martha gave a mock laugh. "Well, honey. We're all waiting for *someone* to go in first. Looks like no one wants to go."

Oh boy. "Huh." Looked like even the big, burly pack leaders were afraid of the house, of ghosts and poltergeists.

Martha's eyes went wide. "How about *you* go first? You're a Merlin. You know how to deal with ghosts and death."

"Death?"

"Yes. Howard Crane and his wife both died in that house."

"I didn't know that." I looked over to the front door. We came here because we were invited, yes, but I came here to get a scoop on this Benjamin. And I wasn't going home without going through that door and meeting him.

I glanced at Marcus, my aunts, and then Iris and Ronin. "I'm going in." At my words, the group outside seemed to relax, as if they were all soldiers being given the command to "stand down."

"I'm coming with you," whispered Tinky, and I felt a tug on my hair as she settled on my shoulder.

Like a stone in a stream, the guests parted, giving me a wide berth as I walked along the walkway and climbed up the steps to the porch.

I caught a glimpse of Marcus following behind me along with my friends as my aunts brought up the rear.

Was I nervous? Little bit. I had no idea what to expect. Over the past year, I'd grown some serious lady balls (not that kind, but you know what I mean). I could do this. Having dinner with a demon, or whatever he was, was simple.

Getting him to swallow some of that potion would not be.

I let out a breath, feeling the same energies in the air near the door as when I'd come here with Iris earlier today. I could hear faint music playing on the inside. Okay, so he was here. Good, I wanted answers. And behind that door were my answers.

Demon or not, I was going in.

I made a fist, raised my hand to knock—

The door swung open.

A man in his mid-fifties stood on the threshold. He was fit and tall with broad shoulders under a white shirt tucked into a pair of black dress pants. He'd rolled his shirt sleeves to expose beefy forearms marked with tattoos. His hairstyle looked almost military—short and gray in a neat cut.

Icy blue eyes watched me. His piercing gaze raked over me for a few beats and then scanned the area behind me, taking in every detail. His presence was imposing. He smiled, but there was no warmth behind it.

"Ah. You're all here. Good. Very good. Welcome to my home," said Benjamin Morgan in a rough voice that echoed his stature. "Please come in."

I smiled. *Here we go.*

CHAPTER

6

Without a word, I followed the large man into the foyer. The last time I was here, the interior had been covered in darkness, and we had to use flashlights. Now, the entire entrance was basking in soft yellow light.

I glanced around. The marble floors sparkled and looked newly polished. Unfortunately, the enormous chandelier that hung from the ceiling with the heads of children with light bulbs coming out of their mouths was still there. And functional, as the gleaming bulbs shot illumination from the children's mouths like water fountains spouting water from their apertures.

The pricks of energy were still in the air but different from the last time I was here. These were warmer and more inviting, like how the house was presented now, not cold and sinister.

I quickly moved away from the front door as Marcus, my aunts, Ronin, Iris, and finally all the guests piled into the foyer. I used that as an excuse to get closer to Benjamin.

I sidled next to him, sending out my witchy senses to feel some demonic energies from him. No demonic pulses, but I did get a feel of something. Looked like he was wearing a powerful glamour. He could be a damn wizard for all I knew or a werewolf with deep pockets. But that's why I was here. I was going to find out.

"I'm Tessa Davenport," I blurted.

Benjamin Morgan's icy gaze slid over me, and I felt a shiver roll up my spine. His eyes held a trace of a predator, something I'd seen many times in Marcus's gaze when he was staring at an enemy.

He blinked, and it was gone. "Yes. I know." He stepped forward, that false smile returning to his lips like it was something he'd practiced, and now he was an expert at it.

I held out my hand, and he shook it. Usually, I like a good firm handshake, but he squeezed my fingers, almost crushing them, like he was *showing* me who was in control. I pulled my hand away, still smiling and refusing to show him that he'd hurt me. Bastard. At least now I had a good reason to dislike the guy.

When I looked away, I spotted Ronin with a frown on his otherwise smooth, handsome face. He was looking around the manor, obviously still ticked that he didn't get to purchase it. It was a spectacular house.

Marcus watched Benjamin in silence, his expression dark though calm as he sized up the host. Benjamin flicked his gaze over the chief as though he'd sensed him watching him, his face hard, but I saw a bit of humor in it like he wasn't at all intimidated by the large wereape. It was like watching two alphas glaring at each other from across a room, waiting for some internal signal to start fighting to see who was the strongest. Marcus was slightly taller, but both men had so much muscle that it was almost ridiculous.

"Tessa," whispered Iris, giving me her wide eyes and staring at my breasts.

Staring at my breasts?

I looked down.

Holy fairy tits.

The potion vial was sticking out of the top of my dress like it was happy to see me. I crossed my arm over my chest, pretending to fix my hair, spun around, and pushed the vial down, tucking it into my bra properly. Damn. Had Benjamin seen it? No, I didn't think so. Well, I hoped not.

Heat rushed to my face from both anger and embarrassment. The evening was not starting out very well.

"Welcome, welcome," came Benjamin's voice, and I turned to look at him. "I'm delighted you all could join me tonight. Let's take this opportunity to get to know each other better. Drinks are being set up in the den before dinner. If you'd follow me this way." Benjamin motioned for everyone to follow him as he walked out of the foyer and down the hall.

Surprising me, Gilbert pushed his way through the hunkering crowd. Martha went flying into the wall as he rushed up to be at Benjamin's heels like a good dog. Curses flew from Martha's mouth. With her red face, she pulled down the fabric of her dress and followed behind Nancy and the others, still adjusting her hat.

I shook my head. "Gilbert is a fool."

"Gilbert was always a fool," said Dolores as she, Ruth, and Beverly huddled around me. "But he's our fool."

"You can keep him," I said, feeling some tension along the back of my neck. I looked at Iris. "I'm not getting any demon vibes. You?"

"Just the usual pulse of wards and echoes of magic," answered the Dark witch. "Nothing unpleasant. Sorry."

"Iris is right," said Dolores, her voice low so only we could hear. "Nothing here is cause for alarm. Just a beautiful house that someone took great care of restoring. You have to accept the fact that perhaps you are wrong, Tessa."

I didn't think I was. "I'll be the first to admit it if I am. Don't worry."

"Shall we go in?" Beverly pushed up her breasts and walked away, swinging her hips like they were weapons. Maybe they were.

"Yes. Let's go. I'm curious to see the rest of the house," Dolores said, following Beverly.

"I want to see the ghosts," commented Ruth with a smile as Hildo leaped off her shoulders and landed expertly on the floor. "Maybe we can be friends?"

Yep. Ruth was a weird one, but I loved her for it.

I knelt next to the black cat familiar. "Okay, guys," I whispered to Tinky and Hildo as the fairy flew off my shoulder and hovered next to the cat. "You know what to do. See if you can find anything suspicious or anything that will give us a clue as to who he is and what he wants."

Tinky gave me a soldier's salute. "Yes, boss."

I laughed. "Just don't get caught. We don't know who else is here."

"I don't plan on it," said Hildo. "Come on, Bug. Let's go."

I opened my mouth to scold him for his comment, but Tinky grinned, seemingly thrilled at his new nickname for her. I watched as they both rushed forward down the hallway without a sound, like ghosts.

Once Hildo and Tinky had disappeared around a corner, I stood up and joined the chief as he waited for me.

"Ready?" He reached out and took my hand, his grip strong but soft, nothing like the way Benjamin had crushed it when he shook it.

"Ready," I answered, checking the vial again to make sure it was staying down.

As we made our way through a long corridor with doors leading to other chambers, I noticed the bright tapestries on the walls, the Oriental carpets covering the marble floors, and the large wooden staircase that went up to the upper levels. The heavy furniture from the 1700s had been intricately carved into bizarre, misshapen figures.

Miles of crafted wood paneling extended in every direction, all polished and glowing.

Benjamin Morgan hadn't changed a thing. He'd even kept the eerie portraits with the same odd, soulless eyes that seemed to follow you wherever you went. Well, that's what it looked like to me. He'd kept all the old furniture from the previous owners. But somehow the furnishings looked… new. Just like the exterior of the house. Creepy. And I didn't like it.

We stepped into a room left of the staircase. It had a very masculine feel with lots of brown leather sofas, chairs, and dark polished wood, which stood out handsomely against the white walls. An antique Persian carpet in deep shades of wine, blue, and gold contrasted the dark wood floors.

At the end of the room was an enormous limestone fireplace, which was empty at the moment but could have been suitable for roasting a moose.

The room was sparsely populated with witches, shifters, and weres standing in little knots, talking while sipping their drinks. Some even sat in comfortable chairs as soft music played with a steady rhythm. The smell of cigarettes reached me, and somewhere in the middle of all that, I felt a quiet, quivering pulse—magic.

It hummed through the walls and the floor like a living, breathing beast, as though the house itself was made of magic, like Davenport House. But this wasn't from the home. It came from wards.

Somewhere inside this house was a secret that Benjamin didn't want us to know.

But I was going to discover it.

Male waiters balanced trays with drinks and offered them to the guests. Martha seemed to have recovered from her altercation with Gilbert as she chatted happily with Ruth. Dolores and Gilbert were in some heated argument, gesturing at the ceiling and the side moldings. I didn't know what that was about. I didn't care.

Beverly stood next to Benjamin, a glass of red wine balanced in her left hand while her right hand was carefully placed on the man's large biceps. The host stared at my aunt like he wanted to throw her over his shoulder and take her upstairs. He was into her. That much was obvious. No warm-blooded man or demon could resist my aunt if she put on her A-game. If she could keep him this distracted, I might have a shot.

She turned her head, and our gazes met. She winked.

Yeah. Beverly was awesome. She was putting the moves on for me. This was going to work.

Benjamin smiled at Beverly, a cigar in one hand. It wasn't cigarettes I'd smelled earlier but his cigar. I didn't know how Beverly could stand the smell. Even at this distance, it was giving me a headache.

She was a real trooper.

Marcus pulled me closer. "You know how you're going to do it?" His eyes landed on my boobs. Too bad it was because he was referring to the vial and not my average cleavage.

"Not yet." I was tense. The more I thought about it, the more it sounded insane. Stupid. How the hell was I going to dump the contents of the green potion?

A waiter stood next to me. "Can I offer you a drink?" Feeling a little better, I grabbed a glass of red wine from the tray. "Thank you." As he walked away, I couldn't help but notice that he didn't give off any paranormal energies. He was human. That wasn't a huge shocker. We sometimes hired humans for these types of events.

Glancing around, I noticed that all the waiters were male and were a bit rough around the edges, like pro wrestlers in waiters' outfits. Not experienced like you'd expect them to be. Something was strange about them, but I just couldn't put my finger on it at the moment.

Ronin stepped my way. "Is it me, or do the waiters seem off to you?"

"No. It's not just you."

"They're human," said Marcus. "But I don't recognize them. They're not the regular humans we usually work with."

"Right." They definitely didn't look like the ones I'd seen at the Sisters of the Circle's, Cocks and Broomsticks party, with their too-tight clothes and their manhoods tightly packed. Still, I had no idea we had a "regular" group of humans for hire.

"All this could all have been mine." Ronin took a swig of his drink, an amber-looking liquid.

"Still pissed about that, huh?" I asked, giving Iris a look.

Ronin frowned. "Nothing's legal about how it was done." He turned his head and glanced at Benjamin, who was laughing at something Beverly was saying. "I'm going to figure it out." He walked away, his entire body tight with tension.

"Why is he so upset?" asked Marcus. "I'm sure it's not the first house he missed out on."

A sad smile appeared on Iris's face, her cheeks a little flushed and her eyes glassy as she spoke. "Because he was going to buy it for us. For me. It was supposed to be a surprise."

"Ah. I understand now." I stared at the back of Ronin's head, my heart heavy as I felt for my friend.

"I told him it didn't matter," said Iris. "I don't need a big house. I just need him. But he's not hearing me."

I reached out and grabbed her arm. "He'll get over it. Eventually. I'm sure he'll find another house."

"Not like this one."

She was right about that. Apart from Davenport House, this manor was probably one of the most beautiful homes in Hollow Cove. Ghosts and all.

"Tessa!"

I blinked at the fairy who came zipping past my head. Her wings tickled my neck as she settled on my shoulder.

"We didn't find anything. I'm sorry," she said in my ear just as Hildo bounded into the den, his tail pointing to the ceiling. I looked over to Benjamin. He smiled at Beverly, but his eyes were on the black cat.

I leaned down to scratch the cat under his chin. "Nothing?"

"The place is clean, too clean," said the cat. "We checked every room. The guy keeps his place immaculate. Nothing personal about him either. No records that we could find."

It didn't surprise me that they could search a house of this size that fast. Both were magical, and both were in their element.

"Except for one room," said Tinkerbell, and the warning in her tone had my heart thumping.

"It was locked," said the cat familiar. "And no matter what we did, we couldn't get in."

I knew it. "He's hiding something in there." And if we could get inside, I knew we'd discover the truth about him. "Where's this room?"

"Top floor," said Tinky. "I think it has to be one of the bedrooms—likely the master bedroom. It's the only room on the top floor with double doors."

I felt the tingling sensation of eyes on me, and when I looked up, Benjamin was watching us. "I don't think we'll be able to get through tonight," I whispered to them. "Not with the host watching us."

Looked like it was going to be my turn now. I didn't have a choice.

"Well, if that's it for tonight," said Hildo. "We've got some hunting to do."

"Fireflies?"

"Crickets," answered the fairy as she leaped off my shoulder and hovered beside Hildo.

I didn't want to know. "You guys can go. Have fun with…whatever you're doing."

Tinky beamed. "We will."

I watched as the black cat and the fairy left the den and disappeared. They didn't need me to open the door for them either. Magic and all that.

I straightened, wondering if Beverly was enough of a distraction for me to sneak up to the top floor and try to open the door.

"Was that your cat?"

Shit. I flinched as I recognized the roughness of Benjamin's voice.

Yup. I turned around, and the large man was just standing there. "Yes. He's my familiar. Likes to follow me around. You know… cats." I gave a fake laugh. "I told him he could go home. Wouldn't want him to soil your beautiful home with his fur. He's molting right now."

"I don't care much for *animals*," he said, and I didn't care much for the annoyance in his tone at the mention of my furry friends. "They stink. Bring in fleas and disease."

My face flamed. "Yes, well, he's gone now." It was one of my rules I'd had since I hit my twenties. If you didn't like animals, I didn't like you either.

"Good." Benjamin took a puff of his cigar, watching me. The smoke made my eyes water. I blinked, waiting for him to comment about Tinky, but he didn't.

Marcus stood just off to the side, flexing his hands with power and strength radiating from him. It was like he was waiting for Benjamin to insult me so he could take a swing at him.

"I like what you did to the place," I told the host. "How did you manage to restore it so quickly?" I knew this question was on everyone's mind.

I looked behind the big man, seeing if Ronin was near, but he was sulking near the fireplace, staring at the contents of his drink. I turned my attention back to the host.

Benjamin arched a brow. "I can't share all of my secrets."

"Why not?"

He sucked on his cigar. "Because I'd have to kill you."

I flinched, and so did Marcus. Was that a threat? Benjamin took another drag from his cigar, a smile on his lips. If Marcus didn't punch him, I was going to kick him in the meat clackers.

"Just kidding, of course," said the host, the cigar between his teeth.

"Of course." I stood there with my heart nearly jumping out of my chest.

There was no humor in the way he'd said it. It was a threat. I felt it in my witchy bones. But it's not like I could blast him with my demon mojo. Not yet. I needed answers first.

Then I'd blast his stupid ass.

"Ah, there you are." Beverly arrived with two drinks in her hands. "Here's your whiskey, darling," she said, holding a short glass with amber liquid inside.

The host took the drink without so much as a thank you. "Your niece is interested in my house."

"I think everyone is interested in your house," purred Beverly, running her fingers over his large tattooed forearm. Her green eyes flicked to me for a second and then to the drink in his hand. "But I'm more interested in you." She traced her fingers up his arm, leaning so close that her breasts brushed against him. "Tell me more about that trip to Peru," she said. "It's making me all *hot*… and *sweaty*." At that, Benjamin lost all interest in me, as his eyes were focused solely on Beverly and her cleavage.

Okay, this was the distraction I needed. It was now or never.

Giddy up.

I reached into my bra, yanked out the vial, and gripped it tightly, hiding it from view. Taking a breath, I thumbed the top, leaned forward a bit, and tipped the contents into his drink.

When I leaned back, Benjamin was still absorbed with Beverly and her perky boobs. He'd never seen me.

Ha! That was easier than I'd thought.

But my little victory died as I stared at the glob of green goo floating *above* the liquid.

It wasn't blending.

Holy gremlin poop.

Panicked, sweat broke out on my forehead, and I could feel a droplet drip down my back. I was screwed. I met Iris's eyes. They were practically bugging out of her head, reminding me of the goat she was once cursed to be.

Shit. Shit. Shit. This was bad. I was going to get caught.

Beverly glanced at Benjamin's drink, and her features went tight.

And then he turned his head.

I couldn't breathe.

Beverly's hand whipped out and cupped his jaw, turning his head toward her. "Tell me, Benjamin, you never said if there was a *Mrs*. Morgan."

I barely heard his response as all my attention stayed on his drink. And then, lo and behold, the green gob sifted and then broke apart, disintegrating into the alcoholic beverage until it disappeared completely.

And just in time, as Benjamin laughed at something Beverly was saying and then took a swig of his drink.

I was still holding my breath as he swallowed, watching his face for any traces of detection of something amiss in his drink. But as I stood there like a fool, watching my aunt put the moves on the host, he didn't notice a thing. So far so good.

A flicker of movement caught my attention. I turned my head to see Ruth waving at me, and then she started to mimic…yup… she was sniffing her armpits. I knew what she was trying to tell me, but now everyone around her was giving her a wide berth. They thought she was mad.

After what felt like an eternity, it was time for the smell test.

How does a witch covertly sniff a male host without him knowing?

Very discreetly.

I grabbed my wine glass with both hands to hide my trembling fingers and stepped forward. I angled my body so I was positioned the same as Benjamin. I was so close to him that my shoulder nearly brushed his arm.

And then, as stealthily as I could, I inhaled deeply through my nose and … nothing. Just a musky scent of whatever cologne he was wearing.

Damn. I wasn't close enough.

I looked up. Iris was staring at me with an expectant expression. I shook my head. I had to get closer.

This was probably one of the weirdest positions I found myself in. But a witch's gotta do what a witch's gotta do.

I leaned over, closer still, until my nose was practically in Benjamin's armpit—and sniffed.

"Are you smelling me?" Benjamin's eyes narrowed as he stared down, looking at me like I was mental.

I felt like lava had been poured over my head. Maybe I was mental. I had to be a little crazy to try and sniff my host to see if he was a demon.

"Huh? Of course not. It's just allergies," I gave a laugh and a mock sniff. He wasn't laughing. He was still watching me suspiciously. Did he know what I was trying to do? If he did, he didn't say anything.

"Dinner is served," called one of the waiters.

"Oh, good, I'm starving." Beverly hooked her arm around Benjamin's and pulled him away with her to the dining room, I presumed, though I hadn't seen it yet. But not before she looked over her shoulder at me, raised a perfect brow, and mouthed, "So?"

I watched them walk away. Dolores and Ruth joining them as the guests all filed out of the den. Only Marcus, Iris, and Ronin remained with me.

Yes, I'd looked like a big ol' fool. But my embarrassing experiment did tell me one thing.

Benjamin Morgan was not a demon.

So what the hell was he?

CHAPTER

7

"**Y**ou're sure he's not a demon?" Marcus stood next to our cottage's kitchen island, his big, manly hands splayed on the marble counter, his expression stiff.

I grabbed a glass and poured water from the filtered water pitcher. "Not if Ruth's potion worked properly, he's not. And I'm sure it did." My heart sped up just remembering how close I got to being caught. "He's not a demon."

"Then what is he? He's not a werewolf or a shifter. I didn't get a sense of that."

"I don't know." I knew Marcus's wereape abilities enabled him to get a *feeling* of what paranormal race a shifter was in their human form.

"He could still be a witch or a mage. That could explain how quickly he restored the manor."

"Is that what you think?"

I shook my head. "I'm just not sure anymore. He was wearing a powerful glamour, though. And Ruth's potion was supposed to reveal if he was a demon or not. Not."

"And you didn't get a sense of anything when you…" a smile spread over his face. "When you *smelled* him?"

"Ha. Ha. No, I didn't."

Marcus leaned back and crossed his arms over his chest. "So why hide it? If he's a witch or whatever, plenty of them are here in Hollow Cove."

I shrugged. "No idea. He kept playing it off and changing the subject whenever anyone asked him at dinner."

The dinner had been a strange event. The food was delicious, and obviously Benjamin had gone all out, to the delight of many including Beverly, who sat next to him the whole time. The man knew how to entertain. I'd give him that. But he'd remained tight-lipped about who he was, where he came from, and why he chose to move here, of all places.

"I wanted a change," was all he'd said on the matter. And then he'd said he'd hired more than a hundred people to refurbish the manor. Even then, I knew enough about renovating since I had done some renovations in the house I'd shared with my ex to know that you couldn't restore a home that size in under twenty-four hours. No matter how many workers you hired. It was impossible. Magic was the only answer here, even though he didn't want to admit it. He'd used a hell of a lot of it.

When we'd left the dinner, Ronin was still in a brooding mood and left without saying goodbye, Iris waving at us as she hurried to catch up with him. My aunts were just as surprised and confused as I was about our host. Though my dislike of the man was reaching new heights.

"Not a demon, eh?" Dolores had said as she climbed into the back seat of Marcus's Jeep.

"I didn't get a foul smell from him," I told her.

"If he didn't smell like rotten eggs, he's not a demon," Ruth concluded.

"He smelled like sophistication, male and rich and handsome," crooned Beverly. "I loved the way he said *Beverly*."

Ruth made a face. "But that's your name, silly. What else would he call you?"

"I can give you a few suggestions," sneered Dolores.

A sensual smile pulled over Beverly's lips. "But it'll be much better when I hear him *scream* my name." She giggled. "Over and over again."

"I wouldn't touch that man with a ten-foot pole," commented Dolores.

"I'd let his pole touch me whenever he wanted," purred Beverly.

Yeah, that didn't sound right.

"The point is," continued Dolores, her face flushed. "Something's sinister about him. The way he was observing us the entire night."

I shared that sentiment exactly.

"He's hiding something," said Marcus suddenly, pulling my thoughts back to this moment in our kitchen. "He wasn't trying that hard to make it less obvious."

"What do you mean?"

Marcus stared at the countertop in thought. "I had the impression this was a game to him. The dinner party. Him buying the house. It's all part of a game."

I hadn't thought of that. "What kind of game?" It made sense now, come to think of it. And those he invited to his party were the players, the pawns. I hadn't told Marcus about how hard Benjamin had squeezed my hand. If I had, he would have decked him.

The chief let out a long sigh. "I don't know. This guy is a ghost. He comes here, buys a mansion, and then invites a few people to his dinner party, but he chooses not to be open about his reasons. You could tell he was lying. He wasn't even making an effort. And I want to know what those reasons are."

"Me too." Benjamin Morgan rubbed me the wrong way. Even if he hadn't crushed my fingers in that handshake, I wouldn't have warmed up to him.

"Did Tinkerbell and Hildo discover anything?"

I glanced back at the chief. "Nothing that would tell us who he is or what he wants. But a door on the third floor was locked and protected by magic. They couldn't open it."

"What are you thinking?"

"That behind door number one lies all Benjamin's secrets. Why else would he lock it? Because there's something valuable, important behind it." I thought of something. "Can you search his house? You're the town chief. Can't you get a warrant or something similar? I bet you could get that door open."

Marcus shook his head. "We don't have warrants like the humans. And I can't just barge in there. I need a reason. Has to be a security reason. And it's not."

"Too bad."

"I know types like him." Marcus's face was blank, but I could see the anger seething behind his eyes. What was that about? "The wealthy, powerful types, the untouchable ones. You can't imagine the horrors they get away with."

"Oh, I can imagine." I just didn't want to think about that now. I had enough on my plate to deal with.

"He's up to something," continued the chief. "He came here for something. We need to figure out what."

"We will." I moved forward and touched his arm. "This is just the first night. We have all of tomorrow to keep looking into this guy. Beverly seemed an expert at charming him. We could use her talents again. Maybe we'll invite him to dinner at Davenport House." And toss him in the basement if he doesn't cooperate.

Marcus looked down at me. "I don't think I want him in your aunts' house. We don't know anything about him."

"Maybe," I said, leaning closer until I was facing him. "But better to be in our house and our rules. Maybe this time, we'll be able to figure out what he is and what he's hiding. You know, a few spells might do the trick."

"And you know what else can do the trick?" said Marcus, his voice deep, carnal.

I swallowed. "What?"

"This." He angled his head and kissed me. When his tongue slipped between my lips and tangled mine, my nether regions screamed, "Halleluiah!"

He grabbed the back of my head and pulled me closer, kissing me slowly at first and then harder. A spike of desire ignited in my core.

I gasped as I sank into him, one arm hooked around his neck and the other hand playing with his hair. His grip on my waist was tight, hinting at the desire coursing through him, and it was all I could do to keep from ripping off his clothes.

Scratch that. I *am* going to rip off his clothes. You just watch me.

I pulled away, my hands reaching for his belt and yanking it off. "Take off your clothes," I ordered.

The chief gave me a smile that had my panties combusting. "Your wish is my command, *wife*."

Wife. There was that word again that sent a jolt of electricity throughout my entire body. My Lady V pounded like it was an engine starting. Vroom vroom, baby.

A ring came from Marcus's phone sitting on the counter. We both stilled and stared at it, our hearts pounding. After the fourth ring, it stopped.

Grinning like a fool, I hauled myself out of my dress, standing in just my bra and somewhat melted panties. I noticed a slight gut protruding from my abdomen, no doubt the result of eating a sizeable plate of Portuguese chicken, rice, and veggies—and let's not forget dessert. A polite guest never refuses dessert, which was, to Ruth's delight, raspberry, and chocolate marble cheesecake. Benjamin was a douche, but his cook was fantastic.

The gut thing wasn't sexy, but there you have it.

In one swift move, Marcus tugged out of his dress shirt, pants, and briefs and tossed them on the floor. Those damn wereape abilities still amazed me.

It was hard not to salivate at the naked man standing before me. He stood there, his body glistening in the light, the hard muscles and skin looking as if sculpted from marble. The look on his face was intense and feral as though he was ready to devour something. Me.

Dessert seconds. Yay!

Again, Marcus's phone rang, and I glared at it like an annoying mosquito, contemplating whether to smack the hell out of it or not.

"Come here, *wife*," growled the wereape as he crushed his mouth on mine again. He reached out, grabbed my waist, and pressed my body against his. I slid my hands over his chest, exploring the hard muscles of his back. His skin was hot and smooth.

His tongue searched my mouth, and every thought of his phone and whoever was trying to contact him vanished from my brain. There was only this gorgeous man's desire and my pounding lady bits.

I blinked, and his hands were on me again, jerking on my bra and panties, and the next thing I knew, my bra had performed a disappearing act along with my partially melted panties.

"One of these days, you'll have to teach me that."

The wereape let out a lazy growl. "No. I'll keep that for me. *I* should be the one to undress you."

Okay dokie. Who was I to complain? The man was smokin' hot, this glorious, strong beast of a man who was also my husband.

Another ring came from Marcus's phone.

"I swear I'm about to take a swing at your phone," I teased. Talk about killing the mood.

"I better check. Might be important." Marcus sighed as he pulled away from me, and I felt the loss of his heat immediately.

"Mmmhmm." I watched as the wereape slid the phone to his ear, listening to whoever had left a voicemail. Then his jaw clenched, and his eyes narrowed. I knew that look. Something had happened. And it wasn't good.

"What's going on?" I asked as he pulled the phone away from his ear.

"Joe Whitemane's gone missing," he said. "His wife's hysterical. He never came home from the dinner at the manor."

I wrapped my arms over my chest, feeling a little chill. "Maybe he went to the pub? I know he likes his pint of beer."

"No. She called. It's a small town. She's called all the pubs still open at this hour. According to her, he doesn't go off like that without telling her first. Even for a beer."

"So, she thinks something happened to him." I understood her worry. I'd be frantic, too, if Marcus went missing. But like he said, it was a small town. He'd show up eventually.

"I should check it out," said the large wereape, scooping up his discarded clothes from the floor.

"Right." I tried to hide the disappointment in my voice, but when Marcus snapped his head in my direction, I knew I had done a poor job.

He pulled me for a kiss. "I'll be back before you know it," he said, his voice low and his gray eyes flashing with desire. "Don't go anywhere. We need to finish what we started."

Even though his pants were back on, they did nothing to hide his tented front.

"Hurry up," I said, nibbling on his bottom lip. "A husband is supposed to satisfy his wife's needs."

"Oh, this husband is all about satisfying his wife." He planted another kiss. "Be back soon."

I watched him leave, disappointment filling me, even though I knew he would be back. I just didn't know when. I picked up my clothes, went to my bedroom, and pulled on a clean pair of undies, a bra, a large T-shirt, and some gray joggers.

Just when I stepped out of my bedroom, the front cottage door swung open.

"Ah, good. She's here," said Dolores as she marched into the cottage.

"I thought she'd be having sex," chuckled Ruth, coming up behind her.

"By that flush on her face, I'd say she's already had some," said Beverly as she stepped into the cottage, smiling and looking like she would have loved to walk in on us.

I was about to ask them why they didn't knock, but I never knocked when I barged into Davenport House. My face heated at the thought that if Marcus hadn't gotten that phone call and left, this situation would have been extremely awkward.

"What's going on?" I asked as my aunts all gathered around the kitchen island.

"Nancy Farleap is missing," answered my tall aunt.

My chest tightened. That was weird. "Isn't she the werewolf who owns Hairy Dragon Pub?"

"The very same." Dolores's features were tight. "Her husband just called. She never came home from the dinner party."

My mouth fell open. "Okay, *that* is really weird."

"That's not weird," said Beverly, picking at her nails. "I'm sure there's a good explanation. Maybe she has a lover. Elias is a bit of a bore, you know. He likes to *garden*. Ugh. I think this is just him overreacting."

"Maybe she went for a walk? Or mushroom picking," offered Ruth with a smile.

Dolores glared down at her sister. "In the middle of the night?"

Ruth shrugged. "It's the best time to find Mycena mushrooms. They glow in the dark."

"Joe Whitemane's missing too," I blurted before the sisters started arguing about the best way to cultivate mushrooms. "Marcus's gone to look for him."

"That can't be a coincidence," said Dolores, her hands on her hips.

I shook my head, feeling a ribbon of dread wrapping around my middle. "No. It can't. What are the odds of two of our townspeople going missing after attending that dinner party?"

Dolores raised a brow. "Remote."

"What do you suppose happened?" Ruth looked at each of us, her cute face screwed up in worry.

"I'm not sure," I told her. "But I have a feeling it has something to do with Benjamin. That's the one thing these two people have in common. They both attended his party."

"But you said in the car that he wasn't a demon." Beverly stared at me like she wanted me to be wrong about him.

"He's not. But that doesn't mean he didn't have something to do with this."

Beverly wrapped her arms around herself. "Oh… I don't like this. Not one bit."

"Hopefully, it's nothing," I said, though I didn't believe a word. "Like Ruth said, maybe she went out for a midnight stroll. But we better go and look for her. Just in case."

"Right. We'll need to get changed." Dolores made her way to the front door, which had been left open. "Let's go, girls."

I didn't believe for one minute that Nancy went for a walk in the middle of the night alone. The two missing persons were connected. Connected to Benjamin. Though I couldn't prove it. Yet. I'd deal with that later.

First, we needed to find her before something terrible happened to her. And I feared the worst.

CHAPTER

8

"What's taking Ruth so long?" I stood in the front yard of Davenport House, adjusting my bag.

"You know Ruth," commented Dolores. "She might have gotten lost again."

I laughed, though I really shouldn't have. "The sooner we get out there, the better." Because the longer Nancy was missing, the odds of finding her alive grew smaller.

"If Benjamin turns out to be in the clear, I'm dating him." Beverly walked down the stone walkway, her heels tapping the stone. Those tight jeans looked like they'd required a team of experts to pull them up.

"You'd date him?" I'm not sure why I was surprised.

"Why ever not? He's handsome. Rich. Single. And he couldn't take his eyes off of me the entire evening." Beverly giggled. "Did you see the size of his hands? Imagine what they can do to my glorious body."

Dolores gave her sister a disdainful look. "You look ridiculous with those heels and that blouse. We're tracking a missing person, not working every street corner as ladies of the evening."

Beverly gave out a frustrated puff. "This is how I usually dress. There's nothing wrong with wanting to look your best."

Dolores made a sound of disbelief in her throat. "If you want to look like the best prostitute money can buy, I'd say you've accomplished that goal."

I yanked out my phone and quickly texted Marcus.

Me: *Did you find Joe?*

Three dots appeared straight away. Seemed like Marcus had his phone handy.

Marcus: *Not yet.*

Me: *We're off to look for Nancy. I'll let you know if we find anything.*

Marcus. *Okay. Be careful.*

Me: *I will.*

I'd called him right after my aunts all had returned to Davenport House to get changed and told him about Nancy Farleap having also gone missing.

"Ruth!" shouted Dolores. "If you're not down here in the next two minutes, we're leaving without you!"

The front door swung open, and a shape stepped out.

The height and build matched Ruth's, though I couldn't see her clearly in the darkness. But when she stepped into the porch light…

"Oh dear," breathed Beverly. "It would have been better if she'd gotten lost."

A black beanie hat covered her head, concealing most of her wispy white hair. She wore a pair of black pants and a striped black and white top with black gloves covering her hands. And to finish the look, she had a pitch-black eye mask shielding her eyes. She reminded me of the cartoon thieves back in the 1930s and 40s.

"Ruth? What the hell are you wearing? Halloween's not for another two months," growled Dolores.

Ruth climbed down the steps, a proud smile on her face. "I made it myself. I'm a thief," she whispered. "Hildo and Tinky have matching costumes too. But they're still not back from their hunting. We would have been triplets!"

I bit my lip to avoid bursting into laughter, though I knew my expression must have given that away. Ruth always made me smile; she was always the life of the party. I loved my Aunt Ruthy.

Beverly rolled her eyes. "Yes, well, you don't look inconspicuous at all."

Ruth made a face. "Well, if I wanted to be obvious, I'd dress like a slut like you."

Oh dear.

I cleared my throat. "Okay. Let's focus, people. We're supposed to be searching for Nancy." I waited for Ruth to join us and said, "Any ideas where we should begin?"

"We should retrace her steps and go from there," offered Dolores.

That sounded like a plan.

The four of us made our way down Stardust Drive, and after a few minutes, we hit Gallows Hill, arriving at Benjamin's manor.

"The lights are on. He must still be awake." Beverly stood on the tips of her toes, staring at the house like she was contemplating whether she should go to him for a little midnight dessert between the sheets. "If he's in there, that means he had nothing to do with those disappearances. Maybe I should go check, just in case." She started forward.

"No," I warned, making Beverly halt. "We don't want him to know that we're onto him. If he's not involved, we'll know soon enough."

"He might not be in there," said Ruth, yanking down her beanie. "The lights are on, but that doesn't mean he's there."

I stared at her, trying to take her seriously, but it was really hard in that outfit and eye mask.

"See?" Beverly waved a hand at Ruth. "I think we should check."

"Tessa's right," said Dolores. "What would you tell him if he opens the door?"

A wicked smile spread over Beverly's lips. "Oh, don't you worry. There's plenty I could tell him and *show* him."

"We don't have proof that he's involved," I said, though my witchy instincts all said he was, "and we don't even know if anything bad happened to Joe and Nancy. Let's stick to the plan."

Looking disappointed, Beverly spun around and walked back.

"So…" I exhaled, looking down the street and seeing shadows and darkness except for the few streetlights that gave a bit of illumination. "Which direction would she have gone?"

Dolores pointed down Gallows Hill. "That way. It's only a fifteen-minute walk to her house from here."

Dolores started forward. We all lined up behind the tall witch and followed her down the street.

"Look for any clues that could help," I said as I scanned the ground next to the sidewalk. "We're sure she didn't get into a car?"

"I asked her husband," came Dolores's voice from up ahead. "And he said she walked to the manor and would walk back. She's a werewolf. Nothing out here would scare her or challenge her if they didn't want to end up in shredded pieces."

"Right." Which made this all the more eerie and confusing.

"It's too dark to see anything," said Ruth.

Dolores halted, reached into her bag, and muttered a few words under her breath. Then she tossed what looked like a white, glowing globe into the air. Witch light.

The tiny sphere the size of an apple hovered over our heads and cast a blast of illumination enough for us to see through the dark.

I pursed my lips. "Good call."

Dolores straightened. "I know."

I laughed as we continued. Now, with the witch light following us like an oversized fairy, I was able to see the sidewalk clearly as well as a bit of the houses that lined the street. But it did nothing to put a damper the dread that was creeping inside me.

After a five-minute walk and finding nothing, I noticed the houses were sparser until more trees and clumps of forests replaced the houses.

"That's Aurora Park up ahead," indicated Dolores.

From where I was, the line of trees looked ominous and treacherous. I wouldn't even go in there during the day.

"You think she went through there?"

"Yes," said Dolores over her shoulder, "cutting through the park saves her a twenty-minute walk if she went around it. She lives just on the other side of the park."

"I hate that park," said Beverly. "The mosquitoes are enormous. It's like they know my blood is hot, and they can't keep their hands off me."

"They're bugs, you idiot, not men," growled Dolores.

I saw a tiny smile spread over Beverly's face. She loved to pick on her sister.

I tripped over a crack in the sidewalk. Cursing, I looked down and halted.

"Guys… is that… blood?" I stared at a dark maroon stain on the concrete sidewalk.

At that, the three sisters all huddled around me.

Ruth knelt and stuck her finger in it. She lifted it to inspect it, rolling the substance between her fingers.

"If you lick that, I'm going to be sick," said Beverly.

Ruth ignored her sister. "It's blood."

"Look." I pointed to what appeared to be more drops of blood. "There's more. And they're leading all the way down…"

"To the park," finished Dolores.

We all stood in silence for a second, realizing what this could mean.

"If it's Nancy's blood," I said, cutting the silence but not the tension, "then she's in trouble. She needs help." I started forward at a semi-walk run, following the blood like a bloodhound on a trail. At the loud tread behind me, I knew my aunts were right at my heels.

The blood splatter continued, and then the small beads became bigger drops of blood, all leading into the park's entrance.

I hit the park at a run now, the witch light hovering a few paces ahead of me. Thank the cauldron since without it, I'd have smacked my face right into a tree right about now.

The sidewalk disappeared, and I was running on a gravel path, trees flanking me on either side. The wind hitting my face and lifting my hair was chill, carrying the scent of wet earth, decomposing leaves, and growing things. I could still see the blood. And it was still leading us deeper into the park.

"It doesn't mean this is her blood," I heard Beverly say behind me. "Could just be an injured animal."

"Maybe." I panted. "But let's find it to make sure." My witchy instincts told me this was too much blood for a tiny animal. We didn't have large wild animals in Hollow Cove. The largest were the red foxes, and even then, that was too much blood for such a small animal.

The forest grew denser around the path. The blood trail stopped suddenly, and I halted.

"Wait," I said, spreading out my arms like a baseball umpire. "I can't see the blood anymore." I got lower to the ground, looking, but the blood trail just ended.

"There!" Ruth pointed to the left of the path. "There's blood on the leaves here. And there." She stepped into the cramped forest. "It keeps going this way."

And we were off again, wafting through shrubs and branches as we followed Ruth. I didn't know how she spotted the blood in the darkness, even with the witch light. That was incredible, and I didn't care. I was glad she was with us.

The pine and fir forest pressed close on either side as I ran down the dirt-packed trail, which really wasn't a real trail but more of a break in the forest tree line.

Panting, I leaped over a tree trunk and kept running. I wasn't a werewolf or a wereape, but I still enjoyed the freedom and the high of a run. Who am I kidding? It was more of a wabble-halt-stumble kind of run.

My thighs burned with every step, and my feet throbbed from the blisters forming inside my shoes.

"My heels aren't made for running long distances." Beverly panted from somewhere behind me. "They're made to look sexy. I have very desirable feet."

"You should have thought of that before you put them on," Dolores snapped back.

Beverly mumbled something in reply, but I couldn't hear it over the thrashing of my heartbeat in my ears and the crushing of dry leaves under my feet.

Ruth halted suddenly, and I would have nearly crashed into her if I hadn't been paying attention at the very last moment.

I stumbled past her. "What? What is it?" I didn't have to look much farther. The witch light hovered over it, giving us all a very good view.

A body lay just fifteen feet from us, eight arrows perforating from its back.

And the head was missing.

"Cauldron, help us," hissed Beverly, coming around to stand next to Ruth. "Is it…"

"Those are the clothes she was wearing," said Ruth, her face twisting like she was going to be sick.

I understood the feeling. Not every day do you get to see a decapitated body.

"It's her." Dolores braved a step forward and stopped. "Ruth's right. I recognize her clothes. She was wearing that pretty fuchsia top. It's Nancy."

Following Dolores's example, I moved forward until I stood beside the body. A large amount of blood pooled next to the stump where her head would have been. It told me that whoever did this had cut it off here and… taken it? But somehow, the arrows made me feel worse.

"She fought hard." Bile rose in the back of my throat. "She tried to escape. She was tough and strong if she could run away with eight arrows sticking out of her back." I didn't think I could run with only one arrow. She had eight.

"Why didn't she shift?" asked Beverly. "She could have defended herself."

"She couldn't," answered Dolores. "Not with so many arrows. Don't think she didn't try. I'm sure she did. But she was shot in the back. Probably never saw her assailant until it was too late."

"How horrible," whimpered Ruth. "She was my friend." Ruth sniffed as she pulled off her eye mask and tossed it to the ground.

"This is sick. Deranged." Dolores's voice was loud in the forest's silence. "They killed her and then took her head? Who would do such a thing?"

I had to agree with her. This was sick and twisted.

"Why arrows?" Beverly stood away from the body, staring at it like she was afraid it would suddenly jump up and come alive. "Why not just kill her and be done with it?"

Good question. At that moment, my phone buzzed with a text message.

Marcus: *Found Joe Whitemane. He's been killed.*

An image popped up below his text. I tapped it so the image filled the screen of my phone.

Oh shit.

"Uh, guys," I said, looking up and meeting their gazes. "They found Joe. He's been killed. And in the exact same way as Nancy."

"What? Give me that." Dolores grabbed my phone from me. "Cauldron, save us. I can't believe it. What is happening in our town?"

Ruth let out a whimper as she kneeled next to her dead friend. My heart ached for my beloved Aunt Ruthy. I was overcome with anguish and rage at whoever had done this terrible deed.

"I'll tell you what is happening. Benjamin," I said. "He did this."

"But what proof do you have?" Dolores handed me back my phone. "Apart from the fact that these deaths coincided with his moving here. Nothing indicates he did this."

Beverly sighed loudly. "We'll have to wait for the forensics team to go through the crime scene. Maybe something will turn up."

Our forensics team was just Marcus's deputies who had additional training in scientific techniques to examine evidence.

"I doubt Benjamin would be stupid enough to leave his DNA here," I said, staring at Ruth as she wiped her eyes. Her lips moved as she said a prayer for her dead friend. "No. He's smart."

"Then how?" asked Dolores, the question high in her expression.

"I'll prove it." I clenched my jaw. "I know he's involved. Something's off about the guy. Demon or not, he's vile. He invited us to his home for a reason. I don't know what that is yet, but I am going to figure it out. I'll prove he's responsible."

"But how?" Beverly was yanking a twig out from the front of her shoe.

"Easy," I said as a plan formulated in my brain. "The proof is in that locked room. I know it."

"And how, exactly, are you going to search it?" asked Dolores. "Are you going to ask him nicely and hope he'll let you in?"

"Of course not. I'm going to break in. I'm going to break into that room and get us the proof we need to stop this bastard."

Because if we didn't, I had a feeling this was only the beginning.

CHAPTER

9

I paced in Davenport House's kitchen early the next morning, a cup of coffee in my hands and my mind contemplating my plan. I barely slept a wink. I dozed off for a few minutes, dreaming of dozens of *my* severed heads floating in the air, only to wake up in a panic, my hands going to my neck.

Said plan was to break into Benjamin Morgan's manor and somehow get through that door on the third floor. I knew it wouldn't be easy, but no matter what, even if I had to break it down, I was getting through that room.

"Sit. You're giving me a migraine with all your pacing," ordered Dolores, watching me over her reading glasses. Her glasses did nothing to hide the bags under her eyes. Guess she didn't get much sleep, either. None of us did after finding a member of our little town beheaded and discarded like her life meant nothing.

And now, with Marcus's confirmation, there were two. Two victims. Both had died with arrows in them, and both were missing their heads.

Damn.

I didn't get the head part. It was disturbing. The only plausible reason was that the heads were taken as trophies. Sick, yes. But plausible.

I sighed, pulled out a chair next to the kitchen table, and sat beside Dolores. The tall witch had been immersed in one of her large tomes since I came in this morning and told her about my plan.

I motioned to the book. "And you'll find me the spell that'll break the ward? I'll be able to get inside that door?"

Dolores made a sound in her throat and pulled her eyes away from the tome. "It'll get you through the front door, yes. But you'll need Ruth's help to get into that bedroom. Different spells for different doors. You know the drill."

"Right." I glanced toward the potions room where Ruth was concocting a potion to help me get past the bedroom wards. I had no idea what to expect, but Tinky warned me that the wards were powerful, dark, and different from the front door wards we encountered when we visited the manor yesterday morning.

I wanted to ask her more about the bedroom door. But when I spotted Hildo curled up in a ball in one of the armchairs in the living room, I figured Tinky was still sleeping.

Dolores grabbed a piece of paper and started to copy words down. "You're still convinced Benjamin is responsible for those deaths?"

"I am." I was ninety-nine percent sure. The way he crushed my hand last night was almost like he was challenging me, wanting to see if I'd figure it out. "Aren't you? He moves here, and the very next night, two people are found dead. It's a hell of a coincidence."

And he was the arrogant type. He wasn't even hiding. Like he wanted us to know. The previous night's events were swirling around my head like a maelstrom, threatening the coffee I'd drunk to come right back up.

"Well, we need proof before we convict the man of such horrible crimes. It still might not be him, though I'm starting to see it your way."

I yawned and rubbed my eyes. "Don't worry. I'm going to get you that proof."

"How's Marcus doing? Did he inform the families?" asked Dolores as she kept scribbling. "I hate that part of the job. And I'm glad we don't have to do it this time."

My heart gave a tug when I thought about how excruciating it must be for him to tell the families that their loved ones were dead. Not just that but *how* they died.

I drummed my fingers over my hot mug. "He did. He's been out all night. He came in for a quick shower this morning and went straight back out."

For some strange reason, which I believed had to do with his wereape blood, the chief didn't look like he'd been up all night, like us witches. He looked rested and fine. You wouldn't have guessed anything was wrong if not for the dark storms brewing in his eyes and the clenching and unclenching of his fists.

As the chief of our town, part of his job was to keep the residents safe, as it was for us Merlins. I knew he was taking it hard.

"Any DNA from the bodies yet?" I'd asked him as he pulled on a clean pair of jeans back at our cottage this morning.

Marcus's wet hair clung to his forehead. "Still waiting. I've asked to put a rush on it. I should have something this afternoon." Worry etched his handsome face, and part of me wanted to kiss it better. Hell, I'd have kissed him everywhere if he hadn't had to leave in such a rush.

"Be careful," I told him instead as he headed toward the front door.

The chief turned around. "They won't attack during the day."

I stared at him, surprised. "They won't? How can you be so sure? And you think it's a *they*? You think there's more of them? Not just Benjamin?" I hadn't thought about that. I was so convinced that the stranger had done it that it never occurred to me he might have had help.

"It might not be him," said Marcus. "I know you dislike him, but don't let that cloud your judgment. This could be something else. An attack from another group. Once we gather all the evidence, we'll know."

I frowned. "What group?"

"I know these types. I know how they think. How they operate." Marcus's gray eyes met mine, and I could see the echoes of some distant memory there.

"Have you seen this before?"

The chief looked away momentarily like he was sorting out what he wanted to say. "I've heard rumors of similar killings, but I don't want to say anything before I can confirm it."

"Did the lab give a time of death?"

"The deaths occurred roughly about a half hour apart from what the lab was able to tell me."

"Which gave Benjamin plenty of time to do both. It's not a very big town. And you said you found Joe behind The Siren's Song music store. That's not that far from Aurora Park."

"Maybe," answered the chief. "But it's more likely that this was orchestrated by more than one person."

I'd watched the chief go, leaving me standing in the doorway with more questions and uncertainty.

A loud boom resonated from the potions room, shaking me out of my thoughts. The walls shook, and the toaster quivered like a message card had popped out but didn't.

Ruth came sliding into the kitchen like a pro curler. Her white hair was smoking like it had been on fire moments before.

"No worries. Everything's under control," she said, her face smeared with soot and some orange paste.

"You need any help?" I offered, not that I knew much about potion making, but she was doing this for me. I might as well help if I could.

Ruth pointed at me, and that's when I noticed the pink kitchen gloves over her hands. "No. You just sit there. It's almost ready." And with that, she rushed out and disappeared back into her potions room.

Dolores shook her head. "One of these days, she'll burn down the house."

I snorted. The house was magical. I doubted Ruth could burn it down, though it had been destroyed by fire once, by that horrid group of Dark wizards, and then had been magically restored by Lilith. But I had confidence in Ruth. She knew what she was doing.

"Girls!"

Dolores and I turned at the sound of Beverly's voice.

"Holy shit," I said as my Aunt Beverly waltzed into the kitchen, and I had to do a double take. Not because she walked into the kitchen but because of what she was wearing—or rather—what she was *not* wearing.

Beverly stepped into the kitchen wearing gold heels and a string gold, bejeweled bikini. The tiny triangles hid her nipples, her Lady V, and a bit of her butt. I'd never seen so much of my aunt's skin before. It was uncomfortable, but it was hard not to stare. She looked incredible.

Even though I was younger than my aunt, I'd never wear something so revealing and exposing. But Beverly's body was incredibly fit. Nothing bounced or flapped when she stopped walking. Everything was perky and in the right places. Go, Bev.

"How do I look?" asked Beverly.

"Like a Vegas slut," snapped Dolores, giving her sister a disapproving glare.

I spat some of my coffee and wiped my mouth with my hand.

"Why thank you, Dolores," she said, grinning from ear to ear. "I'm feeling fabulous today. And I wear my fabulousness as a shield. Your words mean nothing."

Dolores flicked a finger in Beverly's direction. "Why not just go naked. Not like it would make much of a difference."

Beverly put a hand on her hip. "I would, but the judges said it wouldn't be appropriate."

I burst out laughing. I couldn't help but smile along with her infectious energy. My aunt had always been a free spirit, but seeing her so carefree and happy was a sight to behold. "Well, you certainly look fantastic," I said, admiring her toned figure. "You look great. Seriously."

"Thank you, darling." Beverly twirled around, showing off her teeny-weeny bikini. "I've been hitting the gym lately," she said, striking a pose. "Gotta keep this body in working shape, if you know what I mean." She winked. "So you think this is good enough for the pageant swimwear?"

"That's not swimwear. That's a string," said Dolores.

Beverly giggled and did another practice twirl.

I leaned forward. "Wait. The pageant's still on? I would have thought Gilbert would put a stop to it after the murders. Does he not know?"

"Of course, the pageant's still on," said Beverly, losing a bit of her smile. "I've been waiting a year for this. I won't let a few murders stop me from getting my crown."

At the mention of a crown, I couldn't help but think of when Beverly had crossed over to

Storybook and had become the Queen of Hearts. If I looked closely enough, I could still see a little bit of that fierce queen in her.

"He knows." Dolores pulled off her glasses and rubbed the bridge of her nose. "He doesn't want to scare the town. We don't want a panic on our hands. So pageants and other festivals are to continue."

I frowned. "But is that wise when we know two people are dead and there might be more? This isn't going to stop." Not when this psycho saw how easy it was to kill two of us. I was sure he was going to do it again. And according to Marcus, that when was tonight.

I looked at Dolores, waiting for her response. She rubbed her chin and adjusted her glasses before replying. "I understand your concern, but we can't let fear control us. We have to continue living our lives. Otherwise, the killer wins. Don't you see?"

I shook my head. "No. Not really." But I had to agree with her about not alerting the town just yet. I didn't want a panic on our hands; people did stupid things when they panicked and always got hurt. Plus, I didn't want Benjamin to know that we—that I—was onto him just yet. I needed to get into that room first.

Beverly nodded and smiled again, her excitement for the pageant returning. "Tessa, darling. Nothing will happen. And besides, we have security measures in place. Marcus and his team will be there, and I'll make sure to have extra security at the pageant. We'll be safe."

Only two days were left before the pageant. And two days was an enormous amount of time for Benjamin to do more harm in our town.

I couldn't argue with their logic, though, and felt myself starting to relax. Maybe they were right. I couldn't let fear control me. I had to be smart.

"Here you go!" Ruth came rushing into the kitchen, her bare feet slapping on the hardwood floors. Her white hair was still smoking, but now so was her blouse, which was black, but I swore it had been light blue moments ago. She handed me a small jar.

I took the jar. "What's this?"

Ruth wiped her nose, leaving a streak of black across her face. "You need to sprinkle some at the foot of the door and say this spell," she added, reaching inside her skirt pocket to retrieve a folded piece of paper.

I unscrewed the lid of the jar and stared at the orange, glittering powder-like substance. "And this will open that bedroom door?" I screwed back the top and took the paper from her.

Ruth beamed. "It will. Oh—but make sure you stand back while saying the spell. You don't want to be caught in the blast."

I swallowed. "Right. What would happen if I did?"

Ruth gestured with her hands and said, "Poof."

All right then. Good to know.

With Dolores's ward-breaking spell and Ruth's magical power, I was feeling more and more confident by the minute. I was going to stop Benjamin before tonight. He wasn't going to kill or hurt anyone anymore under my watch.

The bastard was mine.

"I'm hungry," said Ruth, looking around the kitchen, and that's when I spotted a rather large bald spot at the back of her head. "I think I'll make—oh. What are you supposed to be?" It seemed Ruth had just spotted her sister in her barely there bikini.

"A wanton slut," said Dolores.

Beverly laughed, not bothered at all by being called a slut yet again. "It's the bikini I'm wearing for the pageant. Don't I look fabulous?"

Ruth made wide eyes. "Oh. I get it. Why don't you just go naked?"

Dolores snorted. "That's what I said."

I laughed. I was so happy to have such a wacky family. It was never boring at Davenport House, and I loved it.

Suddenly, the toaster rattled, and a message card flew out. Dolores snatched it up before I had time to blink.

I sucked in a breath as I watched her eyes move along the card, her lips parting in what I could only describe was sudden shock.

"What? What is it?" I stood up, not liking the worry that crept over Dolores's features.

My tall aunt looked at me and then at her sisters. "Brian Halfclaw is missing. So is Percival Kingsley and Boris Bravebird."

Ruth let out a muffled cry and covered her mouth with her hands.

"Oh, no," said Beverly, losing all of her glamour and amusement in one instant.

Dread filled my gut until I thought I might be sick. I didn't know them well, but they were all alive last night at Benjamin's dinner party. But now I feared the worst. "Let me guess. They never came home from the party?"

Dolores's face paled as she lowered the card. "No. They never did."

"We should go look for them," said Ruth, her eyes brimming with tears. "They might still be alive. They might need our help."

"Ruth's right." Beverly stared down at herself. "I'll go and change. I'll be too much of a distraction in this." She caught me staring and winked.

"Wait." Dolores looked at her sister. "We're supposed to be helping Tessa. Getting into that house is important. In any event, it'll prove Ben's innocence or guilt."

I set my empty coffee mug down. "No. Ruth's right. You three go. Iris and Ronin will come with me to the manor."

I hadn't told Marcus about my plan to go to the manor this morning. I'd barely had a chance to talk to him as he'd rushed home to shower. I could text him, but I didn't want to add to his mounting stress. And now, with three more missing townspeople, Marcus would lose it.

Guess Beverly's pageant would be canceled when Gilbert got word of more missing people. I wanted to believe my aunts would find them alive, but I knew that wasn't the case.

"Do me a favor and call Marcus," I told them. "Tell him about the missing people."

"We will. Here." Dolores handed me the piece of paper with the spell she was working on. "That should break the ward at the front door. The rest is up to you."

I took the piece of paper and stuffed it in along with Ruth's. "Thanks."

"And Tessa…" said Dolores, the warning in her voice giving me pause.

"Yes? What is it?"

"Be on your guard. We still don't know what Benjamin is. He's not a demon. We know that now, but the fact that he hasn't disclosed his paranormal race doesn't sit well with me. He doesn't want us to know, and that can't be good."

"No it can't." I looked at my aunts, seeing the fear and worry on their faces. "We'll get to the bottom of this. I promise. When you see me again, I'll have your answers." I turned around and walked out the kitchen's back door.

It was a bold statement, and I knew it. But now, with three more people missing and presumably dead, I felt an urgent duty to uncover Benjamin's secrets.

I *was* going to discover them.

And sometimes we have to be careful what we wish for.

CHAPTER
10

I stood on the front porch of the Crane family manor, which now belonged to Benjamin Morgan. No landscape workers were around this time as far as I could tell.

The front door gave off the same cold pulsing of energy. And if you looked closely enough, you could see the complex network of multicolored runes and sigils marked over the door's frame. Wards. The wards that kept intruders away for fear of being infused with great amounts of pain.

I wasn't afraid. Hell, I was pissed. Yet I was nervous. Anxious about what I would find. What if I was wrong? What if Benjamin had nothing to do with these murders? I'd been so sure that it was Benjamin, but now that Marcus had mentioned some group that could be responsible, something that he'd heard about or even been involved with, there was a chance I'd been wrong this whole time.

"What if he's home? Then what?" Iris stood next to me, her dark hair pulled back in cute pigtails that made her look like a teen girl.

"I'm going to make him answer my questions," I said, glaring at the door. "I don't think he is. No cars are in the driveway, though, and he wouldn't have set up this ward if he was inside."

"True." Iris looked over her shoulder. "Ronin!" she hissed. "What are you doing?"

I turned and saw the half-vampire standing in the front flowerbeds, inspecting the window ledge.

"Just admiring the details." His face was hard, and I knew he was still very upset about losing out on the manor. Now that I knew he'd planned to buy it for Iris and him, I understood his frustration. I would much rather have Ronin and Iris be the owners of this old manor than some stranger.

Iris moved toward the door, her nose an inch from the doorframe as she inspected the runes and sigils. She raised her hands and closed her eyes for a moment. "This is your usual trespassing ward." She opened her eyes. "We can't get through unless we want to end up like fried chicken."

"It reminds me of the time my friend Claude was chased by his harem of witches," said the half-vampire as he climbed up the porch. "They tied him up to a stake and danced as he burned. Poor bastard."

"I've come prepared," I told Iris. "If anyone can break this ward, it's Dolores's uber ward-breaking spells."

"True." Iris stepped back to give me space, holding on to her bag, which I assumed had her precious Dana and DNA collectibles she never left home without.

"Let's do this." I let out a nervous breath, pulled out the piece of paper with what I recognized as Dolores's handwriting, and made sure I didn't use Ruth's by mistake. Anger and nerves finding their release, I tapped into my will and the elements around me, pulling on the energy and holding it until I had a large enough amount to break the wards, hopefully. Then I said the incantation.

"Door unlock, no magic block. All I have to do is knock."

Magic coursed through my body as the spell's energy spilled over me, humming as a tingle ran from my fingertips to my middle. But I felt no pain, no burning. I felt it gather around me, and with a sudden push, it hit the door.

The runes and sigils over the door's frame glowed a bright red. And then their luminescence diminished until they faded into a dull black.

"Guess I didn't have to knock. Thank you, Dolores."

"I'll have to ask Dolores if I can borrow that spell," said Iris, clearly in awe of my aunt's high-level magic. Yup. She was awesome in that department.

Still feeling the tickling effects of the spell, I took a deep breath, grabbed the door handle, and pushed open the door.

I went in first in case some of the wards were left. I didn't want my friends to get fried, but as soon as I crossed the threshold and stepped into the foyer, I was still alive and still in one piece.

"Ben!" howled Ronin, making Iris and me jump.

I punched him on the arm. "Why the hell did you do that?"

The half-vampire shrugged. "Just checking to see if he's here. What?"

I sighed and looked around, my heart still thrashing like I'd just jogged around town for fun. Yeah, like that would ever happen. "He's not here. The place feels deserted."

"Smells deserted, too," added Ronin. "I'm not getting any odors that people are here. Just the usual smell of floor polish and cleaning products."

I screwed up my face. "You can smell if people are here?" Of course, with his vampire side, I knew he had sensitivity to certain things that we witches had not. Not sure smelling bodily odor was something I envied.

"I can." Ronin glanced around the foyer. "Right now, it's just us."

I walked into the hallway, seeing it in daylight for the first time. It was cozier than last night, and with all the natural light, it was quite beautiful. "I'm not getting the impression that he sleeps here."

"So, where does he sleep?" asked Iris.

"Not here." I just didn't know where. Another red flag rose to the surface.

"I don't get it," said the Dark witch. "Why go through all the trouble of buying this house and fixing it up if you're not going to sleep in it?"

Good question. "That's what we're going to find out."

"What a waste." Ronin was shaking his head. "I'd sleep here. And I'd sleep here with you, baby," he purred, making Iris blush. "Imagine all the places we could *sleep* in?"

Iris slapped him on the shoulder. "Be serious."

His eyes danced with desire. "Oh, I'm *very* serious."

I snorted. "Okay, you love birds. Let's see what's inside that room." I walked over to the grand staircase and started climbing, Ronin and Iris behind me.

"Did you hear that?" came Iris's voice behind me.

My leg muscles locked, and I was rooted in place. "What did you hear?" I whispered to her, looking over my shoulder at her.

"Did you hear something?" asked Ronin.

Iris shook her head. "That's just it. I don't hear or feel or smell anything. Not like the last time we were here when you disappeared through that portal. I didn't sense them last night either, but there were too many guests and people to get a reading. But now I'm sure. There're no more ghosts. He got rid of them."

"He did some sort of exorcism?" Ronin glanced around the staircase as if expecting to see a ghost or a spirit.

The Dark witch nodded. "Probably. But not an exorcism. It's a spirit-removal ritual. A spiritual cleansing. A complex weave of spells. Only a very skilled and knowledgeable witch could remove the resident ghosts that were here."

Ronin flashed Iris his pearly whites. "Like a modern ghostbuster."

"I guess, yes," answered Iris.

"Man, I get so turned on when you speak witch geek," said Ronin, reaching out and pulling her closer. "The things I could do to you right now."

I rolled my eyes and continued to climb the staircase. "Only you could get horny at a time like this."

"It's always time to get horny, Tess," said the half-vampire, a smile in his voice.

We reached the second landing after a few moments. It was strange to see it so alight. Windows across from the staircase let in bounds of natural light, bouncing off the white walls with the occasional artwork. It truly was a glorious house.

The landing branched out into two long hallways broken up by several doors.

"Which way?" asked Iris, stepping next to me.

I pointed to the right. "Tinky and Hildo said the doors they couldn't open were off to the right of the staircase. The only set of double doors on this floor."

The hallway opened up into a spacious room. Large doorways hinted at equally spacious rooms down the corridor.

One, two, I counted the doors as I marched down the hallway. When we reached the double doors, I halted.

Like the exterior front door to the manor, I could see the runes or sigils. An intricate lattice of glowing, green-and-red runes and sigils covered every inch of the door's frame. Energy rippled through and around the door, pulsing around us in great heaps of waves. I felt the pulsing of the wards rubbing against my face like static electricity. Yeah, these were much more powerful.

"Whoa." Iris took a step forward and raised her palms to the door, closing her eyes as she tapped into her witchy senses. "There is really strong energy here… the most powerful wards. I'm not surprised Tinkerbell and Hildo couldn't get through."

"Like the motherlode of wards," I said.

"Exactly."

"Then how do we get in?" Ronin angled his body like he was ready to kick down the door. "Can we break down the door?"

"If you touch it, it'll kill you."

Ronin stepped back. "It's all yours."

I pulled out Ruth's spell and the jar of that orange powder.

The half-vampire leaned over my shoulder. "What's that?"

"Explosive magical powder." I didn't know what else to call it, and Ruth had said to stand back after sprinkling the stuff.

Ronin grinned. "Nice."

Iris was leaning over my other shoulder. If I didn't know any better, it looked like she wanted to grab some of the powder for herself. I'm sure she did.

My heart sped up. There was only one problem. Ruth didn't specify how much of the stuff

I was to use. Damnit. I should have asked for more details.

"What is it? What's wrong?" Iris's shoulder bumped into mine.

I shook my head. "I don't know how much I'm supposed to use. I mean, if I don't put enough, it might not work, and I don't know if I can repeat the spell. I don't think I can."

"And if you put too much?" Iris questioned, her voice high with tension and nerves.

I looked at my friends. "Boom?"

Ronin laughed. "Just call her. She'll tell you."

"Right." I put the jar and the paper on the floor, grabbed my phone, and called my aunts. But after the fifth ring, it went to the machine. I hung up. "They're not home. They're out looking for the three missing people. And before you ask, no, they don't have cell phones." I let out a frustrated breath. "Looks like we're going to have to wing it."

Slipping my phone back in my bag, I set it next to the hallway, beside door number four. Then I stuffed the paper in my mouth and grabbed the jar of explosive magical powder.

"So? How much are you going to put?" asked Ronin. "The suspense is killing me."

I thought about it for a moment. "All of it," I said, around the paper clamped on my teeth.

The half-vampire rubbed his hands together. "Excellent. I love blowing up stuff."

I'd never known he did, but then again, he was male.

"You sure?" Iris looked at me, her pretty face twisted in worry.

"No. But we can't afford to mess it up. Better put too much than not enough." Because I needed to stop Benjamin, like yesterday. I waved my free hand at them. "Stand back."

"We got you, boss," said Ronin, pulling away his girlfriend with him and moving to stand next to my bag on the floor.

"All right then." I stepped forward and faced the doors. My pulse was rocketing, and I could feel sweat breaking all over my body. This was my chance. I couldn't mess it up. Not now.

Resolute, I knelt, unscrewed the lid, and poured the entire contents of Ruth's powder on the floor at the base of the doors. I wiggled my nose at the strong, bleach smell. What the hell was in this stuff? I set the jar aside and moved back, standing just a foot from my friends.

"After this, he'll know someone's been inside," said Iris, and I saw Ronin yanking her behind him. So very gallant he was.

"I know," I told her, unfolding Ruth's spell and recognizing her squiggly handwriting. "But it's too late to change my mind. Let him know. Maybe it's better that way. Maybe it'll stop him."

"But what if it's *not* him," said Iris, and Marcus's words flashed back into my head.

"We're about to find out." I swallowed hard, readying myself mentally and physically for the spell. Knowing Ruth and what I heard from the potion's room back at Davenport House, it was about to go *boom*.

I willed the power of the elements around me again, felt the tug of power, and released it as I read the spell. "Wards be gone, wards no further, hear me now and blow away this sucker."

The first thing that happened was that I smiled after reading the spell. Only Ruth would come up with something like that.

And then the explosion happened.

A blazing, orange light exploded around me, blinding me for about a second. And then, a sonic boom blasted throughout the hallway, making me jump. The light subsided, and I blinked rapidly, trying to rid my vision of the orange spots.

The power of the blast had knocked me from my feet, sending me sailing back into the hallway along with Ronin and Iris. I went hurling back violently to the ground, hit by an invisible force. I slammed on the hard floor and rolled to a stop next to the staircase railing.

"Did it work—"

A ripple of energy washed through me as orange light swept down the hallway. The rush of blinding and wild light went through my head to my toes. My eyes swam with color as my ears rang from the explosion, and the smell of burnt hair reached me.

I heard a horrible, wrenching sound, a shriek of protesting metal, and then a thundering blast as something heavy slammed into the floor, vibrating beneath me.

I tried to stand, but the world shifted, so I sat on my butt, waiting for the room to stop spinning.

"You guys okay?" I looked over to Ronin and Iris, both with their hair and clothes disheveled like they'd driven around in a convertible with the top off, but otherwise they looked unscathed.

"Oh, no, Tessa," cried Iris. "Your eyebrows!"

"Huh?" I reached up. Sure enough. I was as bald as an egg when it came to eyebrows. "Shit. That's not good."

Iris stood up. "I have a great eyebrow pencil you can use to draw them in until Ruth can use her hair regrowth ointment."

Having no eyebrows was the least of my problems. Finally, I managed to reach to my feet without falling on my face and walked back down the hallway to the double doors. Only there were no more doors.

"Whoops." Guess I'd used too much of Ruth's magical powder. But at least now we could get inside.

Ronin stood next to me and held out his hand. "Ladies first. Or are you a lady without your eyebrows?"

I growled at him, making him laugh more, and stepped through.

Tinky was right. It was a master bedroom or something similar.

The bedroom was the size of Davenport House's first floor and large enough to get lost on your way to the bathroom in the middle of the night.

The furniture was the same as the rest of the house, the original pieces I imagined. In the middle of the room rested a bed that could have fit the three of us comfortably.

A grizzly bear's head was mounted over the bed's headboard. I flicked my gaze around. Two more heads, one a tiger and the other a wolf, were mounted across the room.

Anger rushed through me as I strolled into the room and went straight to the large mahogany desk. A dozen frames sat on the top. Not of Benjamin's family. But of him and other men with hunting rifles and the cliché picture of him standing over the body of a dead lion.

My insides twisted. Motherfracker. I hated this guy.

My gaze glanced over to the other series of frames. Pictures of Benjamin in military uniform and gear standing before a unit of soldiers.

Human military.

"He's human," I said, the words feeling strange coming out of my mouth, but once they were out, it all made sense. It started to click. "The bastard's human."

"He's human?" Iris grabbed one of the frames. "So, he's been pretending to be one of us? Why? That doesn't make sense. And how did he find Hollow Cove? I thought your aunts said it was protected and hidden from humans with glamours and spells."

"I think he knows of places like ours," I said as Marcus's words came back to me. "I think he's done this before and has friends or spies in our communities." I would bet my life on that.

"But that still doesn't prove he killed those people in our town," said Iris.

"Guys," came Ronin's voice. "Look at this."

I turned to the sound of his voice and saw him standing at the other end of the room next to a target dummy I hadn't noticed when I rushed into the room. A series of arrows perforated its hide.

Ronin wrapped his arm over the dummy's shoulder with a goofy grin. "If that's not your proof, I don't know what is."

I rushed over. "I'm no expert, but these look like the same arrows." If we had his bow or crossbow, that would be even better, but I couldn't see it anywhere. Maybe he kept his weapons with him or in his car.

"He must really hate us," said Iris. "A human who hates the paranormal. You don't hear of that too often. But I've heard stories. It's usually because they're jealous."

"If he's human," said Ronin, moving away from the dummy. "It means he paid a witch to do all the wards and shit."

"Yes, probably." I felt sick staring at the dummy, the images of Nancy's beheaded body coming back to me in spades, but it didn't explain why he was doing this. Why did he want to kill us? And why only a certain group?

"Hey. Look at this." Ronin stood next to a tall, wooden cabinet a few heads taller than the half-vampire.

"It's locked," said the half-vampire. "You want me to open it?"

"Yes," Iris and I chorused.

"As you wish, my ladies." With a soft click and using his vampire strength, Ronin yanked open the cabinet door, the lock hitting the floor at his feet with a clang.

I rushed over, not knowing what to expect but not expecting what lay before me.

Skulls.

Human and animal skulls sat on every shelf, nestled on satin cloth like expensive jewelry you'd see on display at Tiffany's. There must have been at least fifty.

"Yeah. Okay. The dude's eccentric, I'll give him that." Ronin reached out and grabbed one of the human skulls. "He's a freak. But aren't we all?"

Iris reached out and grabbed what looked like a feline skull, like a cougar's or maybe a leopard. She raised it to her nose and took a sniff.

"They've been boiled and cleaned. And there's a substance on it that I can't identify. Maybe some sort of preserver. I don't know." My lips parted as she dropped the skull in her bag and reached for another.

"Uh… right." I looked away and glanced at the human skulls, an eerie feeling waking up in my middle. There was something here. Something I was missing. "Human skulls, animal skulls…"

"It's obvious he's some kind of exotic hunter," said Ronin as he picked up what looked like the skull of a great bird. "He's probably been all over the world. Hunting wild animals."

"But why is he here?" Iris had her hand over the skulls, her fingers twitching like she was trying to decide which one to grab next. "There's no game here. Apart from some deer."

My eyes fell on a certain skull that had my knees shake. And then bile rose in the back of my throat as my heart pounded in my ears.

I reached out and grabbed said skull. The skull of what I could only guess was a gorilla.

A wereape.

I held the gorilla skull in my hand, its weight heavier than it should have been and said, "Because he's hunting *us*."

CHAPTER

11

I didn't feel any better after Marcus and his deputies showed up ten minutes later. The idea that a human man had infiltrated our town, our community, so that he might hunt us for sport had me on edge and my temper loose like one of those wild animals he'd killed. I felt crazy mad. And I wasn't sure I could control myself the next time I saw Benjamin.

Part of me wanted Benjamin to show up so I might grab him, jump a ley line, and drop him in the middle of the Atlantic Ocean to see if he could float. Or better yet, let the sharks get him. Good visual.

But the bastard hadn't shown up yet.

Marcus had been really quiet after he'd arrived at the manor. His shoulders were steely with tension. Rage, fury, and a number of emotions I couldn't read sparkled in those gray eyes as he stared at the two wereape skulls in his hands. Yup, there were more. His posture shifted, and the muscles on his shoulders and neck bulged. His stare became vicious and primal, and cold licked up my spine.

He oozed ferocious power and strength. This was the reason the town had chosen him as their chief. He was also their alpha because Marcus was the strongest, the fiercest of them all.

I also knew this situation was affecting him deeply. As the town's chief, he was responsible for keeping the inhabitants safe. And now two were dead with three still missing. It didn't look good.

"Marcus. Here's the arrow from the evidence you wanted."

I turned to see Lori, a tall, no-nonsense werebear female who had all the vibes of a human city cop. Her chiseled cheeks and chin were as sharp as her tone. Her brown hair was pulled back in a braid that hit her waist. She'd been hired a few weeks after Scarlett's disappearance into Storybook.

Lori walked into the bedroom holding a transparent plastic bag with what I presumed was said arrow.

Marcus laid the skulls back on the shelf and took the bag. I watched as he moved over to the target dummy and yanked out the arrow from the bag. He pulled out one of the arrows in the dummy's chest and compared them.

"So? Are they a match?" I'm not sure why I asked. My witchy instincts told me they were.

The chief said nothing for a while, his chest rising and falling as he studied the arrows. "Yes."

"I could have told you that," said Ronin, sitting on the edge of the bed. "This asshole is hunting us. A freaking human special ops or some crap like that. Can you believe this?"

The fact that Benjamin was a human was still a bit of a shock. But it explained why he hadn't commented on Tinky at his dinner party. Because he *couldn't* see her. Not without some magical help, which I believed he had in spades.

"Bag this up," Marcus told Lori as he handed her the two arrows.

"Yes, boss," she said, taking the arrows and pulling out the others in the dummy's chest.

Two more of Marcus's deputies, whom I'd never seen before, were busy putting the skulls into bags and labeling them. Iris was standing next to Ronin, looking innocent and not at all like a thief. Her bag was full and heavy with the skulls she'd stuffed inside, but I wasn't about to tell on her. Besides, she'd get more use out of them than leaving them to collect dust locked away in some evidence room.

The chief walked over to me. "What happened to your eyebrows?" Marcus inspected my face, seemingly only now having noticed.

I reached up and touched the bare skin where my eyebrows should have been. "They fried when I busted down the door." I probably should have put a bit less of Ruth's go-boom powder. Too late now. "So?" I exhaled. "How do we catch this bastard? I doubt he'll be back here, not with all of us inside now." I had the strange feeling either he or some of his friends were keeping eyes on the manor.

Marcus's muscles popped along his shoulders and neck, his jaw clenching. "I've stationed some guards at the foot of the Hollow Cove bridge." And at my questioning brow, he added, "Called for reinforcements early this morning from Lockwood Village. The chief there owes me a favor. No one goes in or out without permission. He can't come back in. Not unless he wants to get caught."

"No," I said. "He's too smart for that." Something occurred to me. "Unless he never left," I offered. "He might be hiding."

"You think he's still in Hollow Cove?" Iris made her way closer to us. The bed groaned as Ronin shot to his feet, following behind her.

I shrugged. "Maybe. Maybe not. But we should look. Try to flush him out somehow. He can't hide forever."

"No," answered the chief, "it's not a big town, but there're many places he could hide." Marcus nodded, his eyes darkening. "You're right. We need to flush him out and fast. We'll split up and search every building, every alleyway, and every hiding spot. I want him found by nightfall. I don't want any more deaths on my hands." His voice held a steely edge that left no room for argument.

"More deaths?" My pulse throbbed. Oh, hell no. "You mean more than the two we already know?"

Marcus's eyes pinned mine. "I was with your aunts when you called. They found the bodies of Brian, Percival, and Boris. Two were shot with arrows, the other with a twelve-gauge rifle. And in Brian's house."

"Oh my god." Iris pressed a hand to her stomach. "I think I'm going to be sick."

Ronin was next to her in the blink of an eye. Damn, that vamp speed. "I've got you, babe. I've got you."

I understood Iris's sick feeling. Hell, I shared it. But right now, it was squished, replaced by only fury.

Rage soared, and I trembled with it. "In his house. He killed them in Brian's own home?" I really hated this guy.

Marcus's expression was cold. "He did."

"When?"

"Last night. Same as the others. Just not all at the same time. Maybe an hour apart. From what we know, he killed Joe and Nancy first and then went to Brian's house and killed the others."

My eyes went to the target dummy, watching as Marcus's team pulled a bag over it and hauled it out of the bedroom. "And he hasn't killed anyone during the day. When the sun is up?"

"No," I heard Marcus say. "Only at night."

"But why?" Iris wrapped her hand over her bag as though the contents inside were her safety blanket. Maybe they were. Her eyes filled with concern. "You said he was a human. He *is* a human. Why at night? I don't get it?"

"Maybe he works during the day?" offered Ronin. "It would explain why he's not here. He could be somewhere else in another city nearby."

I glanced at the half-vampire. "Maybe that explains why he's not here now. But I know why he hunts only at night."

"Why?" Iris's dark eyes were round.

"Because," I said, the puzzle pieces coming together in my head. "It's a challenge for him." I walked over and picked up one of the frames that Marcus's team hadn't bagged yet, staring at Benjamin's smug smile. He held some heavy gun that looked like it belonged in a video game.

"It's harder at night. Being human, he doesn't have the night vision that a shifter or a were has. He *wants* it to be hard. He loves it. The thrill of the chase and all that crap." I knew it in my witchy bones. This guy was demented, and he took pleasure in hunting us, the paranormals. Because to him, we were nothing but beasts.

"What does this mean? Why is he doing this?" asked Iris, terror high in her voice. "We don't bother the humans. We keep to ourselves."

"I'll tell you what it means," I said. "It means this sick bastard has a list of kills. And everyone who was invited to that party is on it. Me. You. My aunts. It means we're all targets."

"That's it," said Ronin. "He's dead. He's fucking dead." Ronin's talons shot out from his fingertips as his eyes went black. "I'm not going to be a sitting duck. If I see him come near me or Iris, I'll rip him to shreds." I didn't doubt it. "Better we kill him before he kills one of us."

"It's not that simple."

We all looked at Marcus. "He's human..." began the chief. "It complicates matters."

As the tension in the room rose, I could sense the fear and anger emanating from my friends. They were right to be afraid of this hunter, but I knew that killing him wasn't the answer. Violence only begot more violence, and we needed

147

to find a solution that wouldn't result in more bloodshed.

Or maybe we just offed him, just this once.

I pressed my hands to my hips. "How so? We can't just let him continue. And if he comes at us, we will defend ourselves."

"Hell yeah," said Ronin, his eyes back to their normal brown, though his talons were still visible as he flexed his fingers like they were kitchen knives about to tear into a meaty steak.

The chief's expression was hard. "This guy is well-protected. He's got money, and he's well-known. If we kill him, that'll bring more attention to us. He's not alone in this. Others know about us and this town. If he goes missing… more will come. And these are not the ignorant humans with nine-to-five jobs, three kids, and a puppy. These are trained killers with military experience. Trust me, you don't want to make Hollow Cove a bigger target than it already is."

True. My heart sped up at the sense of familiarity in his tone. "You've heard of this before? Of humans hunting the paranormal?" It was crazy when I thought about it, but crazy people did crazy things.

The wereape shifted on his feet, tension visible all over his body as he tried to contain his rage. He looked like he was about to punch a few holes in Benjamin's master bedroom. Not that I would mind.

Marcus was programmed to protect those he cared about, to protect me. And not being able to do that was seriously messing with him.

But this wasn't just about me. It was about all of us—those who'd come to that dinner party. Those Benjamin Morgan had handpicked specifically.

"I have. Just not as sophisticated," answered Marcus after a moment. "I've never heard of a group that actually bought property in one of our communities and pretended to be one of us. He's very well-organized, and I have a feeling he's been planning this for a while now. He's playing with us, seeing how far he can go before getting caught."

"Pretty far, if you count the five dead." I looked at Marcus. "And their heads... you think..." I couldn't bring myself to say it, though I knew what the chief was about to answer.

"He kept them as trophies," answered the chief.

"Sick bastard," cursed Ronin. "I can't believe he stole my manor. Why the hell did Pauline sell it to him?"

"He probably offered *a lot* more than you," said Iris, reaching out and patting his arm.

Marcus let out a long breath of tension. "He's been at this before." His eyes moved to the cabinet, its shelves now empty. "He's prepared. And he won't stop."

I turned to the group, my muscles tense and ready for action. "We can't just sit around and wait for him to strike. If we can't kill him… then what?"

Ronin wiggled his taloned fingers. "I say we find this bastard and make him pay. Send him off to the human world in little asshat pieces."

Marcus raked a hand through his tousled dark hair. "We can't kill him," he repeated, with enough primal authority that Ronin recoiled a step.

"I agree with Marcus," I said, stepping forward. "Killing him won't solve anything. And we don't want another group of these murderous humans here seeking retaliation. We need to find a way to stop him without resorting to his untimely death."

Ronin snarled, his claws still extended. "What other options do we have? We can't just let him keep hunting us like animals. How are we going to make him to stop? Say, please?"

I frowned at my friend. "Look. I know you're upset. I am, too. But if we kill him, more will come. Is that what you want?"

Ronin's mouth clamped shut, his eyes narrowing.

"What do you suggest we do?" asked Iris, her voice trembling with anger.

I took a deep breath, thinking quickly. "We need to change his mind. We need to make him and his group…forget about us."

"I'm not following?" Ronin watched me with a confused expression.

"It's like Marcus said." I looked at the chief before continuing. "If we kill him and his team, it'll only alert whoever else he's told. And we don't want a war with the humans. But… if we can make them *forget* this town exists… we're safe."

"Like a memory charm?" Iris eyed me curiously. "That would work. Your aunts can do that. But what about the other paranormal communities? He'll be onto them if not ours."

I nodded. "I know. But for now, it's all I've got. We can think of something else for them. Maybe my aunts can share whatever spell they come up with that can camouflage the towns better from these humans. Make them forget that they're there at all."

"You think your aunts can start on this memory spell right away?" asked Marcus. The tension in his voice was palpable.

"Yes. I'll go straight away and tell them. It'll take time, like all spells. What do we do in the meantime? To protect ourselves?"

Marcus made a noise in his throat. "First, we need to find him."

Iris spoke up, her voice low and even. "I think I may know a way to find him." She glanced between Marcus and me, and I could see the determination etched onto her features.

"Go on," Marcus prompted, folding his arms.

Iris reached into her bag and pulled out one of the skulls she'd taken. I cringed, but Marcus didn't say anything or even look surprised that she'd nicked one of Ben's skulls. "I can make a locator spell with this. It's got his human imprint, or DNA, on it. It'll be harder than, say… locating a paranormal, but it's doable."

"Good. That's good." I smiled at the Dark witch, holding what looked like a canine skull in her hand. "That'll tell us if he's still here in town or not. How long will it take to prepare?"

"I'll need at least an hour," answered the Dark witch, dropping the skull back into her bag.

"So, we'll just have to be on our guards 'til then," I said, feeling less nervous and tense now that we had a solid plan. "And all those on the list need to be told. They have to know what's happening."

Marcus nodded. "I agree. The whole town needs to know."

"So…" Ronin rubbed his hands together. "How do we hit these motherfrackers with the memory charm?"

I stared at the half-vampire, seeing a glint of excitement in his eyes. "First, we need to figure out if he's still here. If he is, and we know his location, the rest is easy."

"And if he's not?"

"We beat him at his own game," I told him. "We set up a trap. He's hunting us. Right? So let him. Let him come to us."

"You're insane," said Ronin with a smile. "I like it."

My heart thrashed with anticipation at the thought of getting this bastard at his own game. Ronin was right. It was crazy. But we had to try something if we were going to get out of this alive without arrows prodding out of our backs.

"I don't know, Tessa." Marcus scratched his chin, something he did when he was nervous or just very angry. "That's dangerous. So many things could go wrong."

"And so many things will go wrong if we don't try," I countered. "He needs to be stopped." I stared at the chief, but he looked away like he knew despite it being dangerous, it was the only way he could see this working.

Ronin still seemed somewhat hesitant. "I'm all in. But if this doesn't work, we do it my way."

I watched as Ronin and Iris headed out, feeling marginally better now that we had a plan. And it was a good plan.

We would get this sonofabitch. We would.

He was hunting us. But not if I hunted him first.

I'm coming for you, Benjamin.

CHAPTER
12

I took a sip of my coffee, letting the bitter taste warm my throat as it went down. With my second cup, I was already jumpier than a kangaroo on caffeine. Not sure that was the brightest idea.

Sitting at the dining room table, I watched as my aunts poured over old leather tomes and files as they worked on a spell or charm that would make Benjamin and his team forget that we ever existed.

They'd been at it for almost forty-five minutes. I'd given them a recap of what we'd discovered back at the manor and finally proved that Benjamin was indeed responsible, that he was human, and that he was hunting us.

They were all very quiet with solemn expressions. It must have been quite the shock, discovering not one but three more bodies. Three more *decapitated* bodies, no less. My heart tugged at what I saw on their faces, but we couldn't let despair take hold. We needed to work on getting rid of the evil humans to keep our town safe.

"I've spoken to Pauline," I heard Ronin's voice from the living room.

I glanced over to the living room where Iris was kneeling beside a granite mortar and pestle. My eyes swept over another mixing bowl stained with blue powder to the large Hollow Cove town map that was stretched out before the Dark witch. A skull sat on the map, and a black cat lay next to it, his tail lashing behind him and his eyes on the skull. If I didn't know any better, it looked like the cat was about to pounce on that skull.

"And?" Iris sprinkled some powder into her bowl.

"And she told me her hands are tied," said the half-vampire. "That he's still the rightful owner, human or not."

"We'll find another house," Iris said, focusing on her locator spell.

Ronin grumbled something that I couldn't catch. Obviously, the half-vampire was still angry about losing the manor to a human. And he didn't look like he was about to give up either.

"How many humans are in this group?"

My eyes flicked to Dolores, seeing her brows high as she waited for my answer. "No idea. Ten. Fifteen. I don't know. But I do think those waiters were part of his team." Come to think of it, they looked like the military type. Not waiters.

"And how many waiters were there?" asked Dolores.

"Six," answered Beverly. She caught me staring and wiggled her eyebrows. "I make it my mission to know how many men are in a room at any time."

"Isn't that the job of a tramp?" asked Ruth, looking serious.

"But that doesn't mean there aren't any more." Dolores tapped the paper of her tome. "Without the precise number, we can't know how much of the charm we need. Too little, and it would only work for, say… a few days. Then they'll remember everything."

"Can't you just make more, just in case?" I asked.

"Sure we can." Ruth beamed, her eyes wide. "We'll make it a triple dose! A super batch!"

Dolores let out a sigh. "This isn't your famous spaghetti sauce, Ruth. This is serious."

Ruth's face went hard. "My spaghetti sauce is *very* serious."

I laughed at Ruth's enthusiasm. "It sure is."

"Ooooh. That sounds like fun." Tinkerbell fluttered above the table and landed on Ruth's shoulder. "Can I help?"

Ruth reached up and yanked out one of the pencils that was holding her bun in place on the top of her head. "Sure you can. We'll need all the help we can get." She scribbled something that looked like an equation on her notepad.

Dolores stared at the page of her tome. "Say that we do make a larger amount. But we would still need to dose them all at the same time. Can we do that? Can we make sure we get them all at once?"

Good question. "I can't know for sure. But we'll try. I mean, do they all go hunting at the same time?"

Ruth cringed at my use of the word *hunting*, and I immediately regretted using it.

"I think they go on the *chase* as a unit," I tried again. "At least, that's what I think."

"If that's true, it will work." Dolores grabbed her coffee mug and took a sip. "These bastards will never remember us. Never remember Hollow Cove."

"Sounds like a complicated spell," I said.

"Indeed, only the most talented and experienced can cast such advanced magic," Dolores boasted, her exaggerated attitude prompting Beverly to roll her eyes.

I leaned forward, curious. "How does it work exactly? Like amnesia?"

"More like a lobotomy," said Beverly, a compact in her hand as she checked herself in the mirror and gave her reflection a few kisses.

"You're kidding?" I stared at my aunts to see if Beverly was exaggerating or not.

"She's right," said Dolores. "The spell will erase all memories of time spent here in Hollow Cove. It will also remove any thoughts or mentions of our town and people. It will spread into their minds, removing them piece by piece, part by part, until nothing is left of us. Until it will be as though we never existed. And never will."

"Wow." My aunts were truly amazingly capable witches. The town was lucky to have them.

"Like cute little worms inside their brains eating away those memories," said Ruth with a smile as though the prospect excited her or she just liked worms in general.

I smiled at Ruth, not sure how to respond to that.

Dolores's expression turned sour. "Those miserable humans will never bother us again. What they did to us…" I knew she wanted to say more, but it was as though the memories of what they found this morning were just too raw, too soon to talk about it.

"I'm sorry you had to see that," I told them, my throat tight at the moisture in Ruth's and Beverly's eyes, even Dolores's.

My tall aunt cleared her throat. "Let's not talk about that. Let's focus all our efforts into this spell."

I grabbed my phone to see if Marcus had texted. He hadn't. "How long will it take?" We had the spell, but I still didn't know how I was going to set this trap for Benjamin. Not yet. But if I was right, and he only hunted at night, I still had plenty of time to figure something out.

"Well…" Dolores pushed back into her chair. "Once we get the incantation right, and we still have a few hours of work in that area, there's still the question of working the potion."

Damn. "Do they have to drink it?" That would be a problem. How did I make a group of men all drink the same potion? It's not like we'd be invited to another one of Benjamin's parties where I could slip some of the potion in their drinks. How the hell could I pull this off?

"No, they don't," said Ruth as a smile crept over her cute face. "That's the beauty of it. Think of it like a gas bomb. Whoever is in a five-foot radius when it goes off will be submerged by smoke, by the spell."

Ruth never ceased to amaze me with her potion-making, or rather, bomb-making. Apparently, Ruth liked things that went boom.

I grinned at my aunt. "Well, that'll work."

"Of course, it'll work," snapped Dolores. Her friend, the scowl, returned to her forehead. "Who do you think we are? The

Wanderbushes?" She laughed and then snorted like that was some inside joke. I didn't get it. I thought her cousins were quite capable witches.

I tipped my coffee mug and finished off the coffee. "So, a few hours?"

"About six hours should do the trick." Dolores looked over to Ruth, who nodded her confirmation.

Good. That gave me plenty of time to prepare and brainstorm a plan of action.

Beverly let out a dramatic sigh and dropped her compact on the table. "Guess I'll have to reschedule my date with Carlo."

"I'm sure you'll be able to go on a date with him soon," I offered. "We should have all of this mess wrapped up in a day or two." Or so I hoped.

"That's just it. I don't know if I can wait that long." Beverly's green eyes met mine, and she waved her hands over her body. "Look at me."

"Okay. I'm looking. What am I supposed to see?"

"Can't you see the plague of rashes over my body?" said my aunt, making Ruth snort.

"No. Should I?"

Beverly flapped her hands over her body again. "It's the *dateless syndrome*. Usually, only the ugly women get it. Must have caught it from Dolores."

My tall aunt pointed a pen threateningly at Beverly. "Watch it."

Beverly shook her body. "I'm filled with these flutterings and hot flashes. I feel like I'm about to burst into flames. My body has needs, you know. As all irresistible, gorgeous women do."

"*Irritable* women," grumbled Dolores.

Beverly glowered at her sister. "You're just a grumpy old spinster."

"Aren't spinsters unmarried older women?" Oops. By the venomous glare Beverly was giving me, I guessed that was the wrong thing to say.

"You take that back, Tessa Davenport," hissed Beverly. "I choose to be unmarried. That way, I can date any men—all the men—I desire."

"Like a whore," offered Ruth. "We all gravitate to what we're good at."

Instead of being offended, Beverly flashed her perfectly white teeth. "How right you are, Ruth. I'm very good at sex. I excel at it. In fact, they should be writing books about my experiences. Maybe I should teach."

"Teach sex?" I laughed. "You can't be serious."

"Yes," said Beverly. "Sex education. I'll teach them the pleasures of the mortal bodies. Why keep all this knowledge packed into a perfect little body when I could share it with the world? I'll make sex soldiers."

161

This was a very weird conversation. "Right. Have fun with that."

"Ignore her, Tessa," said Dolores, reading my expression. "I'm afraid when her vagina is involved, it all comes out in slut."

Ruth stood up, walked over to the kitchen, grabbed a cloth from one of the drawers, and returned. She leaned over me. "Okay. Time to check your eyebrows."

"Right." I'd forgotten about them. I'd given Beverly quite a laugh when I showed up at Davenport house without eyebrows. Ruth smiled and said, "I've always said never trust an electrician with no eyebrows."

Right. Good point.

She'd patted my shoulder and added, "I've got just the thing to grow them back. They'll be just as bushy as before."

Not sure how I felt about that comment. But I'd let her put some ointment on my eyebrows anyway. Ruth was the expert in all things potions, magical lotions, and creams.

I sat patiently as Ruth pressed the cloth over my brows and rubbed the ointment off.

When she was done, she leaned back. "Oh, no."

My breath caught. "Oh, no? What do you mean, oh no?"

Beverly glanced my way and laughed. "Now *those* are some fiery eyebrows."

I reeled in my emotions, trying not to panic. "Ruth?"

Ruth shrugged, looking confused. "Must have forgotten to add the blue coloring to the mixture."

I stood up. "What the hell does that mean? Tinky?" I stared at the fairy still sitting on Ruth's shoulder.

"You should take a look in a mirror," she said, looking apologetic. "It's not that bad."

"Anyone who says it's not *that* bad means it *is*."

"Here." Beverly handed me her compact.

I lifted it to my face and cursed. "Holy shit. My eyebrows are as red as tomatoes."

"Tomatoes are good for ya," said Ruth.

I sighed. "Can you make them like they were before?"

Ruth nodded. "Be right back."

Okay, so I had red eyebrows. Big deal. Lots of redheads had red brows. Right? Or dark auburn. Had I been in my twenties, I would have been mortified. But by now I'd been through so much. My brows were the least of my worries.

"It's ready!" called Iris from the living room, and all thoughts of eyebrows disappeared.

I rushed into the living room with Beverly and Dolores right behind me.

Both White and Dark witches had their own versions of locator or tracking spells. Iris's Dark witch old version was excellent, but it required hours spent on pre-spells and aura-detecting spells—not to mention adding the compass link to the skull. Then we would need to add all the mix and link it to an amulet that would act like an actual compass, which would then lead the way.

But we didn't have hours to mess around with spells. I needed to find Benjamin like yesterday. The longer we wasted time working spells, the further away we would be from discovering where Benjamin was hiding.

But Iris, being the clever Dark witch she was, had improved her locating spell by adding her special touches. Which I assumed were borrowed from the White witches' method.

It meant we didn't have to wait long to locate the bastard.

"That was fast," I said, smiling at her. She stared at my eyebrows but was kind enough not to say anything. Ronin just flashed me a smile.

Iris beamed up at me. "Yes. It was more complicated than I first thought. Since Benjamin's a human, their energies are different from ours. They're more… faint. It occurred to me that I needed more of his human aura. Once I understood that, I had to double my spell."

"And it'll work?" Dolores stood with her hands propped on her hips.

"It should. Yes," answered Iris, looking slightly offended.

"It'll work," announced Ronin, coming to his girlfriend's rescue. Man, these two were so cute.

"I had to *change* the spell around a little to adapt it to a human." Her eyes met mine, and she smiled. "It'll work. I promise."

"You don't need to promise. I believe you. Dolores better watch out," I added, glancing at my aunt, who looked mildly impressed.

Dolores frowned at me. "Please, do your spell, Iris. We're all anxious to know where he is."

The Dark witch beamed. "Yes, ma'am."

With my adrenaline spiking, I watched as Iris tucked a strand of dark hair behind her ear, took a container the size of a jam jar, twisted the top, and sprinkled some ashes or dirt over the map. Was that grave dirt? I didn't want to know.

Next, she took a slow breath, her eyes narrowing as she tapped into her Dark witch magic, which was more or less borrowing from some demon in the Netherworld. Hopefully, she'd moved on from Gigi. That poor little creature had helped enough.

"Power of the Netherworld, I summon thee," she chanted in a clear voice. "I seek your help in finding the human called Benjamin Morgan."

Power surged. I stiffened, and my breath hissed in through my nose. The outpouring of energy from demons filled the air, cold and familiar.

A burst of dazzling light flashed before our eyes as magic tore through the room. On the map, the wolf skull rose a few inches and spun around on its axis in a blur.

"It's working," said Ronin.

"Of course, it's *working*," snapped Iris, which only made Ronin grin, seemingly pleased he was irritating her.

I stared at the skull. "It *is* working," I whispered, having seen this before with a pen when I was looking for Marcus. Soon, we would know where that bastard was hiding.

"This reminds me of the time when Timothy and I were playing Twister with no clothes on," commented Beverly. "That man was incredibly flexible. What he could do with his toes…"

No idea what she was talking about, and I didn't want to know.

"What do we do when we find his location?" asked Ruth, stepping into the living room with Tinkerbell looking anxious on her shoulder.

"Well, first, let's see where he is," I said. "Then we'll make plans." The truth was I hadn't thought that far ahead yet.

With another flash of light, the skull stopped spinning, still hovering over the map. I watched in amazement as the wolf skull zoomed to the left, all the way *off* the map, and then dropped near the front entrance.

"Holy shit," I breathed, just as Hildo chased after the skull like it was a furry squirrel.

166

"Holy shit on a stick," expressed Ronin.

I walked over and picked up the skull. It was warm. Pushing away the creepiness of it all, I turned to Iris. "The skull didn't fall on the map. Is that normal?"

"Yes," Iris said as she leaned back, a proud smile on her face. "It means he's not here." She gazed around my aunts, Ronin, and me. "He's not in Hollow Cove."

CHAPTER

13

"**A**nd you're sure he's not in Hollow Cove?" Marcus sat on the edge of the couch, his elbows on his knees, looking like he wanted nothing more but to release some pent-up tension on Ben's face. I could oblige.

"Positive." I let myself fall next to him. "I trust Iris's abilities. And we all saw the skull shoot right off the map. Wherever he is, it's not in Hollow Cove."

Marcus grunted a sound of acknowledgment, but he sighed in relief.

"What's that? I don't speak gorilla grunt."

The tiniest of smiles pulled at the corners of his lips, but then it was gone in a flash.

I hated seeing him like this, like he was carrying the weight of the world on his shoulders, or in this case, Hollow Cove. The five deaths were hitting him hard. They were hitting us all hard. It was a tragedy—a ruthless, mindless murder of decent people. They didn't deserve to die like they did, hunted like animals, and then desecrated by removing their heads. My insides twisted when I thought of their families. Benjamin Morgan was a killer. But not just any killer, a killer of paranormals, of us.

The chief stared out the living room window. "I'll let my people know. I've got some teams scouting the town looking for Benjamin and his crew in case they were hiding somewhere. They'll be better served at the bridge." He grabbed his phone, and his fingers swept the screen as he started to text someone. "How's the spell going? The memory one?"

"Good, I think. I'm pretty sure it'll be ready in a couple of hours. They were halfway through when I left. So, maybe another two?"

Marcus set his phone down. "Good. We're going to need it."

"You think he'll be back?" I also shared that sentiment. It was just too easy to think that Ben was done with us. And in my life, things were never that easy or simple. They were complicated. Very complicated.

The only good thing I had going for me was that Ruth had managed to change my eyebrows back to their normal color after applying an additional ointment to them for only a few minutes this time around.

"I do. He's not done." A muscle twitched on the chief's jaw, tension rolling off his posture in spades. "Someone that organized, someone who paid lots of money for that manor and who lived here, even for a short while, and has a team of what I suspect are highly trained individuals, won't give up that easily."

He had a point. "I hate to say it, but I agree."

"I think he goes somewhere during the day. Somewhere close. Possibly somewhere in Cape Elizabeth. And comes back at night…to…"

He didn't have to say it. We all knew what that bastard was up to. The thought that Benjamin was so close, only a few minutes' ride away, had my adrenaline pounding through me. A crazy part of me wanted to jump a ley line and look for him. But that could take all day, and then what? Bring him back here so my aunts could dose him with their spell? That would solve him but not his crew.

"But you're protecting the entrance to the town," I said. "You've got your people stationed at the bridge."

"I do."

I leaned forward a bit to see all of his face. He wouldn't look at me. "But you think he'll come."

"He might not be aware that we broke into his house and discovered his... trophies," he added that last word with a growl that had the hairs on my arms standing at attention. "He might not know."

"And that's what you're counting on? You want him to show up. At the bridge. To pound in his head a few times?" I added with a grin.

Marcus flexed his fingers, his lovely, big and rough man-hands. "I do. Wouldn't mind a one-on-one fight with this piece of work."

I loved it when he was all protective and showing his alpha side. It had my hormones doing a jig.

Marcus let out a low growl, his eyes flashing with anger. "He's just arrogant enough to show up and challenge me. And I'll be waiting for him."

Fear bubbled up at the thought of Marcus fighting that crazy human. It might be inevitable, but it didn't mean I had to like it. It's not that I didn't think Marcus could take on the human. I was certain he could, and not even in his gorilla form. But I didn't trust Benjamin and knew he was the type to fight dirty. Like Marcus said, he was resourceful and knowledgeable about our kind, so he'd probably fought a wereape before and knew their weaknesses. Hell, I knew he had, and he'd killed it. The proof was in his cabinet of skulls.

I let out a breath, only now realizing my hands were shaking, and immediately stuffed them under my thighs. "Don't forget you're on his list of kills."

"As are you." Marcus spun his head so fast that I had to blink a few times to make sure it was real. "I hate that this guy has you on his list."

"I can take care of myself."

"I won't let anything happen to you, Tessa. I promise." His words were meant to be reassuring, but they only served to heighten my desire for him.

"I know you won't," I said softly. "But I can take care of myself."

"You're my wife now, my mate," he growled, and the way he said it with such ferocious protectiveness made it difficult not to jump his bones right there and then. "It's my job to protect what's *mine*."

"I love your caveman talk. Gives me the *feels*."

I watched a smile spread across his face, illuminating his handsome features. Marcus was everything I ever wanted in a mate and more. He was strong, loyal, and protective but also gentle and caring. Being with him made me feel alive in a way I never thought possible.

"I can say the same thing about you." I reached out and placed a hand on his arm, feeling the bulge of his muscles beneath my fingertips and giving them a comforting squeeze. "We'll take care of this," I said softly. "We always find a way."

A muscle in Marcus's jaw twitched as he stared off into the distance. I knew he was thinking about the danger we were both facing, the possibility that one or both of us might not make it out of this alive. But he didn't say anything, just took a deep breath and turned to me.

"We need to be ready for anything," he said, his voice low and serious. "If he shows up, we need to take him down fast."

"You know," I said, ideas running around in my noggin. "The bridge. That would be the perfect opportunity to set up my trap."

"*Your* trap?"

Whoops. "Yeah." I watched as his face went rigid. "With the memory charm. When he comes to the bridge, he'll be with his team. Right? We can get them all together and dose those sons of bitches." It was perfect. Just when Benjamin and his crew showed up, right before they thought they're about to fight—wham— we hit them with my aunt's memory charm. Strangely enough, I felt better and less nervous that we had a sound plan. Hell, it was going to work.

Marcus nodded, a smirk forming on his lips. "You look very excited at the idea."

"A chance to lobotomize Benjamin? Yes. Yes, I am."

I couldn't help but feel a rush of excitement at the thought of finally getting the upper hand on Benjamin and his crew. It was about time we took matters into our own hands.

"You heard about the town meeting tonight?" asked Marcus.

"Yeah. Gilbert wants to discuss our options. How to protect those still on the list, mainly him." I snorted. "News of the murders had probably reached everyone by now. I'm sure we have a lot of scared townspeople who want answers." And I didn't blame them.

"They have a right to be scared." Marcus went silent, his eyes flashing at some internal struggle.

"You haven't touched your food," I said, pointing to the plate of freshly baked lasagna—from Ruth, of course—that rested on the coffee table next to a beer that hadn't been touched. "You haven't slept, and you're not eating. Don't think I haven't noticed."

Marcus looked at me. His features were carefully guarded. I knew he didn't want me to know how worried he was. But the beginnings of dark circles were showing under his eyes. The dire situation was starting to take its toll on the chief.

"I thought I'd try fasting for a while."

"Ha. Ha. Seriously. You should eat. At least have a bite. Ruth made this especially for you. Said she put some extra hot spices in the sauce."

Marcus reached out and grabbed my hand. "I'm sorry we haven't gone on our honeymoon trip. I know you were looking forward to going to Europe."

His tender voice had my throat throb. I shook my head, hoping it would shake off that rush of emotions or at least hide it. "I don't care about that right now. We'll go later. No rule says we have to go right after we get married. Besides, we've been married for over two weeks now. It won't kill us to wait another few weeks."

"You're my wife." His rough voice was making my skin tingle. "You deserve a honeymoon. I want to give that to you. You did save me from Storybook. I owe you," he added with a smile.

"That's right. You owe me plenty." I laughed. "But seriously. You should eat something. A big, burly man like you needs his protein. You don't want all that muscle to go to waste."

Marcus's gray eyes searched my face. "I'm a wereape, Tessa. My muscles won't go anywhere."

"Right." Guess that explained it all.

Marcus's phone rang, and he picked it up from the coffee table. "Yeah."

I eyed the lasagna. It was pretty. Can lasagna be pretty? The smell was intoxicating, and it was making me salivate.

"Are Kev and Brett at the foot of the bridge?" Marcus was asking whoever was on the other line. "Where's Jonas?"

The lasagna was staring at me. It *wanted* me to eat it.

"…turn them away," Marcus said, an edge to his voice. "I don't want anyone coming in that's not a resident. No. I don't care."

My stomach grumbled like I had a gremlin living in there.

It was a sign.

"No one comes in or out." Marcus's voice had gone all alpha. I did not want to be the guy on the other side of that phone call. "Get it done."

That's it. I'm going in!

I reached out, grabbed the fork, and cut me a big bite of Ruth's infamous lasagna. I moaned as the flat pasta, cheese, spinach, and her spicy sauce hit my tongue. Oh, my. If I had a tail, it would be wagging.

Marcus hung up, his eyes settling on me.

I swallowed. "Sorry. It was too damn hard to resist."

The chief smiled. "I've got to go."

"What? Wait."

"I'll see you later at the town meeting," said the wereape.

"Okay."

He stared at me for a long moment, his dark eyes boring into mine. "You've got some sauce on your face."

"Where?" I wiped my mouth with my fingers.

The tiniest of smiles pulled the chief's lips. "Here." He stepped closer until his chest was rubbing against my breasts. A finger scraped my left cheek. And then his tongue. "It's gone." His voice was low and rough.

The way he was looking at me made my heart race, and I couldn't help but feel like I was about to combust.

I leaned in closer to him, needing to feel the heat of his body. I pressed a finger to my lips. "I've got more sauce here," I said, as the clever witch that I was.

I didn't have to wait long as the wereape's lips brushed mine. The kiss was electric, igniting a fire within me that I couldn't control. Marcus's hands were on my waist, pulling me closer to him as our tongues danced together in a wild frenzy.

I knew I was lost when we finally pulled apart, panting for breath—lost to this man who had become my protector, my confidant, my lover.

"You know," I said, tracing circles around his bulging biceps. "It's kinda hot when you go all alpha male like that. I kinda like it."

"Do you, now?" He pressed his hard body against me and grinned. "How much do you like it?"

"A lot."

He brushed his lips over my neck and kissed my collarbone softly. "Like...this?"

My skin tingled with pleasure, and I felt my breath hitch as he pulled me closer to him. I pushed him away playfully. "Are you trying to seduce me," I teased.

The chief winked at me mischievously. "Is it working?"

"Maybe..."

He was still looking at me with absolute desire when I captured his lips with mine, giving him a playful bite on his lower lip. His eyes filled with ravenous hunger, and his hands, grasping for more of me, explored my body. It was exhilarating to be kissed and caressed by a man who obviously desired me so fiercely and ardently.

He pulled back slightly. "I don't have to go just yet... I think I have some time for a little..."

"Doing squat thrusts in the cucumber patch?"

Marcus burst out laughing. "You are a strange one."

"That's why you *loooove* me."

"It is."

The wereape's growl of pleasure rumbled through my lips as he kissed me. We laughed, and with unsteady hands, we started undressing each other, eager to make it to the bedroom without tripping.

I ripped off my clothes and flung them across the room. Marcus lifted me off my feet and laid me down on the mattress, positioning himself between my legs. He pressed his body against mine so closely that I could feel his heart thudding against my chest, and he breathed heavily with desire. His lips met mine, and my worries seemed to dissolve in that moment as our kiss grew passionate.

His hands roamed my body as his tongue waltzed with mine, and we moved in perfect harmony as if our souls were made for that exact instant. I felt like I was soaring away from reality, engulfed in the sensation of being so cherished by this remarkable man. I wanted to savor this moment of sheer pleasure and intimacy forever.

Which should have prepared me for what followed. But it didn't.

CHAPTER
14

After my round of mind-bogging sex with my *husband*, I took a quick, five-minute shower, ate the rest of Ruth's lasagna—why waste a perfectly good meal—and headed to Davenport House.

My aunts sat at the dining table, and they all looked up as I entered. Iris was there, a few pink spots coloring her cheeks, and I noticed the empty glass of red wine beside her.

"Where's Ronin," I asked as I walked in, grabbed a wine glass from the upper cabinet, and stepped over to the table, seizing the open wine bottle and pouring myself a drink.

"Said he had some—" Iris made finger quotes. "Stuff to do before tonight's meeting."

I took a sip of the wine, enjoying the fruity taste. "He went back to the manor."

Iris sighed. "I know. He's still angry about the whole thing. I think he's angrier at the fact that he lost the house to someone who's trying to kill us."

"That's Ronin for you." I took another sip, glancing at the large dish of lasagna that was missing its other half.

"Are you hungry, Tessa?" Ruth caught me staring at the lasagna. "I'll get you a plate."

I raised my hand. "No, thanks. I ate Marcus's piece."

Ruth's face fell. "Oh. He didn't like it." Her eyes went to her stove. "I can make him something else if he would prefer. I know. I'll make him some veggie fajitas!"

"That's not it," I said quickly before she got up and started to cook up another meal. "It was amazing, and I'm sure he would have eaten it all. But he's just not hungry." Just hungry for my body. "He's too… upset with the murders. He blames himself."

"It's not his fault a mad human decided to play target practice with us," said Dolores, and then she tipped her wine glass to her lips and finished it. "No one could have predicted this."

"We weren't prepared for it," offered Beverly. "I thought he was a handsome stranger looking for a good time." She smiled. "And I would have given it to him if he wasn't a murderous bastard."

"His version of a good time is not you naked," snapped Dolores, her cheeks flushed as she reached for the bottle. "It's your head in one of his cabinets."

Beverly reached up and clasped her neck. "I do have the perfect-shaped head. Claud told me so. He's an artist. Uses my body as inspiration. I'm his muse." She giggled.

Okay. "Do you know what Gilbert wants to do? Has he said anything about the meeting tonight?"

"Well." Dolores poured herself another glass of red wine. "We told him that Benjamin is not in Hollow Cove, and that seemed to bring him some relief."

I'd noticed that my aunts were visibly less tense now that Benjamin wasn't in town. But I was with Marcus on that score. I had a feeling he'd be back.

"And the memory charm," added Ruth.

"Yes, we told him we would retaliate with the memory charm should Benjamin return," added Dolores. She laughed. "That seemed to lower his blood pressure."

I doubted that. The little shifter was high-strung. Stepping in gum might give him a stroke.

"I still can't believe we're on a kill list," said Ruth, her face losing its cheeriness and making her look tired and old. "Doesn't feel real. Feels more like a bad dream."

"Believe it because it is *very* real," said Dolores, her voice rising. "A human hunting us. *Us*. Feels like the witch trials all over again, only this time we're not burned at the stake. We're hunted down like beasts and beheaded."

I wanted to point out that witches weren't the only ones on said list, but I decided to shut my mouth.

Ruth made a face and stabbed her half-eaten piece of lasagna with her fork.

"You okay, Ruth?"

Dolores waved a hand dismissively at me. "Don't worry about her. She just tried to cut the tap water with scissors again."

"It's not what I was doing." Ruth glared at her older sister. "I was rinsing the scissors."

A smile inched across Dolores's lips. "Sure you were."

Suddenly, the sound of the front door slamming reached us.

"Marcus?" Iris looked at me.

"Doubt it."

We heard the sound of shoes scuffing the hardwood, and then a pretty fifty-year-old woman with dark hair and matching eyes stepped into the kitchen.

"There you are," said my mother as she crossed the kitchen and stood by the table. "Your father's worried about you. I was just at your cottage, and you weren't there," she said, sounding annoyed.

"No. As you can see."

"I have to say I'm glad I didn't get invited to that dinner party," my mother went on. "I'm not a target like you."

"Thank you for that, Amelia." Dolores glared at her younger sister.

My mother ignored her and walked over to the same cabinet I'd used, where she grabbed a wine glass, returned to the table, and poured herself a drink. Just as I had done.

Whoa. That was eerie.

She took a sip of the wine and made a face. "You need to invest in better quality wines."

Dolores sighed. "How about you buy your own the next time."

My mother gave a one-shoulder shrug and took another sip as her eyes met mine. "I'm not on that psycho's list, but you are."

"Apparently."

My mother propped a hand on her hip. "Well?" She stared at me expectantly, swirling her wine.

"Well… what?"

"What are you going to do about it? Your father suggested you stay with him until this problem is fixed."

I loved my demon father. And I knew he loved me. My middle warmed at his concern for my well-being. However, staying in the Netherworld wasn't my idea of a nice, comfy trip, and I wasn't about to run away and hide when my aunts and the town needed me.

"Thanks. But I'm not going anywhere."

"Why not?" My mother's eyes rounded with concern. "It's the safest place for you. And your father would love to have you."

"No doubt he would," I answered. "And the demon realm is probably safer for me." I can't believe I just said that. "But I can't leave now. The town needs me. I'm a Merlin. It's my job."

My mother gave me a skeptical look. "You haven't been a Merlin long enough to be considered one."

"I can always count on you for the lovely compliments."

My mother let out an exasperated breath. "I just don't want you to get hurt. There're already two dead. Do you want to be the third?"

Obviously, she hadn't heard of the recent three additional deaths, and I was going to keep it that way. "I'll be fine."

"Why don't you just blast these idiot humans with your magic? That'll solve it," suggested my mother.

If only we could. "We can't. Marcus said that if we do, it'll only alert more humans. More of the same kind of humans. The murdering-para-normal-kind."

"We don't want that." Ruth hugged herself. "I thought humans were nice. Stupid, but nice."

"You know, I'm disappointed in you, Tessa," said my mother again with that dissatisfied tone to her voice that I'd grown accustomed to in my teenage years. It was like a third parent.

"I'm used to it."

"I never thought you'd be one of *those* married women. You know, who *do* as their husbands *tell* them. I thought you were made of stronger stuff."

Anger rushed into me, and I was surprised at how fast it hit. I knew it wasn't as much as my mother had said, but more due to the situation. My body vibrated as my demon mojo surfaced. Funny how it seemed to feed on my emotions. I wasn't about to blast away my mother, though I had thought about it in the past. Instead, I took a calming breath and downed the rest of my wine in one go.

"Did you just come here to insult us, Amelia?" Beverly shot a glare in her sister's direction. "Because if you did, you know where the door is."

My mother scoffed. "I'm just trying to look out for my daughter's best interest. Unlike *some* people."

Beverly's face hardened. "You mean *us*?"

Ruth laughed. "We're your sisters, silly. Not some people."

"Whenever she's involved with this Merlin business, she gets hurt," said my mother. "Why can't you three figure it out? You're *much* older than her."

Iris let out a cough and recovered with a sip of water. But I suspected she was enjoying the hell out of this.

"I appreciate your concern, Mother, but I'm capable of making my own decisions," I said firmly. "Have been for a very long time."

"Sure you are," my mother rolled her eyes. "What you should be doing is enjoying your honeymoon. Not trying to get yourself killed."

"Still alive the last time I checked."

"You know what I mean." Frustration lined my mother's features. "Let them take care of it for once. Why does it always have to be you."

"It's not," I told her. "I've never gone through anything alone. My aunts, my friends, we were always together. We fight and then shoot the shit together," I added with a smile.

"This is not a laughing matter." My mother was shaking her head and making a clicking sound with her tongue. "You've put on weight."

That was it. I was going to kill her.

"If you don't watch out, it's all downhill from here," continued my dear mama. "The older you get, the harder it is to lose weight."

"I haven't gained weight." Total lie. My jeans did put up a hell of a resistance when I tried to pull them on. I blamed it on the dryer.

"That's not what your ass says," replied my mother.

"Enough, Amelia," Beverly spoke up. "Don't you have things to do? Like clean your house or something?"

"Fine, I know when I'm not wanted," my mother huffed. She looked at me. "Just… be careful. It's all your father and I ask."

It was hard to stay mad when I knew she cared in her own way. "I will. Tell my father I'll be careful."

My mother nodded, left the room, and disappeared out the front door.

As she left the room, I let out a sigh of relief. Dealing with my mother was never easy, especially when it came to all things magical.

"You okay?" Ruth asked, placing a hand on my shoulder.

"Yeah." I nodded. "Just tired of the drama."

"Amelia was always such a drama queen," said Beverly.

Dolores snorted. "You're the drama queen. Amelia was always the runner-up."

Beverly smiled as she stood up with a dramatic flourish and struck a pose. "I am a *queen*."

Oh boy.

Although my mother had left, and there were some smiles all around the table, I could still feel the tension in the air, the weight of everything that had happened to us in the past few days. It was like we were all hanging on by a thread, waiting for the next shoe to drop. But in the midst of all that fear and uncertainty, there was something else. Something that made my heart race and my palms sweat. It was the feeling that it wasn't over yet.

And that was one of the reasons why I wanted to come here.

My eyes found the Dark witch sitting at the table, who'd been silent this whole time. "Iris. You think you could perform your locator spell one last time for me?"

I'd noticed the map still spread out on the living room floor, next to her mixing bowl and other magical instruments.

Confusion flashed over my friend's face. "You don't think it worked?"

"No. I mean, *yes*. I think it worked. But that was a while ago. I just want to make sure he's still not in Hollow Cove."

"You think he's back?" Dolores's mouth hung open like she wanted to say more.

I pushed my chair back and stood. "I want to make sure he's not."

"Why?" Dolores pressed.

"Just… give me a minute," I said. "And I'll explain everything." I glanced at Iris. "Can you do it again?" I hoped she would say yes and not that we'd have to wait twenty-four hours. You never knew with magic and spells. Sometimes, you couldn't do the spell twice in a row. It didn't always work that way.

"Of course," said Iris. "I gathered more than enough grave dirt to do the spell again another four times if you want."

I cringed on the inside but pulled a smile on my face. "That's great."

The Dark witch beamed, leaving the kitchen table with her glass of red wine to sit on the living room floor next to the Hollow Cove map.

I followed her. The sound of hurried bustling and feet told me my aunts were right behind me as I settled on the floor next to Iris. Beverly took one of the armchairs as Ruth and Dolores sat on the couch.

The sound of wings caught my attention just as Tinky flew into the living room, and a black cat padded behind her.

"Oooh, are you doing another spell?" asked the tiny fairy, hovering over the map.

"We are. Same spell as before." I eyed the odd pair of pals. "Let me guess… going after fireflies again tonight?" I wasn't sure I wanted to know what they did with them after they were killed. Did they eat them? Yeah, I didn't want to know.

Tinky gave an excited flap of her wings. "Not exactly."

"We're going to catch some sand crabs on Sandy Beach." Hildo licked his front paw and rubbed his face. "They only come out once the sun sets. So we've got a half hour before the first batch crawl onto the beach."

"Yay!" clapped Tinky. "Fun times."

Yuck. Just thinking about hundreds of crabs creeping up the shore had the hair on the back of my neck rise. "Right. Have fun with that."

"We will. See you all later!" Tinky flew out the open kitchen window as the back door opened magically, and Hildo tottered out.

"Aren't they cute?" said Ruth, beaming. "I thought for sure Hildo wanted to eat her. But look at them now. They're eating *other* creatures together, not each other!"

I snorted. "Yes, very cute." I loved that Tinky was living here with us and not in her home world, Storybook, where I knew she was hunted by whatever beings Samael had created.

I shifted to get comfortable on the floor and watched as Iris grabbed some of that grave dirt and sprinkled it over the map like it was cinnamon and she was about to bake an apple pie.

I didn't have to wait long this time around. Once Iris placed the skull back on the map and said the chant, the skull rose in the air, hovered over the map, and then shot across the room to land near the entrance.

"Satisfied?" Dolores asked. "He's not here."

"Yet," I said. "Thanks, Iris."

"No problem," said the Dark witch. "I'll keep the rest of the grave dirt here in case you need me to perform it again."

"Thanks."

Dolores stood from the couch. "What do you mean *yet*? You think he's coming back tonight?"

"Yes. But that's good."

"Good that a murderous human hunter wants to cut off our heads? Are you crazy?"

I pursed my lips. "Little bit."

Ruth laughed. "You're funny."

I beamed. I loved my Aunt Ruthy.

"Okay, let me explain," I said, walking over to pick up the skull and handing it back to Iris, who stuffed it in her bag for safekeeping.

"This better be good," said Beverly, crossing her legs.

"The thing is, with Benjamin out of our town right at this moment, we'll know where he'll be when he comes back because—"

"There's only one way on this island, and that's with the bridge." Dolores narrowed her eyes at me. "You mean to intercept him."

"Exactly. We might not know the exact time he'll come, but it'll be tonight. And now we have the location. He'll be trying to cross the bridge," I told them. "Perfect to hit them with that memory charm. You following me?

Ruth leaned forward. "But you haven't moved."

I glanced at my aunts. "Is the memory charm finished?"

Dolores nodded. "We've done our part."

"Yes," said Beverly. "Ruth?"

192

"Yes." Ruth nodded. "I just need to fill up the bullets we're going to use in the gun."

"The gun?"

Ruth's eyes widened in delight. "A *big* one. We're going to blast these bad humans," she said and punched her open palm.

"I like the way you think."

"Let me go get it!" Ruth leaped into the air and rushed out in a blur of white hair and limbs before vanishing into the potions room.

Beverly leaned back into her chair. "Too much sugar again."

I smiled at Ruth's atomistical energy. But also because we had a good, sound plan.

Like Ruth said, we were going to blast these bad humans tonight.

CHAPTER
15

I sat in the first row facing the city council, which consisted of Mayor Gilbert, sporting a plaid bow tie and brown corduroy jacket, and two other council members, Martha and Marcus, on either side of him. As I settled into my chair, I watched as our mayor fiddled with his bow tie in an attempt to straighten it out.

I tried to get Marcus's attention, but his eyes were fixed on the floor before him, his expression pinched in deep concern and his eyes far away.

As I shifted in the hard seat, trying to avoid numb-butt, I couldn't help but feel an eeriness to the situation.

And it was strange, very strange.

This wasn't my first town meeting inside the Hollow Cove Community Center. I'd been to many—some good and some not so good. Only this was the hall's first time as silent as the Hollow Cove cemetery.

Like I said, very strange.

The Hollow Cove Community Center was filled to the brim with locals. It felt like the entire town had come out for the occasion. All these people and not enough chairs—most of them were wedged in next to the walls, shuffling around trying to make room.

"This is like one of my recurring nightmares," commented Beverly, sitting next to me to my right. "I'm naked, and I walk into a room filled with men."

I looked at her. "I'd think that would be a good dream, not a nightmare," I said, knowing her.

Beverly shook her head, looking troubled. "You would think, but the men just stand there, watching me, without a word about my magnificent naked body. Like they don't want to touch it. Like I'm not *desirable*," she added, her voice filled with horror.

It took a lot of effort not to laugh. I guess for my aunt, having men not find her attractive was a nightmare.

Gilbert cleared his throat. "Yes, well, I will have order," said the mayor, tapping his gavel on the desk and looking just as puzzled and ill-prepared to face the silence as I was.

"There *is* order, idiot," grumbled Ronin, sitting in the seat next to Iris, who sat on my left.

Gilbert gave the half-vampire a death glare, his cheeks now a rosy shade of anger. His face scrunched up in an array of wrinkles, making it look like he was a prune about to burst.

I sighed loudly and took in my surroundings. Fear had taken over the small town, and all the townsfolk seemed to have the same wide-eyed, anxious expression as a litter of scaredy cats. I could understand why; something strange was happening, which certainly wasn't pleasant.

Like a human hunting us.

I leaned forward, resting my elbows on my knees, my fingers laced together. My eyes scanned the room, taking in all the frightened faces. I knew what they were feeling. I had felt that palpable fear that seemed to cling to your skin and eat away at your insides.

The air smelled of perspiration, fear, and too many bodies stuffed inside a limited space.

Iris wrinkled her nose. "What's that smell?"

"Sorry, that was me," murmured Ruth, her face turning a darker shade of pink. "I have gas when I'm nervous."

I laughed. "Me too."

"I see that anyone who's anyone in town is here," Gilbert's voice echoed throughout the room as he eyed the crowd. "Let's begin tonight's council meeting with the issue that's on everyone's mind." He made a show of his grim expression. "Benjamin Morgan." He raised a hand as if silencing a sudden outburst, though there wasn't one. "I know. I know. He's not what we thought he was."

"More like what *he* imagined him to be," I whispered, making Iris laugh.

"Is it me, or does Gilbert look shorter?" questioned Ronin.

Gilbert raised his hand again, signaling for silence that was already there. "I know this news is hard to swallow. But we must remember we are not alone in this world. Humans are out there who would do us harm. But there you have it. A vile human *imposter*." The room was silent, and all eyes turned to Gilbert as he continued. "This imposter has been living among us for weeks."

"What?" My mouth fell open. "Is that true?" I asked to no one in particular.

"It's true," said Dolores. "Well, from what we know, he bought the house two weeks ago. He restored it a few days ago, but it's been his for a while."

So my theory of him walking around among us, studying us, came to light. The bastard had been here for weeks without us knowing. Watching us, analyzing our habits. It creeped me out, but it also angered me.

"Pretending to be one of us while secretly hunting us down like prey," continued Gilbert, his eyes exaggeratedly large. "Humans cannot be trusted!"

"Here we go," I muttered.

A murmur of agreement rose from the crowd, and I could sense the fear growing stronger within them. This was not the way to go. We all knew most humans were good, like most paranormals. This wasn't the time to start blaming all humans for the actions of one asshole.

"He's making this worse," said Iris. "Everyone's already scared out of their minds. What's the matter with him?"

"How long do we have?" I answered.

Gilbert raised his hands. "But, I'll be happy to tell you that we've seen the last of this Benjamin."

My heart pounded as I leaned forward. "What the hell is he doing?"

The mayor smiled at his constituents. "The Merlins have *guaranteed* that he cannot cross the bridge into our town. We are safe. I am happy to say that the threat… is over."

The room erupted in a wave of murmurs, whispers, and gasps. Some people looked relieved while others were simply confused.

I was pissed.

"That little shit," cursed Dolores, her hands gripped into fists. "It's time to make owl pot pie."

"I'll get the pot," said Ruth, her cute face pressed into a scowl.

I was about to stand up to correct the owl shifter, but Marcus beat me to it.

"That's not exactly true," said the chief, speaking loudly, his commanding voice bouncing off the room's walls. "The threat is not over. Benjamin and his crew are still a danger to us."

Gilbert rounded on the chief. "But you said he wasn't here and that he couldn't cross the bridge. Did you purposely lie to me?"

"He really knows how to piss people off. I'll give him that," commented Ronin with a smile. "Wish I had brought some popcorn and some beer."

I took a moment to look at Marcus. His face was stoic and expressionless, like it had been sculpted from granite. But his eyes were raging with emotion, like boiling thunderclouds.

Uh-oh.

"I said he wasn't in town, and the bridge was his only way in." The chief's voice rose, and I could hear the anger in his voice, the threat clear in his posture. Marcus looked away from Gilbert and addressed the crowd. "The humans might not be here now, but that doesn't mean they're not going to try to get in again."

"But can't you stop him?" Gilbert's voice was playing off the hysteria. "That's why we pay you. To *protect* the town."

Marcus's jaw twitched, and I thought for a second he was about to snap the mayor's neck. "The Merlins and I have a plan in place should Benjamin try to cross into our town."

"What's this plan? I demand to know all the details," said Gilbert, tapping a finger on the desk.

"Gilbert, please. Calm down," hissed Martha, worry written all over her face. She waved at someone in the crowd. "You're upsetting everyone."

The mayor's face pulled into a grimace. "I will most certainly *not* calm down! We pay these people for protection, and so far, *five* of us have been killed. Where's the security we pay so highly for? Where's the protection!"

"We are working around the clock, Gilbert," said Marcus, his voice cold and dangerously low. Gilbert was a fool if he didn't recognize the threat there.

Oh, yeah. Gilbert was a fool.

"Ha!" cried Gilbert. "If you couldn't protect us before, how do we know you can protect us now should he return?"

The crowd seemed to come to a sudden consensus. I could feel the fear and anger radiating off of them like an invisible wave of energy. They were scared, and rightfully so. Benjamin was a dangerous man and had already proven that he was willing to do whatever it took to get what he wanted. I knew Marcus and his team were doing everything in their power to keep the town safe, but I could understand why the people were upset.

As I looked around the room, I saw the desperation and frustration etched into every face. These good people tried to live their lives peacefully, but outside forces constantly threatened them. I knew something needed to be done to ease their fears and restore their faith in their protectors. Us.

When I looked back at Gilbert, I saw a strange smile on his face, which was never a good thing.

"I think…" He gazed at Dolores. "I think I will be *reducing* your wages."

Dolores's intake of breath was as loud as if she had used a megaphone.

Beverly snapped her compact shut. "Can he do that?"

Dolores's face had gone really still. It scared the hell out of me.

"What are we going to do for money?" Ruth looked lost. "And we have Tinky to feed now."

Tinkerbell ate the equivalent of a mouse, probably less, but I didn't say anything. I got her point.

I glared at the mayor. "He's bluffing." He better be. Otherwise, he was going to end up in Ruth's stew.

"That's right." Gilbert smiled. He looked over to Marcus and added, "And you too. I don't care that you sit on the council. What good are you to us if you can't do your job? Why should we pay top dollar for mediocre work?"

"That's it. He's dead," I growled.

Ronin stretched out his long legs in front of him. "This is so awesome. I knew I couldn't miss it."

I narrowed my eyes, feeling the power of my inner demon stirring deep inside me and ready to lash out. I was itching for a fight, any fight, even if it meant roasting an owl in the process. Dolores glared at me with such intensity that it immediately snapped me out of my murderous trance.

Marcus returned Gilbert's smile, though it chilled me. "You can try."

Gilbert flinched as though Marcus had physically assaulted him. "I-I will. Don't think I won't. I'm the mayor. And you do as I say."

"If no one shuts him up quickly, I'm going to slap him," I said.

Dolores stood from her chair. Her expression turned hard. "Let me remind you that you were entertained by the idea of a rich, paranormal moving into our town, Gilbert, and that you were all praises after the dinner party. I remember you cozying up to this Benjamin. You were like a dog, heeling before its master."

Gilbert's face became a bright shade of crimson. "You no-good, useless witch—"

"Now, now," my aunt interjected. Her glare could wilt an entire garden of blooming daisies.

202

"Don't want to lose any more inches down there. Do you?" Her eyes drifted downward to his waistline with her eyebrows raised in anticipation.

Gilbert scowled, effectively shutting his mouth. He looked like he was struggling to think of a snappy retort.

I wanted to jump in and stuff his bow tie down his throat, but my aunt gave me a subtle shake of the head that froze me in place.

"Yes, I was at that party." Gilbert trembled as he strained to control himself. "So were you, and so were many of you. But I'm not in charge of protecting this town. I'm the mayor. I make important phone calls and move paper. That's what I was elected for."

"No one else was in the running, Gilbert," muttered Martha.

Gilbert sent a glare her way. "If they can't protect us, what good are they to us?"

Martha opened her mouth, seemingly about to protest, but it just hung open with the words still in her throat. Maybe she agreed. Maybe they all agreed.

We couldn't protect them.

When I glanced around the room, I could see the anger brewing beneath the confusion on some faces. It was clear that many of them had been taken in by Benjamin's lies.

"He's right," came a voice from the crowd.

"My cousin's dead," expressed another voice from the back of the room. "They couldn't protect him."

I could feel their fear and uncertainty growing with each passing moment. And I understood it. But without us, without the Merlins and Marcus, they'd have no chance in hell facing Benjamin. And maybe he'd kill everyone at that party and then return for more.

Dolores sat back down, Gilbert flashing her a winning smile. He might think he won. But won what? My aunts and Marcus would never allow Gilbert to cut our wages. They were barely enough to cover all our expenses. And without us, the town would be open to all kinds of threats, not just Benjamin's.

Marcus raised his hand, signaling for silence, and the crowd slowly settled down.

"Benjamin's infiltration into our town was unexpected, and we were ill-prepared," Marcus began, his voice steady and calm. "But we've taken measures to ensure he can't return. Our plan is simple. We have stationed guards along the perimeter of the bridge, and they are under strict orders to surround and trap Benjamin and his cronies if they attempt to cross it. Then the Davenport witches will dose them with a memory charm, powerful enough that they will never remember us or this place."

Gasps and murmurs rippled through the crowd at Marcus's words. I could still see the doubt on some faces, but most of the group seemed to believe Marcus. He had a way of making people believe in him, probably because until this point, he and my aunts and now me had kept the town safe. Well, sort of.

"And how do we know this spell is going to work?" Gilbert gave my aunts a skeptical gaze.

Dolores's smile turned cold. "Are you volunteering?"

Gilbert's lips tightened in a knot, looking like a butthole.

I couldn't help but let out a chuckle at Gilbert's expense. It was clear he didn't want to be the one to test the memory charm. If anyone deserved to have their memory wiped, it was Gilbert.

Marcus cleared his throat, drawing the attention back to him. "I understand your concerns, Gilbert. But I assure you, the Davenport witches are the best in the business when it comes to memory charms. No one is better."

"I beg to differ," commented the shifter owl.

Ruth crossed her arms. "I think I don't like him anymore."

I didn't know why, but I burst out laughing.

Gilbert's gaze latched on to mine. "You think this is funny? You think this is a joke?

"I think you're the joke."

I could see the anger in his eyes, but I didn't care. He deserved it. He had always been a pain in the ass, trying to make everyone's life miserable. It was time someone put him in his place.

My retort only seemed to anger Gilbert further, but I didn't care. He had always rubbed me the wrong way with his constant negativity and skepticism. It was clear he didn't trust my aunts and me, even though we had proven time and time again that we had the town's best interests at heart.

Ignoring Gilbert's scowl, Marcus continued, "Now, I understand this plan might seem extreme to some of you. But I assure you, it's the only way to keep our town safe."

I heard murmurs of agreement from the crowd. It seemed like Marcus had won them over with his charismatic demeanor and reassuring words.

Suddenly, a commotion broke out at the back of the room. A man, wild-eyed and sweating profusely, pushed his way through the throng of people, shouting and waving his arms. His words were garbled and incoherent, but I could sense the fear in his voice.

"Something's out there! Something's coming!" he yelled, his voice cracking with terror.

"What's going on?" asked Dolores, standing and turning toward the man.

I was already on my feet as I tensed, pulling on my demon mojo. I looked over to Marcus, who was walking around the desk, his phone to his ear.

At that moment, Tinky zoomed into the great room.

"Tinky? What's the matter?" I had a horrible feeling I knew the answer.

"Boats on the beach," said the fairy. "He's here. Benjamin is in Hollow Cove."

Well, son of a damnit.

CHAPTER
16

I don't know why I didn't think of using the water as a means to reach us. We'd been so focused on the bridge that we all forgot Benjamin could come up on the shore with a boat. Or even a helicopter and drop out of the sky, but that would have brought too much attention to him, which I gathered was not his gameplay.

I glanced at Marcus, seeing his frustration. Damn. We both forgot about the beach.

"Keep calm!" shouted Gilbert as the masses scrambled for the doors. "Don't panic. Panicking will only lead to more chaos. Please exit the premises and return to your homes in an *orderly* fashion!"

But it was too late. People were rushing towards the exits, shoving and pushing each other in their desperation to get out. Within thirty seconds, the community center was empty. Well, except for us.

I heard a pop behind me, and when I looked back, a tawny owl flew across the room and disappeared through an open window.

"Now what?" said Ronin. "Ben's here, and he's not on your bridge."

"He could be anywhere," said Iris, a touch of fear in her eyes.

She was right, of course. "Tinky," I said, my mind racing with the possibilities as I headed for the exit, flanked by my aunts, Marcus, Iris, and Ronin. "Do you know where Ben is right now?" I was hoping she'd followed him for a bit.

The fairy nodded as she floated next to my head. "He was walking up Spirit Lane with his men when I left to come find you."

Marcus strode alongside me. "How many?" He slipped his phone from his ear.

"Twelve," answered the fairy. "All dressed in black. They have goggles, too."

I was jogging now. "Night vision." Which explained how they could hunt us at night. "They probably have other sophisticated gear as well." I didn't doubt that. Ben was very resourceful. "He knew about the bridge and came by boat. Or did he always come that way?"

"Good question," said Marcus, running next to me. "Maybe."

We burst through the doors and into the cool night air. The moon was high overhead, casting an eerie glow over everything. We all poured onto the sidewalk of the completely deserted streets. Everyone was gone, hiding, most probably in their homes, where they felt safest. But that wouldn't stop Benjamin. I had a feeling he knew all his targets and knew them well. Knew where they lived.

But I wasn't about to let this man hurt or kill any more of our people.

"It's going to be hard to apply the memory charm accurately if we don't know where they will be," said Dolores. "This spell is potent and extremely dangerous. We might have been a little overzealous in our mixture. You don't want to hit any innocent bystanders."

Ruth's eyes widened. "No. That would be very bad."

"Why? What would happen?" asked the half-vampire.

I looked at him. "Basically, a lobotomy."

Ronin swore. "You guys don't mess around. I like it."

"There's no undoing of that spell either," said Beverly, coming to stand next to her tall sister. "Better steer clear of it if you still want a functional brain."

It made me think of House, the way the basement removed the memories of the evil men my aunts brought back from time to time to replenish or feed the magical entity with the minds of some bad men.

I looked at Ruth. "How many bullets or those vials with the charm do you have?"

"Three," answered Ruth.

Damn. "It's not enough. It won't reach them all."

"Not unless they're dancing a line dance, it won't," said Dolores. "They need to be grouped together. That's how it's supposed to work."

"So what now?" asked Beverly, adjusting the sleeves of her blouse. "We don't know where they are, and they might be split into groups searching the town."

She made a good point. Our master plan of using my aunts' memory charm wasn't looking so good. How were we supposed to group them now when they were out there, hunting the next on their list?

"I'm still going to end them if they come near me or Iris," threatened the half-vampire. He glanced at Marcus. "I know what you said. But if it comes to it, if it's us or them, I'm *always* going to choose us."

Marcus rubbed the back of his neck. "I'm starting to think we might not have a choice anymore."

"You mean kill them?" I didn't like the idea of killing anyone, but like Ronin said, if it came down to it, I would also defend myself. If that meant killing Ben or one of his crew, then so be it. We were running out of options.

The chief looked at me. The intensity of his predatory gaze said it all. He would kill any, if not *all,* of Ben's men if he thought I was in danger. "I'm not going to let him kill another one of us. We'll deal with the consequences. But right now, the lives of our people are my priority."

I understood his reasoning and Ronin's, too. But the idea of more humans like Benjamin retaliating once we'd killed these humans was a scary thought. They could and had the means to destroy this town and all of its inhabitants.

But maybe…

"What are you thinking?" asked the chief, his gray eyes rolling over my face.

"Well, to avoid massive bloodshed…" I began, my brain working on overdrive. "We know we're on that list." I pointed to my aunts and then to myself as though that wasn't clear enough.

"Yes, we got the memo," snapped Dolores.

"So, I say we wait. Wait for *them* to come to Davenport House. They will eventually."

"And then we blast them," exclaimed Ruth, a fist in the air. "And show them what we're made of."

"Exactly." It wasn't ideal, but it was something.

"That might take a while," said the chief. "They're going after the weaker ones first. I don't think they'll come to Davenport House 'til the very end."

"I get that," I answered, "but right now, it's the best plan we've got."

"We'll get them to come inside the house," Dolores was nodding. "Yes. That might work."

I looked at my aunts. "You guys stay at the house and make sure that spell, charm, is ready."

Dolores pressed her hands to her hips. "Of course, it's ready. Who do you think we are? We are Davenport witches. We always come prepared," she said, making Beverly roll her eyes.

I pursed my lips. "Right."

"And what are you going to do?" Iris watched me. She was holding on to the strap of her bag like a lifeline.

"I'm going to find those left on the list and tell them to leave town." I looked at the chief. "Can you tell your guys at the bridge to let them pass? It would be a hell of a lot safer. They can come back when it's over."

The chief grabbed his phone, tapped a number, and put it to his ear again.

"We're coming with you," said Ronin. "This is my town."

"Okay," I said. "But we should split up. It'll go faster." I grabbed my phone and checked the list of names I'd written. "Thirteen people are left from the ones who came to that party, if you don't count us. I'll go to the six who live on the west side of town. You go to the east and take the rest." I gave my phone to Iris so she could copy the names down. "Try calling first. I doubt they'll answer but try." I took back my phone from Iris. "Do everything you can to convince them to leave."

"We will," said Iris. "We'll drive, are you going to…"

"Jump a line. If I can grab them in a ley line with me and drop them off in the next town, I'm doing it." It was risky, and my aunts had warned me about taking nonwitches in ley lines with me. But if they didn't listen, I might have to do it.

"I'll call you and tell you how we're doing," said Iris.

I watched as she and Ronin walked toward his car.

"We should go too," said Beverly. "You be careful, Tessa. That man is vile."

"I will. Stay frosty. You never know." I watched as my three aunts made their way down the street and turned at the sound of Marcus hanging up his phone.

"Marcus?" I didn't like the look in his eye. It was wild. "Where are you going?" At first, I thought he might want to come with me, but that look in his eye said otherwise. And I didn't like it.

The chief looked away from me. "I'm going after Benjamin."

"But…" I knew I couldn't stop him or try to reason with him. "Don't die."

"I won't."

"We've got unfinished business, you and me."

"I know."

"You better come back to me," I said, my voice a little tight. "Cause I'll kick your ass in the afterlife if you don't."

"I don't doubt it." He reached out and kissed me. It was quick but enough to feel the fiery passion in it.

As Marcus pulled away, I noticed that same heated passion still lingering on my lips. But my mind was clouded with worry. I knew how dangerous Benjamin could be, and I didn't want to lose Marcus. I *couldn't* lose him.

With a sudden flash of light and an influx of magic, his features contorted, and he changed before my eyes. His skin swelled, stretching the boundaries of what was humanly possible. A momentary blur of black fur and a horrible flesh-tearing sound came with the breaking of bones. And then, instead of a man, stood a four-hundred-pound silverback gorilla.

I couldn't help but stare at this majestic yet intimidating creature; his chest muscles flexed as he stood on all fours, his front hands resting on his knuckles. The gorilla opened its mouth wide, letting out a deafening growl and revealing a mouth filled with teeth.

And then the gorilla bowed his head in a farewell before launching himself down the street, disappearing in a few powerful strides.

I watched him until he disappeared from my sight before turning around, ready to face whatever dangers awaited me.

Gathering my resolve, I reached for the nearest ley line, taking a deep breath and squeezing my eyes shut to focus. The force of the ley line was palpable, almost like it was alive.

I stepped forward, gradually increasing in intensity until it felt like a warm blanket.

And then I jumped.

My body surged forward with a rush of energy, and I could feel the power pulsing throughout my mind and body. As I sped down the street, the houses and trees looked like streaks of light, just as if I were traveling at warp speed aboard some spacecraft.

I forced my will on the ley line until I felt a sudden shift as everything became focused. The lights and images appeared more slowly and clearly.

I spotted the white bungalow with the red door I was looking for. Ray Blackfoot's house.

He was a bit of a recluse and a werebear. Strong as hell. No wonder he was on Benjamin's list of kills.

My gaze fixed on the house. I funneled my energy toward the ley line and pulled it to the left. I stretched it out like an elastic band, slowing its speed before jumping back into motion. I slowed the ley line and then jumped.

I landed on the soft grass of Ray's front yard. Without a moment to waste, I rushed up to the door and knocked. After the third knock, and no Ray, I yanked out my phone and called him. It went straight to voicemail.

I sighed. "Should I break in?"

Hell, yeah.

I tapped into the elements, flicked my right wrist toward the door, and shouted, "Inflitus!"

A blast of kinetic force lashed out from my outstretched hands and struck the door, knocking it off its hinges. Bits of wood shards and dust flew as the door was thrown back into the house.

"You can bill me for that." I stepped through the now open doorway. "Ray? Ray? You in here?"

Silence greeted me as I stepped into the dimly lit hallway. The air was thick with the musty scent of old books and something else, something metallic. My heart began to race as I took cautious steps forward, my eyes scanning the shadows for any sign of danger.

I stepped forward, looking for Ray. The air hung thick and heavy with the scent of damp earth and musky fur, a clear indication that Ray was a werebear. My senses were on high alert, my instincts telling me to proceed with caution.

But the more I looked around, the more I realized I saw no signs of a struggle. And no signs of Ray.

"He's not here." Maybe he was smart and had left town. No car was in the driveway. Perhaps he'd gone.

Resolute, I decided to check the next person on my list. I grabbed my phone just as I stepped over the threshold and onto the small concrete platform.

I sensed a presence on the front lawn before I saw him.

A man stepped into my light of sight as I looked up from my phone.

He was dressed all in black, in some sort of tactical gear with a large assault rifle strapped to his back. A black balaclava obscured his face, but his eyes were piercing and cold.

"You're not Benjamin," I said, though from how he was dressed, it was clear he was part of his crew.

The man chuckled darkly. "No. And you're not Ray Blackfoot."

"Your perception astounds me."

"You're Tessa Davenport. The witch." He reached behind his back and pulled out his rifle.

I wiggled my fingers at him. "Is *that* supposed to scare me?" What I really should have been doing was blasting this sonofabitch back to whatever town he came from. But maybe I could get some answers out of him first.

The man's eyes darkened as he aimed the weapon at me. I could feel the tension in the air, the weight of his intention to pull the trigger. But I didn't falter. I stood my ground, staring him down with all the fire I could muster.

"You should be scared," he growled, his finger hovering over the trigger. "We've been watching you, witch. We know what you can do."

"You mean, eating an entire cheesecake by myself?" I smirked, conjuring up the power of the elements around me. "I'm a witch of many talents."

"We'll see."

"I won't go down without a fight."

"That's what I'm hoping for." The man hesitated for a moment, his eyes flickering between me and the weapon in his hands. It was clear he didn't expect me to be this confident, this brazen in the face of danger. But I wasn't about to let him get the upper hand.

"Where's your bow and arrow? Not feeling the Hunger Games theme anymore?"

"We don't use those for witches."

I tapped my lips with my finger. "Let me guess... fire?"

"Maybe." He moved his fingers on his weapon, and I heard a sudden click like he took off the safety or something.

I stiffened, reaching out to the elements as I readied a power word. My pulse quickened, and I felt a sudden relief at the surge of magic, sending my skin riddling with goosebumps.

It was like Ronin said: It was either them or us.

And I chose us.

I focused my will, called forth the magic of the elements, and shouted, "Accendo!"

Twin fireballs hurled from my outstretched hands, flying straight and true right at the man's head.

The man touched a wrist computer with a screen wrapped around his right arm I hadn't noticed before, and a green semi-transparent shield rose from the ground and over his head until he looked like he was floating in a large soap bubble.

The fireballs hit the shield in a sudden blast of hot air before extinguishing into sizzling smoke. The man pulled back his balaclava, and a small, sly smile drew from his face.

Oh shit.

My magic had no effect on him.

Well, that wasn't good.

CHAPTER
17

I was not expecting that, and judging from his smug smile, he knew it.

His shield had magical properties. I could feel the waves of energy wafting off of it, hot like heat from a radiator.

I flicked a finger at the shield. "Did you find that in a cracker jack box?"

"Wouldn't you like to know," sneered the man.

It looked like Benjamin had found himself some witches or wizards to construct some kind of magical repellent shields. Idiots. He probably paid them well, too. Damnit. Now what?

I could either jump a line and get the hell out, or I could try another power word.

I chose the latter.

"Inspiratione!" I shouted, sending a stream of red energy out of my hand toward the man's defense. The magic snaked around him like a rope but soon fizzled away into nothing after a few moments. He barely moved on impact.

The man laughed. "Nice try. But your hocus pocus won't work on us."

Shit. "I thought you humans didn't like magic and witches. Why are you wrapped in a magical protection bubble?"

He grinned. "So I can kill you. You can't touch me. Your magic is useless."

"Not likely." It's not like I couldn't pull on a ley line and fly my ass out of here. I could still feel the pulses of the lines. Whatever he was carrying didn't affect them.

I took that as a sign that they didn't know about the ley lines. In fact, not many paranormals did, so that meant even less with humans.

This situation wasn't ideal. But the fact that this human bubble was here and Ray wasn't told me the werebear had escaped.

I took comfort in that, yet I still had a huge problem to deal with. He was too powerful with that magical sphere wrapped around him. I had to find a way to dismantle it, burst it, whatever. And fast.

"Listen," I said, "you don't have to do this. You can leave us alone. We won't bother you if you don't bother us. How about you call it a night and go about your merry way?" I doubted it, but I thought I'd just throw it out there and see what happened.

His eyes narrowed. "And why would I do that?"

"Because it's the right thing to do. Killing us won't solve anything. It won't make you feel better."

"Yes, it will."

Okay, wrong thing to say.

The man started to tap on the screen of his wrist tech. He caught me staring and said, "Just telling Ben that I found you."

I pressed a hand on my hip. "Benjamin must be paying you a lot of money to go through all this trouble."

"He is. But I enjoy getting rid of the freaks."

I clicked my tongue. "I'm a Merlin, dumbass. Magical Enforcement Response League Intelligence Network. Just FYI." I was very proud of my Merlin license, even though this creep had probably never heard of it.

He sneered behind his bubble. "Ben's got big plans for you," he said as he started to circle me like that was supposed to scare me. It did make me slightly uncomfortable, though.

I moved with him. The green sphere radiated magic. Lots of it. "I thought you said you wanted to kill me."

"I do, but Ben wants you alive. The man who pays is the man in charge."

He kept circling me, and I kept spinning around to keep him in my sight. "Stop moving. You're making me dizzy."

"I had no idea so many freaks were living in our world."

"*Your* world?"

"Yeah, *our* world. You don't belong here."

I didn't have the patience to teach some history to this fool. "I don't know whether to take you seriously in that bubble thing or not."

He approached me, his smile widening with each step. "You really don't know who you're dealing with. Do you?" he said, his voice low and dangerous.

My magic soared through me, and I kept it there. "The bubble man? Nope. Never heard of you. Sorry, did I just *burst* your bubble?"

He frowned, apparently not appreciating my sense of humor.

"It's a shame," he continued, circling me again like a predator. "I was hoping for more of a challenge. The way Ben was talking about you… like you were the one to beat. But you're not much. You're pretty. I'll give you that, but your magic can't penetrate my defenses. I guess this will have to do, though."

I raised my baby finger. "I've got more magic in this finger than you have in that magical contraption."

"Prove it."

I stood there with my hands on my waist. "Oh? Sorry, are you waiting for me?"

Suddenly, he lunged at me, his hand outstretched, and before I knew it, he had grabbed me by the neck and lifted me off the ground. I could feel his fingers digging into my flesh, cutting off my air supply.

He could reach out of his shield, but I couldn't penetrate it with magic. That was new.

"You witches think you're so powerful," he spat, tightening his grip. "Well, let me tell you something, *sweetheart*. You're nothing compared to us."

I hated being called sweetheart. It rubbed me the wrong way. "Well, I don't know about that, *dick*." I kicked out hard and managed to hit his knee. He let go of my neck and stumbled back, laughing but seemingly unfazed by me and my charms.

"Tell me something," I started. I wanted to know more before I pulled a ley line and dropped his stupid ass in the middle of the ocean. "Why? Why are you doing this to us? We haven't done anything to any humans." Well, as far as I knew, but that might not be true for other communities.

"You're animals," said the man in a matter-of-fact tone. "We hunt animals."

I clenched my fists. "We're not animals. Well, yes, some of us have animal shapes. You can think of it like our spirit animals. But fundamentally, we are people. We have thoughts and feelings just like you."

The man laughed. "That may be, but you're not the same as us. You're different. I don't like different. Nobody likes different."

"Being different is a blessing," I said, my magic spiraling inside me, anxious to be rid of this asshat. "Normal is boring."

"You're beasts," said the man, like it was the most natural thing in the world. "And beasts should know their place. So now it's time for you to learn your place, freak."

I shook my head. "Says the dude wrapped in a bubble."

Bubble dude took a step forward, and I had to admit I was impressed by his lack of fear. Either he was extremely powerful in that bubble suit or just really dumb.

"You said Benjamin wants me alive," I asked, keeping just the right distance from him. "Why? You said it yourself. I'm nothing special. Why kill the others? They didn't deserve to die." My rage pounded through me at the memory of the beheaded body and knowing that there had been four more just like it.

"Those were number threes," said the human man behind his magical bubble. "Threes are hunted and killed. You're a ten."

I hooked thumbs at myself. "Me? A ten? Are you flirting with me?"

Irritation flared in his expression. "Ben has big plans for the tens."

"I feel so lucky I could just burst… see what I did there?"

"You're a strange one."

"Thanks. So your boss goes around paranormal communities to collect us? Where does he put us all? In a zoo?"

"Not all. Ben wants to sell some of you. You won't believe how much people will pay for the likes of you."

This conversation was getting more and more disturbing by the minute. "I think I just threw up in my mouth."

He raised his gun. "You're coming with me."

"No." I steadied myself for what was coming. Because I knew it would.

Cold energy coursed through my veins, and the demon mojo I had long kept contained stirred within me. I welcomed it and opened myself to its power, allowing the cold, wild magic to consume me.

And then he pulled the trigger.

It wasn't a bullet I saw coming out of the barrel. But a silver, gleaming net.

Black tendrils of demon energy roared forth from my outstretched fingers and hit the net.

And nothing happened.

My demon mojo withered and vanished.

The net kept coming.

"Oh shit." It was like watching a scene play out in slow motion; a silver magical net came at me.

I wasn't about to let bubble man take me captive.

So I did the only thing I could.

I yanked on a ley line and jumped.

I felt my skin singe where the magical net brushed my fingers. The world blurred as I bent the ley line and spun it around. When I was positioned behind bubble man, I jumped out.

He was shaking his head. I could see it through his protection shield.

"Boo!" I shouted.

The human man screamed and spun around, his gun aiming at me.

"You scream like a girl." From his confused and angered expression, I'd been right about my ley lines. They didn't know about them. It was the only tool I had, and I was going to use it.

The man's mouth hung open as he pointed to the spot where I had been a second ago. "You were just…but… how'd you do that? You teleported?"

It was my turn to grin. "Wouldn't you like to know?"

His expression turned quickly into something that resembled fury and frustration. "You weren't supposed to be able to move like that. Ben never said."

"Ben doesn't know everything. Where is he, by the way? Why are you doing his dirty work?" I knew Marcus was looking for him, and I wanted to find Benjamin before he did. If these guys were equipped with magical nets and magical protection shields, who knew what else they had with them? I needed to find Marcus.

At that, the human man chuckled darkly, which had the hairs on the back of my neck rise. "Collecting the other tens."

I really didn't like the way he laughed. "Which other tens?"

"Your aunts and that little Dark witch."

My blood went cold, and the ground shifted. My aunts. Iris. They didn't know about these bastards' countermagic measures. They weren't prepared.

Damn. I had to warn them.

I made to move, but the bubble man stepped in my way, his net gun pointed at me again.

"I thought we've covered this already." I wasn't in the mood to play games anymore.

"I won't let you go. I'll get you this time. You won't escape me."

"We'll just see about that." I had enough of his crap. I needed to get to my aunts.

I pulled on a ley line just as bubble man rushed me, tripped on the uneven paver stones—I shit you not—and fell hard on the ground.

I heard a loud crunch, like metal crinkling, and then the man's green shield vanished.

But that's when things got weird.

A green gas rolled out of a part of that wrist tech bracelet, enveloping the man in a cloud.

"What is this? Hey! What the fuck? It burns!" he yelled as he moved around on the ground.

The man then let out a horrifying scream as his body jerked uncontrollably one final time. His lips stretched wide as if to utter some kind of plea that might rescue him, and the sound made my hair stand on end.

Then he stopped moving.

Whatever that wrist tech thing was, it had malfunctioned as it broke in his fall, and the dude had paid dearly for it.

I leaned over the body and said, "I'd ask for a refund."

Then I tapped another ley line and jumped.

Chapter
18

I tried not to think about the disturbing images of the human man thrashing on the grass as whatever magical gas he'd used killed him.

I had to get to my aunts.

I could have pulled out my phone to call them, but by the time they'd pick up, I'd already be at the house.

Davenport House rose before me, its white siding gleaming in the moonlight. I slowed the ley line until it was almost at a full stop and jumped off.

I tried to land expertly on the grass, like the seasoned ley line witch that I was. Unfortunately, my aerobatics weren't as smooth as I'd hoped, and instead, I ended up face-planting into the grass and presenting my posterior to the world.

I pushed myself up, feeling a slight sprain in my left ankle, and charged up the front porch steps, ignoring the throbbing ache.

"Dolores? Beverly? Hello? Ruth?" I rushed inside as fast as I could.

The lights were on. I wasn't getting any vibes of an attack happening inside the house. The furniture was the same as it always was. I rushed to the kitchen, seeing plates in the sink. "Is anyone here?"

I took a deep breath, trying to calm the panic that was threatening to take over. Maybe they were out in the garden or the back room working on another spell. I made my way through the house, calling out their names as I went.

I searched every room of the house, but my aunts and Iris were nowhere to be found. Dread began to settle in my chest. The fact that I saw no sign of a fight told me that maybe the human bubble man was wrong. Perhaps Ben hadn't come here yet.

So where were my aunts? Had they sensed something untoward and decided to hide? I took a moment to gather my thoughts, trying to figure out where they could have gone.

I yanked out my phone and called Iris. It went straight to voicemail after the fourth ring. I hung up and tried Ronin. Same thing.

"Damn it." There was no use calling Marcus since he was in his gorilla form. That's when it occurred to me. There was just one other place they could be. And that was the Hollow Cove Security Agency. It made sense. They could be there.

And there was only one way to find out.

I ran down the hallway, more like limped. "House, if my aunts show up, keep them inside. Don't let them leave."

The floor shook as the pipes whined in House's answer. I knew they'd be safe inside.

I'd left the front door open, so as I stepped onto the porch, I reached out to the ley line, felt it rise around me, and jumped.

Jumping ley lines was becoming second nature to me, almost like walking—walking really fast.

Within moments, the gray building of Marcus's office appeared. Yellow light spilled from the windows, and this time I waited for the ley line to make a complete stop before I stepped off.

I pulled open the glass doors, already seeing shapes moving inside.

If I thought people had panicked back at the community center, this was worse.

At least thirty paranormals were jammed into the hallway. The air was thick with the stench of fear, sweat, and magic. The panic was palpable, almost suffocating. I pushed my way through the crowd, trying to get a glimpse of what was happening ahead.

Windows were shattered, furniture was overturned, and the smell of blood filled the air. My heart sank when I finally saw what had caused the chaos. Two paranormals lay on the floor, both with multiple arrows sticking out of their chests. One I recognized as Lara, a female shifter. And both were alive. A group of paranomals was attending to their wounds. When I made my way closer, I noticed another person on the floor. This one was dressed all in black. Blood had pooled from the body. The man's dead eyes stared at the ceiling.

"Tessa! Thank the cauldron."

I looked up to see Martha pushing her way to me. My aunts and Iris were nowhere in sight, but I couldn't let that distract me. I had to find them and warn them about Benjamin.

"What happened here?"

The beauty witch's hair was sticking out on odd ends as though one of her hair-drying stations had malfunctioned. She had a long, bloody scratch across her forehead.

"We killed one of them."

"I can see that. How? The one I fought had some magical protection barrier."

Martha wiped her sweaty forehead with a trembling finger. "I don't know about that. But he put two arrows into Lara before we took him down."

"Where was this?"

"Near my salon," answered the witch. "And Mateo was attacked while trying to get his family out of town. Neighbors saw and managed to fight the human off. We don't know where he went. But we brought our injured here. Your aunts weren't at the house. Do you know where they are? We need Ruth."

I shook my head, knowing Ruth was the town's go-to healer. "No. I was hoping they'd be here."

"Sorry, hon."

I sighed, feeling a weight settle in my chest. I was proud of my community, proud that they'd fought and managed to save two and take down one of these bastards.

Still, things were spiraling out of control faster than I could keep up. I had to find my aunts and Iris before it was too late.

My eyes landed on Lara. "She needs a healer. She's really pale." She might be a shifter and technically could last a lot longer than, let's say, a regular human, but she wouldn't last long with those arrows sticking out of her chest, not to mention the blood loss.

Martha followed my gaze. "Lara's a tough one. She'll be all right for now."

A commotion caught my attention. I'd recognize the high-pitched voice anywhere.

"Are you mad! Those crazy humans are out there!" shouted Gilbert.

A tall, dark-skinned man pointed at Lara. "She needs a healer. And I'm driving to Lockwood Village to get one."

Gilbert rose on the tips of his toes in an attempt to appear more imposing, but it made him look like he was trying out for the ballet. "If you go out there, you'll die."

The man scowled at Gilbert. "Then I'll die. But I can't just sit here and watch Lara suffer."

"You won't know she's suffering because you'll be dead!" Gilbert's voice had risen to a new level of screeching.

"Those are some serious lungs for such a small person."

Martha rolled her eyes and breathed out some words I couldn't catch.

Gilbert's head turned my way. His eyes widened as he spotted me.

"You! Tessa." Gilbert waddled forward, pushing and nudging paranormals as he went. "You're a Merlin. Stop him. Tell him this is madness."

I glanced at the big, muscled shifter. I could see the terror there, the fear he had at the idea of losing the one he loved. I also saw the defiance there that I knew if I tried to stop him, he'd pound my head in.

I glanced back at Gilbert. "I will not." Because I knew I'd do the same if Marcus were lying there full of arrows. I'd travel to hell and back to get my wereape help. Nothing would stop me.

"What? You cannot be serious."

"Never been more serious. He wants to save his wife. And he has every right to do so."

Gilbert spluttered in disbelief. "You're a Merlin, for cauldron's sake. It's your job to stop this kind of thing. It's why I pay you!"

I folded my arms across my chest, staring at him with a stony expression. "My job is to protect the town, not to interfere with people's decisions. Besides, he's right. Lara needs a healer, and if he's willing to risk his own life to go get one, who am I to stop him?"

"You're just going to let him go out there and get killed?" Gilbert's face was turning red with anger.

"I'm not *letting* him do anything," I said firmly. "He's a grown man who can make his own decisions. If he wants to risk his life to save someone he loves, I'm not going to stand in his way." No. I understood him. "Wouldn't you do the same for your mate?"

Gilbert faltered, looking down at his feet. "Well, yes, but…"

"No buts, Gilbert," Martha spoke up. "Let the man go. It's his choice. Leave Tessa alone. She's not going to stop him, and neither should you. He's doing what he needs to do."

Gilbert huffed, looking like a child who had been denied his favorite toy. "Fine, do what you want. But when he comes back in pieces, don't say I didn't warn you."

"I won't."

"He's going to get himself killed," Gilbert muttered under his breath.

"Maybe," I agreed. "But he has to try."

Gilbert huffed, obviously not happy with my response. "This is all going to hell." With that, Gilbert stomped off, pushing his way again through the throng of paranormals, and then climbed up on a chair to be the tallest in the room. Idiot.

My eyes fell on the big shifter. He nodded in gratitude and then glanced over to his wife one last time before turning around and making his way out of the agency. He strode towards the door, his broad shoulders filling the space and his head held high. I watched him go, my heart heavy with the weight of his determination, and prayed to the goddess that he'd return to his wife alive and with a healer.

As soon as the door closed behind him, Martha turned to me with concern etched on her face. "Do you think he'll be okay?" she asked, her voice laced with worry.

I shrugged, not really knowing what to say. "I hope so. He wasn't one of Ben's threes—I mean targets." Damn. I didn't want that to get around.

Martha sighed, her shoulders slumping. "Me too."

We stood there in silence for a moment, both lost in our thoughts. Then Martha turned to me, her expression determined. "Will Marcus come back, you think? I think everyone would feel better if he was here."

"I don't know. But I need to go. I need to find him and my aunts. If I find Ruth, I'll send her this way."

I took a deep breath, trying to calm my racing heart. The situation had escalated quickly, and I knew we were in for a long night. "I'll go look for them. But be careful, Martha. Benjamin and his goons might come here. They have some magical-repellent shields. So your magic or any magic won't work on them."

"We'll be fine." Martha nodded, her eyes filled with fear and determination. "We will. And Tessa?"

"Yeah?"

"Be careful, too."

With that, I darted out of the room and into the cool night air. My ankle still throbbed, but I barely noticed the pain now. I was too high on adrenaline.

The moon was high in the sky, casting an eerie glow over the small town. I could hear the distant shouts and screams, and I knew chaos had spread over our little village of paranormals.

I ran down the street, my senses on high alert. I could smell the metallic tang of blood in the air, and my heart clenched with fear. What if Benjamin had already found my aunts? What if they were hurt or worse?

I stopped and tried my phone again, calling Iris, Ronin, and even Marcus. But none of them picked up, which only worsened my fears.

The sound of wings fluttering snapped my attention up.

"Tessa!"

Tinkerbell zoomed my way, flying in a pan-icky, twitchy pattern until she halted before my face.

"I've been looking for you everywhere," said the tiny fairy.

I took a deep breath, trying to steady my nerves. I couldn't afford to panic now. "Why? What's happened? Is it my aunts?"

Tinky nodded. "I'm sorry. I couldn't help. I tried and tried, but my magic didn't work. It's all my fault."

"Tinky!" I was shouting. "What happened? Where are my aunts?"

The fairy's eyes met mine, brimming with tears. "He took them. Benjamin."

I swallowed the fear that threatened to take over. I gritted my teeth, cursing myself for not being able to protect my aunts. "Where?"

The fairy hovered before my eyes and said, "To his ship."

Chapter
19

I didn't have to wait for Tinky to tell me where this ship was, or maybe I should have, but before my brain had made up its mind, my hand reached out. I grabbed the fairy, tapped into a ley line—and jumped.

"Balls. Dang. Penis!" screamed the fairy as our bodies rushed forward with the speed of light.

I had a slight moment of panic and regret. I should have thought this through. Taking Tinky in a ley line might get her hurt, but it was too late for that. I cupped her gently in my hands.

"Hang on!" I shouted, bending slightly forward and using my body to propel the ley line.

"I think I peed my pants!" cried the fairy.

The warm salt smell of the ocean hit me first, and the cool sea breeze soothed my sweaty forehead. I could hear the tide rolling in. The breeze from the beach brought a mix of salt and seaweed.

The last time I came to Sandy Beach was during the debacle with Derrick. I pushed the thoughts away. I didn't have time to think of him right now. I had another prick occupying my thoughts.

I slowed the ley line as soon as the outline of the beach came into view. And then I jumped. As we landed, I stumbled—again—and lost my balance before collapsing onto the sand. Tinky flew out of my hands, still screaming obscenities.

I quickly got up and brushed off the sand from my clothes. My eyes scanned the coast, searching for any sign of my aunts and Benjamin and his men. The marina was tucked away next to the town beach, out of sight. Like a floating parking lot, long wharves were draped over the water with yachts and dinghies tethered to them. The air had a certain pungent smell—a mixture of dead fish, algae, and motor oil.

But no people.

Something massive floated a bit out into the sea. It was hard to tell what it was in the darkness, but the moonlight gave enough illumination for me to tell that it could be a ship. A gigantic ship. I could be wrong, but it looked like a freighter. What the hell was it doing here? It was Benjamin's, obviously.

"Tessa," Tinkerbell's voice called out to me.

I turned around and saw her hovering above my head. She had calmed down and was now looking at me with wide eyes.

"That was awesome. I was scared and excited at the same time. What a rush!"

"That's how I felt the first time I rode a ley line."

"Are you okay?" she asked, her concern high in her voice.

"I'm fine," I said. "Where's Hildo?"

"He went to Davenport House, looking for you."

"Okay." I stared out at the freight ship. "They're in there. Aren't they?"

"I don't know," she said, gazing at the would-be freighter. "I left just as they were caught. But they might be there. Yes. I think you're right."

And I was going to set them free.

"Well, well, well," said a male voice behind us. "How nice of you to join us, Tessa Davenport."

I didn't have to turn around to know who had spoken, but I did anyway.

Ben stood at the edge of sand dunes, and about twenty of his men, all dressed in that tactical gear bubble dude had worn and enveloped in that anti-magical shields, flanked his sides.

He was dressed like them but without the anti-magical barrier. I wasn't sure if it was because he thought I couldn't reach him or he was just too arrogant to use one.

With the wind and the waves crashing, I'd never heard their approach.

"I thought you said there were twelve," I muttered to the fairy.

"There were," she answered. "Must have called some reinforcements."

"I knew you would come." The big man walked down the dunes.

"Really. Why's that?"

"Because animals are creatures of habit," he answered, his men moving on either side of him. "If you take something of theirs, they will come and try to get it. It works every time."

"Where are they?" I knew he was speaking about my aunts. "Tell me what you did to them." Rage soared as my body trembled with it. My magic, both White and Dark, vibrated through me. If he killed them… No, I couldn't think that way. They were still alive. I had to believe that.

Benjamin kept climbing down until he was level with me on the beach. "I've gotten them ready."

"Ready for what?" At least by his comment, I knew they were still alive.

He smiled. "For transport."

I narrowed my eyes at him. "Where are you taking them?"

Benjamin chuckled and shrugged. "That's not your concern, Tessa. I will tell you that they'll fetch a good price. Did you know a witch can go for a million dollars these days?"

I felt sick. "You're a disturbed individual." I stepped forward, my fury thrashing. "Where are they? I want to see them."

Benjamin looked at my hands. "Or else… what? You'll do your Shadow magic on me? Yes, I know all about you. I studied you. I know you can conjure both sides of magic. But that won't save you or your aunts. You've lost. I won."

"Won what? You bastard."

"Them." Ben snapped his figures, and more of his men appeared from the darkness, struggling in the sand as they hauled hand truck dollies.

I heard Tinky's intake of breath before my eyes adjusted to the semi-darkness, and I then saw them. All five of them.

Dolores, Beverly, Ruth, Iris, and Ronin were strapped down in an upright position, each on a dolly, their heads, arms, and legs all restrained with leather ties. Green magic, similar to the magic the humans used as their shields, roped around my family and friends. Ronin could have easily broken free from those leather bonds. But not these. These were laced with some kind of magic that kept him from using his vampire strength and my aunts from using their magic to blast them to pieces.

"Excellent," Benjamin said, clapping his hands together, "a family reunion."

Dolores's eyes found mine, and they widened in fear. She couldn't move, but her eyes had enough worry and despair that I nearly lost it right there. Okay, I did lose it.

"Motherfrackers!"

I channeled my inner will and allowed my anger to drive my arcane power. The cold, wild magic surged through me like a drug, stronger than any adrenaline rush I had ever felt before. Opening my eyes, I released the power of my demonic magic. Black tendrils whirled out from my hands like a hurricane unleashed, and I hurled it at Benjamin.

He touched his forearm, and a green, spherical shield enveloped him.

My tendrils hit the edge of his shield, sizzled for half a second, and then dissolved.

Benjamin laughed as if he had expected no less from me.

I gritted my teeth and tried again, pouring even more of my demon mojo into the attack. The tendrils grew larger and thicker, but again, they only hit the shield's edge and dissolved. I was getting frustrated. My demon mojo was my strongest weapon, and it seemed like it was useless against Benjamin's anti-magical armor.

"Stop wasting your energy, my dear," Benjamin said with a sinister smile. "Your magic is no match for mine."

"Yours?" I panted. "You mean some wizard or witch you have on your payroll."

"Perhaps."

I growled in response, staring at him with pure hatred.

He walked over to the human dollies, his eyes flicking over each of my captured loved ones. He pressed a finger on his wrist tech. With a soft *pop*, his shield dropped. "You know, she's a fine specimen. Delicate," he mused, running a finger over Beverly's cheek. "I can ask double for this one. Yes, she'll do just fine."

My hands clutched into fists. "My aunts are not for sale, prick."

"Yes, they are." Benjamin turned around, that smug smile on his face. "I've already started the bidding."

My mouth dropped open. "The bidding?"

At that, some of Benjamin's crew started to laugh. I didn't think I'd ever felt more vulnerable or had more hate for a group of people in my entire life.

Benjamin pulled something from his jacket and tossed it. It landed in the sand at my feet. Keeping my eyes on him and his men, I lowered and grabbed it. It was a phone. I stared at the screen. There were pictures of my aunts, Iris, and Ronin, in their captive states. Above each image was a timer that read 3:26:01. And it was descending. But a dollar value also sat next to each picture, all rising to hundreds of thousands of dollars.

Disgusted, I threw the phone into the water. Well, not exactly. Though I did aim for the water, my upper body strength left lots to be desired, so the phone made a thud as it fell on the sand.

I felt sick and disgusted by these humans who would sell my aunts and friends like objects at an action as though their lives meant nothing. Guess they didn't to them.

I was seriously neck deep in Crapper Lake with no boat or paddle in sight.

How could I save my aunts and friends when my magic had no effect?

"Tessa," I heard Tinky's voice, filled with fear.

"Go," I urged. I didn't want her to get caught in this. "Go. Get somewhere safe. Get Hildo and get to the community center."

"I won't go," said the fairy. "I'm not leaving you."

I looked at her. "You have to. They need to know what's happened."

Something flashed across her face, and then she was gone, leaving behind bits of sparkling golden dust, and for a second, she reminded me of a firefly.

When I looked back, Benjamin was smirking at me. "And I'll get a sweet price for you too."

"Fuck you."

My anger flared again, and I raised my hands, ready to unleash another wave of demon magic.

But the bastard was quick or had anticipated my reaction, and his green armor popped to life just as my black tendrils hit.

Something struck me in the back, and I fell to my knees. The impact of pain took the breath from my lungs, and I felt my hold on my magic release.

"Witch bitch," said a voice. "That's for James." A boot struck me in the chest, and I tumbled into the sand.

I took it that James was the one who had died because his armor turned on him. Or he was the one Martha and the others had killed. I managed to get back on my feet, wobbling. "Your friend's own stupidity did him in," going with bubble guy.

The man's face rippled in anger before he swung his baseball bat—yes, that's what I said—at me.

I leaped to the side but not fast enough.

I cried out as the metal of the bat caught my left side. Agony vibrated through me, and every nerve ending throbbed into a burn. The pain went all the way from my skull to my toes.

Damn it. Every breath hurt. Hot pain throbbed in my side. I was pretty sure he'd broken a few ribs.

I clasped a hand around my middle and staggered away from him, doing my best to remain standing. I felt like I was about to pass out from the combination of pain and exhaustion.

My stubbornness got the better of me, and I stood up and gave him the finger.

He punched me across the jaw, making stars explode in my vision. Damn. That hurt. I could hear Dolores and Beverly scream. Wait. That was me.

Blinking away the tears, I felt someone grab my arms from behind me. I hissed as they yanked roughly, and something hard and stiff—yes, I know how that sounded—hit me across the stomach.

I grunted and fell to my knees, feeling as though my intestines and stomach had been rearranged.

Okay, at that moment, I knew two things. One, if I didn't do something quick, I was going to get beaten to death by that guy and his baseball bat. And two, if I didn't do something fast, I would lose my aunts and friends.

"You're done here," Benjamin said, his tone firm.

"Not even close," I said, though that might have come out as a snarl. Savage fury made its way into my gut and stayed there.

Ben twirled a finger over his head. "Pack it up, boys."

The men started to wheel my aunts and my friends over the beach. The sound of motors reached me, and I could just make out a group of smaller boats making their way to the shore.

Once my family and friends were on that big freighter, I'd never see them again. My loved ones were trapped, and I had no idea where they were being taken or what fate awaited them.

"Wait!" I screamed, thinking up a plan. "I'll trade you."

Benjamin stopped and looked at me. "Trade what?"

"Me." At his cocked brow, I continued, "I'm a ten. Right? I mean, not a *ten*, ten, but you know what I mean. Going with your lingo here."

"I understand." He had a smug look on his face like he was enjoying the sight of me being lost and vulnerable.

"So, then take me instead." I looked at Ruth's tear-stricken face, Dolores's angered frown, and Beverly's shock. I looked at Iris's desperate plea in her big eyes and Ronin's rage that he could not free his beloved. As I saw all of that, I knew what I had to do. What I was *going* to do.

"Take me and let them go," I said again, finding strength in my voice. I hooked a thumb at myself. "I'm a Shadow witch. I'm rare. If you let them go, you can have me." I cringed at how that sounded. I would never let that slimy man touch me. But right now, I'd do just about anything for my friends and family.

Ben pursed his lips in thought. "I admire your love for your family."

"So, you'll let them go?" I wasn't sure how deep in the crapper I just landed. Pretty freaking deep. What the hell did I just do?

Benjamin looked at his crew, and then he started to laugh. The others all joined in like I was the butt of some inside joke. Maybe I was.

"This is funny to you?" I really hated these bastards.

"It is." Benjamin's gaze turned icy. "Why would I trade them for something I already have?"

I narrowed my eyes. "You don't have me—"

A weight pushed me down. It was green and sent off pricks like electricity. A net. I was trapped under one of those anti-magical nets.

My instincts flared, so did fear, and I pushed out with my magic. All of it—elemental and demon. I held on to the net with both hands and pushed and pulled, even kicked.

Nothing happened.

Okay, so we'd established that my magic couldn't break through. But my ley lines could.

I reached out and tapped into a ley line—

And nothing.

Damnit. Somehow, being trapped under this anti-magical net kept me from jumping a line.

Now I was really screwed.

With my head bent with the weight of the net, I looked up through the openings and saw Benjamin walking forward, his shield gone once again, giving me a good look at his stupid, cocky face.

"What have we here?" he mocked. "A witch in a trap."

He had me there. "You've got nothing."

Ben stuck a finger through the net, taunting me. I tried to grab it, but I missed. His smile grew wider.

Buckets of deep fury welled in me. The cocky bastard was enjoying this. His smile widened with sly amusement.

"This isn't over," I seethed. "I'm going to set them free." I just didn't know how yet.

The large man laughed. "What's important is that they're alive, for now. But once they're sold, it's not really up to me. I'm not interested in what happens to them."

"You're sick. You're all sick," I spat, struggling with the net. I felt drained and light-headed all of a sudden, almost like I had a fever, and that's when I realized the magical or anti-magical net was doing that. Almost like it was draining my magic from me, rendering me weak.

I was trapped. My aunts were trapped.

It could not get any worse than this.

Yes. Yes, it could.

"Let her go."

That voice literally had me fall to my knees. I whirled around and peered through a gap in the net.

Marcus stood on the beach. He had on only a pair of joggers and nothing else. And the fury that burned in his eyes could start a fire.

CHAPTER
20

"Now, this is what I call a great turn of events." Benjamin clapped his hands enthusiastically. "The great chief of Hollow Cove. The wereape, Marcus, has graced us with his presence."

"Let. Her. Go." Fury simmered in his eyes, and his hate-filled expression chilled me just a little.

Ooooh. He was mad. I loved it when he was angry, but only at other people.

"Let her go," Marcus repeated, his voice low and dangerous. His eyes were blazing with open wrath as he walked closer to me.

A flutter of wings, and I caught a glimpse of Tinker as she flew past Marcus and came toward me.

"Ah, but why? Why would I do that when she's been caught so willingly?" Ben asked as if he was completely unaware that he was playing with fire.

Marcus stepped forward, each step vibrating with palpable violence. "Because I said so," he said, his voice filled with pure venom.

Tinkerbell hovered before my eyes. "I'll get this off you." She reached out, grabbed a handful of the net, and recoiled.

"Ah! It burned. It burned my hands." She laid out her palms. They were red and blistered. She looked at me, defeated.

I opened my mouth to tell her it was okay, but it really wasn't. "See if you can help my aunts. Maybe the magic's different." I doubted it, but we had to do something. I still believed in my theory that the humans couldn't see Tinky. Maybe they saw a moth or something. At least it would save her from their clutches.

The tiny fairy nodded. "Okay. Be right back." I watched as she flew away, reaching Ruth first.

Marcus raised a finger and pointed it to Ben. "I'm gonna rip your fucking head off."

Benjamin chuckled darkly. "Yes, well. I don't doubt that. They say gorillas have the strength of ten men."

"Twenty," corrected Marcus, vehemence rippling over his body. He looked wild, like he was about to beast out to play Ping-Pong with Ben's head. "You wouldn't last three seconds."

Ben's expression soured. "Well, it's a good thing I've got the upper hand here. I've always been a step ahead of you, monkey man. You welcomed me with open arms when I came to your town. You wanted me to fit in and be one of you, but that was never going to happen."

"I didn't," snarled Marcus, rolling his shoulders.

"I infiltrated your world, and it was easy. I took from you. I took lives. I hunted, and the game was easy. I expected nothing less from a bunch of worthless animals."

"The only animal I see here is you," spat Marcus.

Ben shifted his stance and widened his legs in a more relaxed position. "I've been at this game a long time. I've perfected it. You've lost. I've taken what I wanted from this pathetic little town. And I will take again, and again, from other places just like this one."

An intense wave of dizziness swept through me, and I had to fight not to keel over. The net was weakening me dramatically. Severe pain surged through my skull, like the worst migraine possible, magnified by a hundredfold. It felt like my eyes were about to explode out of their sockets.

Shit. I was going to pass out. I knew I was.

Clamping my jaw tighter, I forced myself to stay standing. But then the world shifted, and I fell to my knees. The net, like a blanket of metal, pressed down on me. I felt frail like all my energy was being sucked into the damn net.

My heart throbbed as I tried to quash the panic from my thoughts. I closed my eyes and focused—on the pain, the fear, and the reason I was doing this.

Marcus made a move to reach me.

"Ah. Ah. Ah." Ben snapped his fingers, and six men pulled out their guns, all aimed at Marcus's chest.

The wereape was fast and powerful, but he could do nothing against bullets. Or maybe he could? No idea.

"You'll be dead before you reach her," said Ben as he crossed his arms over his wide torso. "I guarantee it."

The wereape stood still, his large chest expanding as he panted. Anger and fear cascaded over his body. He knew he couldn't reach me, not if he didn't want to die.

The chief tensed as he attempted to keep his anger in check. His body language showed he was ready to dole out a few blows or beast out into his excellent gorilla form. Marcus had been designed to protect those he loved and ensure they were safe. His inability to do that was unnerving him.

An ache pooled in my core as I saw him like this. It was as though he was in an invisible cage, trapped and unable to defend those he loved.

For Marcus, *that* was his version of hell.

But he didn't do anything. He didn't move. He didn't fight. He just stood there, unrelenting in his determination to protect me. To save me.

Despite the pain, I moved. I crawled over to him on my hands and knees in the sand, stopping just a few feet away. I heard Benjamin laugh. So did some of his men. I didn't care. I just wanted to be with Marcus.

The chief's eyes were locked on mine, and he didn't look away. I saw a sort of wild desperation in those beautiful gray eyes.

The pain was unbearable, but I knew I had to get closer. If I could just close the gap between us… So, I kept going, inch by inch, until I was close enough to touch him.

I poked my fingers through the net just as he reached out and grabbed them with his fingers, squeezing tightly. I felt his warmth radiating from his body, comforting me in a way that nothing else could.

At that moment, I realized something. He wasn't just my protector. He was my everything. He was the reason I was alive, the reason I was fighting.

He was my light in the darkness.

I took comfort in the fact that he was free. He could flee. Run. Get the hell out of here.

But I knew he wouldn't. And I feared what came next.

Benjamin flashed his teeth. They glimmered in the moonlight. "Aw. Isn't that cute? Better make it count. It's the last time you'll see her."

Marcus flinched, pulling his fingers away as though Benjamin had struck him.

Benjamin let out a breath. "I like you, Marcus. I really do. More than any of these beasts here. And if you'd been human, we could have been friends."

"Doubt that." Marcus spat as his neck and shoulder muscles bulged, fighting against each other for dominance.

"But you see… I've got the upper hand. You don't. Yes, you're a mighty, powerful creature, but your strength won't help you here. You've lost."

I peered through the mesh, observing the chief's face as it contorted with rage. His skin was mottled, and his body trembled like he was locked in a battle with himself.

"Let her go. I beg you." Marcus's voice was low, but it carried easily along the beach.

Benjamin's grin widened like he'd been waiting for this all along. Like this whole thing had been part of his plan. "All right."

Marcus's lips parted. "You will? Why? What do you want?"

Yes, I was with him on that. He wouldn't let me go just like that. He wanted something in return, or he was just lying.

"I'll let her go. I will. But on one condition." Ben's smile turned icy, and I didn't like the way he was looking at Marcus like he was the ultimate prize. The real reason why he came to Hollow Cove.

"Name it," said Marcus.

"You for her."

"Done."

"Wait? What!" I stared at Marcus through the gaps of my prison. "Marcus, no! You can't do this. This is crazy. He's lying. He's a lying bastard. Don't do this."

The chief just looked at me. The pain in his gaze was nearly my undoing.

Tears pooled in my eyes. "Marcus... don't... don't do this. Please." I begged, my words coming out between sobs as I tasted the salt from the tears that flooded my face.

Benjamin snapped his fingers, and the next thing I knew, the weight of the net was lifted. I felt like I could breathe freely again. The weakness I felt was still there, and I was still dizzy, but it was lessened. Still on my knees, I watched, horrified, as four men approached Marcus — two with their guns aimed at his head while the other two clamped iron manacles around his wrists and his ankles.

Once Marcus was shackled, Benjamin walked right up to him. The smile on his face, in his eyes, made me sick.

"Now, this is a true prize. The mighty wereape alpha is finally mine." He eyed the chief like he was a rare diamond. "Take him to the ship."

"No!" I lurched forward and landed head-first in the sand. My tears mixed with the sand, scraping my face, teeth, and nose. I didn't care. I pushed myself up on my knees. "Take me! Me. Not him."

"I love you, Tessa," said Marcus, his gaze on me. "Don't ever forget it."

"No. No. No," I cried as I crawled on my hands and knees, trying to get to my wereape. My husband.

"Let's go." Benjamin did a circle thing with his finger over his head, and then he and his group were moving. The ones who had my aunts and my friends were already hauling them in those waiting boats that had reached the shoreline. Two men pushed Marcus forward aggressively.

I'd barely had time to register how quickly my plan had gone down the crapper as I watched the scene, helpless and beaten.

No. I wasn't beaten.

On my knees, I reached into my core, calling up all my magic, everything I had in me, but it didn't answer. It was as though the net had put up a brick wall, not letting me get through to it.

I was useless to do anything as I watched my family, friends, and husband speed away in separate boats, getting closer to that massive freighter ship, the sound of the motorboats ringing in my ears over the hammering of my heart.

I heard a sob and looked up to see Tinky floating in the air, her hands over her face as she cried.

My lips trembled. "This is wrong. This... No. No!"

I scrambled to my feet and ran to the beach's edge, tears streaming down my face as I lost my balance and stumbled onto the coarse sand.

"Marcus!" I screamed, thrusting my arms out in a desperate attempt to grab him. But it was no use. The motorboats were too far away.

He looked back at me one last time, his eyes filled with love and sadness, and then he turned his head away.

My heart hammering in my chest, I collapsed onto the sand, tears blurring my vision. I wanted to chase after them, jump a ley line, but I couldn't. I had no energy left.

My head was spinning, and I could only watch as Marcus was taken away from me.

"No!" I shouted, punching the sand in frustration. I had failed. Failed to protect him, and now he was gone.

Marcus was gone. I'd lost him forever.

CHAPTER
21

I stayed there, on the cold sand, for what felt like hours. Ben's attack had left me drained and powerless. I couldn't even summon the strength to stand back up. All I could do was sob and scream into the empty night.

I sat there on my knees for a moment, gasping for breath and trying to process what had just happened. I couldn't see the small motorboats anymore, couldn't hear them. But I could just make out some light winking at me in the distance, presumably the large freighter ship.

As I lay there on the sand, feeling weak and helpless, I suddenly felt a surge of anger within me. It burned through my veins like a wildfire, fueling me.

"I should have fought harder," I whispered into the dark. "I should…" I took a shaking breath. "Why, Marcus? Why did you do it?"

I knew why. He'd sacrificed himself for me. He didn't even take a moment to think about it. He just surrendered his life without even a thought. He'd just done it.

I would have done the same for him. Hell, I would have traded my life for any of my family and friends. I'd tried. But Benjamin had had other plans.

It's like he'd said. He was always a step ahead of us. And getting Marcus had been his ultimate goal. I didn't think even he realized how his plan had fallen into his lap. Or maybe he knew I'd come for my aunts and knew that Marcus would come for me.

Yeah. I'd been a fool.

"Damnit." I punched the hard, cold sand, feeling my limbs starting to shake. I wasn't sure whether it was the loss of adrenaline or the fact that I was sitting in cold water.

"I'm so sorry, Tessa," sobbed the tiny fairy, her face red and wet with tears as she landed on a large pebble on the beach. "I tried. I… I couldn't save them." She blew her nose with a piece of cloth.

"Not your fault," I said. Seeing her crying was like pressing the on button on my own tears as they started to fall again.

Tinky sniffed. "What do we do now? How can we fight them? Our magic is no use. It doesn't work."

"No, it doesn't." I felt like a failure, as though my magic wasn't good enough. But maybe we were going at it the wrong way.

But then, something inside me snapped. A rage unlike anything I'd ever felt before took over my body. I stood up, wiping away my tears as I glared out at the sea, wishing that Benjamin and I could have a one-on-one. Me with my magic restored, him without his stupid bubble shield.

"I'm not about to leave them to be sold or to die." I wiped more tears away with the back of my hand, my anger intensifying. I knew what I had to do. I couldn't just sit here and wallow in my own misery. I had to take action.

"So, what do we do?" asked the tiny fairy.

"We fight them with everything we've got," I said, my voice shaking with emotion. "We gather our forces and strike back. We'll make them pay for what they've done."

Tinky looked up at me with wide eyes, her tears forgotten for a moment. "But how?" she asked, her face lit with a bit of hope.

"We go back to Davenport House," I said, finding it hard to tear my eyes away from that

itty bit of light I assumed was the big ship.
"Ruth was working on adding some kind of
bullets with the memory charm integrated in
them. We'll use that." I wasn't sure if the
memory charm could penetrate through the humans' magical shield. Guess we'd find out.

"How will you get onto the ship?"

"I'll use my ley lines," I said, realizing that I'd
need some time to recover, to gather up my
magical mojo again. And then Benjamin's ass
was mine.

"Just the two of us?" Tinkerbell looked
slightly deflated at the idea of just me going in
there. "There're so many of them. And I gather
there'll be more on that big ship."

I didn't let her lack of faith in me affect my
ego. "You're right. There'll probably be more of
Benjamin's men on that ship. But I can't do
nothing. I have to do something!" The last part
came out harsher than I'd intended. But I was
losing it. Losing my cool. In one night, I'd managed to lose my family, friends, and my husband.

I couldn't let that stand.

"What about Gilbert, and Martha, and
Tony?" asked the fairy. "They'll come. If we
gather enough people, we'll stand a chance."

I shook my head. "You can forget Gilbert.
And most of the townspeople are frightened.
They're scared out of their minds. Right now,
they want to take care of their own families.

They've never fought someone like Benjamin before. And they're terrified."

"That's true." Tinkerbell's wings drooped. She looked defeated.

I took a deep breath and centered myself. "But we have to hurry. Benjamin's not going to stay here for long. He's got plans. If we lose the ship…" I couldn't bring myself to say the words. I couldn't.

"Can you walk?"

I looked at the fairy. "Yes. I don't think I can run, but I'll do my best."

Together, we rushed back to Davenport House. A wave of energy was building inside me as I kept walking, strengthening my body. I could feel my magic returning. It wasn't quite at full strength yet, but it was like a battery gradually recharging.

I knew what I had to do. I had to get him back. No matter the cost, I would find a way to bring him back to me.

We arrived at my aunt's house about twenty-five minutes later. Panting and sweating, we searched for Hildo, but the black cat familiar wasn't inside.

"He's probably at the Hollow Cove Security Agency," I told the worried fairy.

Next, I hurried into the potions room.

"What does it look like?" The fairy hovered next to me.

"A gun." I searched the tables and found my prize. It looked like a shotgun that had part of its barrel sawed off to make it shorter, more manageable. "Here." I picked it up, getting used to its weight.

"Look. I think those are the three bullets."

I looked over to see what Tinky was pointing at. Three long bullets made of transparent metal stood on a tiny pink plate decorated with kittens. Only Ruth would mix bullets and kittens. Moisture filled my eyes at the thought of my aunt, and I quickly pushed the thoughts away.

I picked up a bullet and examined it. "There's pink smoke in it," I said, seeing it move around the small casing. "Must be the charm." I pocketed the three bullets and hurried back out, hanging on to the gun. It felt strange in my hands. I wasn't fond of guns. But I'd shoot the hell out of it to save my loved ones.

With my pulse hammering, I stepped off the porch and onto the stone path. "Okay, we've got the gun and the bullets."

"Check," said the tiny fairy. "What's next?" She'd tried to sound positive, but I heard the uncertainty in her voice and saw it in the jagged flap of her wings.

"We get to the ship and..." And what? How the hell was I supposed to overcome Benjamin? The more I thought about it, the more idiotic my plan sounded. How could we defeat Benjamin and his crew with just me and a tiny fairy? I couldn't beat him before. Why did I think I could do it now?

I couldn't shake off the feeling of dread that settled in the pit of my stomach and grew like a festering wound. What if I failed? What if I got myself and everyone else killed? We needed help.

"It won't work."

With a scream of rage, I fell to my knees, emotions swelling as I attempted to push away the desperation that tried to take over. This was a fool's plan. And I'd been the idiot who thought it was going to work.

Frustration and fear bubbled up. I pushed myself up, staggered a few steps, and crashed onto the porch. I let my emotions flow, allowing them to tangle with my magic.

Feeling that bit of magic, I went to it, called to it. I called upon all the magic I had in me, shattering the brick wall that had been blocking me from it. The net had underestimated me. It was about to learn its mistake.

I reached out, yanking on my elemental magic, my demon mojo, and the ley lines. All of it. I felt the energy building within me, crackling like lightning. I let it flow through me, letting it fill me with strength and power.

"I need help," I whispered to no one. I was trembling so hard I was physically bouncing on the step.

Wait. That wasn't me…

Suddenly, I was physically thrown off the step as though some invisible person's hand had flung me off.

I landed on the grass, on my ass—yes, it rhymes—and then spun around, pushing to my feet. "What the hell?" I blinked at the sudden bright light that was coming from Davenport House as though a million lights had just turned on from the inside.

"What's going on?" Tinky floated next to me.

"I don't know."

Magic pulsed in the air, making my skin tingle with anticipation. I sensed something powerful had just been unleashed in the house.

"House?" I called out as worry pitched my gut. What if Benjamin had done this? What if he'd put some spell or curse on the house?

The great farmhouse continued to spew light, an internal glow that shifted and expanded until it became frayed at the edges. Still, the light grew and grew. I averted my eyes at the sudden shining blur, which was too bright to look at.

"What's happening!" shouted Tinky.

"Hell if I know!"

Magic cracked all around, thick and heavy. I could feel it pushing against my skin like a gust of wind, as though a living thing had just been awakened, and I reached out to it, extending my senses to see if I could understand what was happening. The magic flowed through me, warm and comforting like a long-lost friend.

The farmhouse shifted, and light exploded from it as it began to fold in on itself.

A sonic boom blasted. The sound rocked the ground beneath my feet and shook the trees around us. I stumbled back, trying to keep my balance as the blast of sound hit me like a physical force. It felt like an explosion, but there was no smoke or debris to indicate what had caused it.

And then, a shockwave knocked me back, flinging me, and Tinky and I tumbled to the ground. When I opened my eyes again, everything was still. The light pouring out of Davenport House had vanished, leaving the place cloaked in darkness. I scrambled to my feet, my heart pounding in my chest.

"What the actual f—" I stopped mid-sentence because I couldn't believe what I was seeing.

Instead of the large, white farmhouse with a wraparound porch and black metal roof that was Davenport House, now stood a man.

Well, shit my pants and call me Franky.

CHAPTER
22

"**A**re you seeing what I'm seeing?" whispered the fairy.

"I am."

"It's a man."

"I can tell."

"Maybe we're having the same weird dream," continued Tinky, her voice low. "I've heard of dream jumping."

"I doubt it." This was no dream. Nope. I was very much awake.

A tall figure slowly emerged from where the farmhouse used to be. There was no evidence of the building, of where it once stood. Not even the rows of Annabelle hydrangeas. Nothing. It was as though it had never been built.

My gaze flicked to Davenport Cottage, standing where it had sprouted through the earth. It was still there. Fear grabbed at my throat as though someone was trying to choke me. I couldn't lose Davenport House, too. It was just too much.

"He's coming this way," said Tinky, her wings fluttering erratically.

"I can see that."

He had a toned physique with wide shoulders and slick dark hair that showed off an angular jaw. His blue eyes seemed to shimmer in the dim light as though they glowed from some internal source. He strode towards us with confidence and grace, wearing a smartly tailored three-piece suit that fit him perfectly.

Tinky flew around me and settled on my shoulder. I felt a tug on my hair as she used it to hide herself. "What do we do now?"

I gritted my jaw. "Well, if he obliterated Davenport House, I'm going to do the same to him."

"He's one of Benjamin's men," said Tinky, her voice trembling. "Possibly the mage responsible for the anti-magic shields."

She was right. I stared at the stranger. "If you're some mage who just destroyed my family home, you're going to regret it, asshole." I yanked on my magic at the thought and felt a sense of comfort as it answered. I was going to fry this sonofabitch if he just killed my aunt's house.

He was a man but not entirely. My witchy instincts told me such. But more than just his appearance was unsettling. An energy about him made my blood run cold.

I couldn't help but feel a sense of awe and fear at the same time. Whoever this man was, this mage, he exuded a powerful energy that made my skin tingle.

"Who are you?" I asked, standing my ground as the stranger came up to me.

The man stopped in front of us and looked down at me with a slight smirk.

"Who *are* you?" I repeated, standing my ground. I would not step back. "You one of Ben's men? Of course, you are. It's not going to end well for you, not after what you did here."

The stranger blinked. "I am not one of Ben's men."

I gave out a mock laugh. "Could've fooled me. I don't believe you." Magic pounded in me, hot and cold, radiating like a fever.

"I'm House," answered the stranger, his voice smooth and articulate.

"Huh?" I stared at him, feeling a thick brain fart moment consuming me.

Tinky shifted on my shoulder. "Did he just say he was *the* house? Like in Davenport House?"

I shook my head and rubbed my eyes with the heels of my hands. "Wait a freaking second… this can't be. This is insane. What's your name?" I tried again.

The stranger tilted his head in a way similar to how a dog does when it is confused by what you're saying. "House. The butler."

Holy. Shit. Lava. Batman.

I blinked. "You're… *the* house. You're *House*?" I'd always considered House as a butler, and now, here he was in the flesh, sort of speaking. He'd transformed himself into a humanoid version.

Holy. Shit. Lava. Batman two.

The thing, the entity, straightened. "I am."

"No, freaking way?" I breathed. "House birthed me a cottage, and now he birthed me you? I mean, you birthed you?" I was going to need a drink after this. Make that a bottle.

I felt a pressure on my shoulder as the fairy leaped off and flew closer to the man, the house, the butler.

"I think he's telling the truth," said the fairy. "I can feel it—him. Yes, he's definitely House." She looked at me and giggled. "This is way better than dream jumping."

I tried to make sense of what was happening. I had always known that Davenport House was a magical place with its own set of supernatural rules, but this was beyond anything I had ever experienced. The House could transform itself into a humanoid shape. It was insane. Crazy.

And it had just happened.

"But *why* are you here? And why do you look like a man?" If my aunts survived this, they were going to kill me. Maybe Beverly would appreciate him being a male, but Dolores and Ruth wouldn't.

"You asked for my assistance. Well, here I am." The butler, or House as he identified himself, gave a small bow. "I'm here to serve you, Tessa Davenport. I am at your service," he said with a twinkle in his eye that made it clear he was fully aware of the surreal situation we found ourselves in.

I took a moment to gather myself, still reeling from the shock of speaking to a living embodiment of a house. "Because I asked for it." I just realized that I had, moments ago, on the porch. I'd asked for help, and House had answered.

This was so weird. Naturally, I was all over it.

"Why haven't you done this before?"

The butler shrugged. "You never asked."

"Hmmm. Why did you...birth yourself into this form?"

Tinky pressed a finger on House's left shoulder and pushed. "Oooh. He feels so real. Touch him!"

"No thanks."

House glanced at Tinky and then back at me. "This shape is much better suited for what you have in mind. In my true form, I'm not able to be of assistance. You mean to kick ass. Correct?"

"Yeah…"

"Then I am at your service in this shape."

I couldn't believe what I was hearing. Davenport House, a magical entity that could transform into a human and was willing to help me kick some ass? It was a dream come true.

Tinky was lifting House's right hand and letting it go like she was testing his mobility. "So, freaking real. Hildo's going to freak out."

My eyes fell on my cottage. "Thanks for the mini version of the farmhouse. It's a nice touch."

"I know. I have exquisite taste." House was staring at the cottage as though making me this structure was no big deal for him.

"How powerful are you?" Hope was coming in fast again. He'd said he was going to help me, and whatever magical entity House was, the air was pulsing with his energy.

House grinned. It was eerie how human he looked. "Very."

Excellent. "How come you speak with the modern lingo?" I remembered that Davenport House was built years ago by my great-grandfather.

He folded his hands before him. "I've had years of practice to familiarize myself with the modern vernacular."

278

"Right."

This was too weird but strangely exciting.

"Do you have all the… *working* parts under your clothes?" asked Tinky, lifting the corner of House's jacket.

"Yes," answered House. "Would you like to see?"

"No," I said just as Tinky said a happy yes.

The last thing I wanted to see was House naked. But then, a horrifying thought occurred to me. "Hey. Wait a freaking second. You've seen me naked. You've seen me pee. You've seen me… *do it* with Marcus!" My face felt like I'd doused it in lava. Kill me now. I'd have to move out.

House didn't look bothered at all by my outburst or my accusation. "Not exactly. Bathrooms are off limits. So are bedrooms. And when your human nature of mating occurs or when you need to mate in other parts of the house or the cottage, I simply look away."

I narrowed my eyes. "Really? You simply *look* away?" I had a hard time believing that. No matter what House was, he was definitely male. He'd appeared as a male butler, not a female housekeeper.

House shrugged like this was no big issue. "I am not a mortal man. I am a magical entity. I care nothing for the naked mortal body or your mating rituals."

It sounded weird, but I believed him. But I couldn't help feeling a little self-conscious, knowing he had seen me at my most vulnerable moments. House was completely unfazed by human nudity and sexuality. It was beyond strange but also intriguing.

I couldn't help but ask, "So you've never been curious about... humans mating? I mean, you must know my Aunt Beverly *very* well. And you know she *mates* quite a lot."

House chuckled. "Yes, she has a very healthy sex life."

"Sure, if you want to call it that." I knew Dolores would call it something else.

"And to answer your question, no," said House. "I have no interest in that."

Tinky, on the other hand, seemed disappointed. "Well, that's a bummer. He's really hot." The fairy seemed fascinated by House's lack of interest in human mating rituals. "So, you've never...done it before?" she asked with a mixture of curiosity and disbelief.

House gave her a small smile. "No, I haven't. I'm not bound by mortal desires."

My face turned red again. "Can we please change the subject? This is getting too weird."

House nodded. "As you wish, Miss."

I stared at House, slowly getting used to his butler appearance. "Call me, Tessa. Okay then. And why did you pick this shape? Why not a woman or an older man? Let me put it this way… why do you look like a hot butler?"

"I can take any shape you prefer." In a blast of white light, instead of the thirty-something handsome butler stood a sixty-year-old man with a large protruding belly in only a pair of tiny briefs and slippers. "Is this better?"

"No," me and Tinky said at the same time.

Another blast of white light and House returned to the previous form. "I guessed this would be more pleasing."

"You guessed right." I propped my hands on my hips. "And how exactly are you going to assist me? You're very good at housecleaning and keeping the house in tip-top shape. The lawns and flowerbeds are always immaculate."

That seemed to be the thing to say as House's face lit up with pride. "Thank you."

"But do you have battle experience? Real combat experience?" I couldn't believe I was talking to House as a makeshift version of a man and wondering if he could fight. But he said he was here to help me kick ass.

"I will learn." He blinked and then said, "How about this?" Twin katana swords materialized in the air. House spun around, the blades twirling as he went, and leaped over to the nearest tree with a spring that was very ninja-esque. We heard the sound of metal whacking wood, saw some sawdust fly up, and then when he stepped back, where once had been a short tree stood a carved wooden bench.

I was impressed with House's sudden transformation into a warrior. His movements were graceful and precise, and he seemed to have an innate knowledge of how to use the swords. I couldn't help but feel a flicker of excitement at the thought of having him fight alongside me. Maybe, just maybe, we had a real shot at getting my family and friends back.

"Impressive," I said, nodding in approval, "but can you handle more than just a tree?"

House sheathed his swords and turned to face me. "Yes," he replied confidently, "I have access to all the knowledge and skills required to be an expert swordsman. I wield the power of a thousand mages."

I raised an eyebrow at that. "A thousand mages? That's quite a claim."

House nodded, his eyes fixed on mine. "It's true. I have access to their knowledge, their skills, and their power. All of it is at my disposal. I can tap into their strength and use it to aid us in battle."

"Unfortunately, we can't rely on magic," I told him. "Benjamin Morgan's got these anti-magical shields." I quickly gave him a recap of the events. "So we need to rely on physical strength." That should be interesting as I had the physical strength and the combat experience equivalent to a bar of soap.

"I will do my best to protect you, no matter what the challenge may be."

I raised a brow at the ninja-butler. "That'll work. You're on, House."

Tinky let out a happy shriek. "We're going to get them back. I can feel it!" she said, spinning around House and sending golden dust looping around him like a rope.

House smiled as the dust settled around him. "We will."

I nodded. "Just FYI, Ben fights dirty. He always seems to be one step ahead all the time. Really annoying. Just stay alert."

House bowed his head in acknowledgment. "I will not let you down."

With House by my side, I felt a renewed sense of hope. Together, we could take on anything that Benjamin Morgan threw our way.

We also had the element of surprise on our side. Benjamin didn't expect me to come for my loved ones. He assumed I was broken, beaten, lying on the ground somewhere, wallowing in the depths of despair.

I might have felt that for a moment. Not anymore.

I wasn't broken. I was hard, strong, fierce, and had grown a pair of lady balls over the year.

And I was coming for Benjamin.

The magical entity that was House beamed. "Are we going to kick some ass now?"

"We are." And now, just maybe, with my new ally, things were about to go my way.

Kicking ass, here we come!

Chapter
23

I parked my aunts' Volvo station wagon in Sandy Beach's marina parking lot and killed the engine. House and Tinky were out before I pulled the key from the ignition.

Part of my magic was restored, and I knew it was enough to jump a ley line at least once. It's not like I couldn't jump a ley line. It would have gotten us here faster. But I needed all the strength I could muster for this fight. And using a ley line, or even my magic, would drain me pretty quickly.

My hands shook as I gripped the wheel, and I took a moment before stepping out of the car.

A lot was at stake here. If we messed up, I wouldn't get another chance like this at rescuing my friends, my aunts, my wereape.

I couldn't fail. Not this time.

I could hear waves crashing against the shore, just beyond the parking lot's limits. House and Tinky followed me as I walked towards the marina, our footsteps echoing in the silent night.

As we walked past the marina, I could feel House's presence behind me, a steady comfort that kept me grounded. Tinky led the way, her tiny frame moving quickly and with purpose. I followed close behind, scanning the darkness for any sign of Benjamin's men. The marina was empty, save for a few boats that bobbed in the water tethered to the docks. The sky was a deep, dark blue, and the air was heavy with the scent of salt and seaweed.

As we walked towards the beach, the air changed, becoming thick and heavy. It was as if the atmosphere itself could sense the impending confrontation. House's hand hovered over one of his katanas, ready to draw it at a moment's notice.

I scanned the area, looking for any sign of Benjamin or his minions. But the only sound was the gentle lapping of waves against the shore. They hadn't come back to the beach.

We made our way down to the sand, and I could see the black silhouette of Benjamin's ship anchored in the distance. It was still there. It hadn't moved.

"He's still here," I said. "The bastard hasn't moved out." No. Because he was still celebrating his victory.

"And he has no idea we're coming for him," said the fairy. "How exactly are we going to reach his boat?"

I stared at the boats that were docked, barely visible in the night. "We could steal one, but it'll take a while to find the keys. Or maybe House can hotwire a boat? But I don't know how silent they'll be."

I'd never ridden in a motorboat myself. I was more of a canoe girl, so I was a loss here. "House?"

I turned around. The butler was kneeling on the beach. "Did you just eat a rock?"

House nodded. "Yes. I have broken it down to its molecular levels." He frowned. "Many dogs have peed on it over the years."

I laughed. "That is nasty."

"Indeed."

House stood up, brushing the sand off his pants. "But to answer your question, Tessa, yes, hot-wiring a boat is not a problem. However, I suggest we take a stealthier approach."

"Why not use your ley line?" asked Tinky. "We can all ride with you together."

I shook my head. "I thought about that. I'm not fully recovered from that net Benjamin's men used on me. I can't use up all my strength. I need it to fight." Preferably to kick Benjamin's ass.

"Right." The fairy's face screwed up in thought. "So, then what? I don't think I can carry you both across. My magic has limits in this world. No offense, House, but you look heavy."

"None, taken," answered the butler. "I am big."

I wasn't sure what to make of that. "Well." I sighed, feeling like my infamous plan had some major holes in it. "If you have any great ideas, let's hear them."

"Can you swim?" offered the fairy.

"I can, but that ship's too far out. I'll probably drown halfway."

"I have an idea," said the butler. "You won't need to swim."

I raised my eyebrows. "Okay. And what's that?"

He grinned. "I'll be your boat."

I blinked.

Tinky fluttered closer to me. "Did he just say he'll be your boat?"

"He did."

"I have many shapes," said the butler. "I can transform into a boat. It's no problem."

My jaw fell open. "No shit."

House made a face. "None whatsoever."

"And you can be a *silent* boat?"

288

"I can," said House. "They won't hear our approach. I promise."

"Okay, then," I said, staring at the man dressed in an elegant three-piece suit. "Let's see it." Yup. That sounded weird.

The butler walked into the water, and when he was knee-deep, he closed his eyes. When he opened them again, they were glowing with an otherworldly light, the same light I'd seen spewing from Davenport House. He raised his arms, and his body started to shimmer and change shape. It morphed and contorted until he was no longer human-shaped. Instead, he resembled a sleek speedboat that could have been straight out of a James Bond movie.

"It's beautiful!" The fairy clapped excitedly as House revved its engine, and I couldn't help but let out a laugh of disbelief.

"I thought you said you'd be a silent boat," I told him.

"Sorry," said House, his voice a low rumble that sounded like the purr of an engine. His voice came from the boat, but I didn't know from which part. It's not like he had a head or a mouth. "I've adjusted it to stealth mode. It will be silent."

I stared at him, boat, whatever, in amazement. "You're just full of surprises, House."

The fairy nodded approvingly. "Isn't he? Can you change into a fairy?" Even though it was dark out, I could see the adoration across Tinky's face. Did she have a crush on House?

"Yes," answered the butler, and I heard Tinky's intake of breath. "Though I don't think that'll help us get to that ship."

"It won't." I stared at the boat. "We should go."

"We should," agreed House. "Now, if you'll just climb aboard, we can be on our way."

I took a deep breath and stepped onto the boat, feeling the smooth, cool metal beneath my feet. The boat, or House, rocked with my weight and then steadied as I found a seat.

I looked over the sides to the dark water churning beneath us. "Are you sure this is safe? You won't spring a leak?" I asked, making Tinky snort.

"Absolutely," said the butler, who was now a boat. "Just hold on tight, and I'll get you there in no time."

The fairy hopped onto my shoulder. "This is so awesome. I can't wait to tell Ruth. She would have loved to ride House."

That didn't sound quite right. "We'll get them back. I promise." It was a *big* promise, but I was going to do everything in my power to get my family back.

"Here we go. Hang on."

We did as we were told, gripping on to the edges of the boat with white-knuckled hands. The water was choppy, but House cut through it effortlessly, leaving a trail of foam in his wake. The night air was cold against my skin, but the adrenaline coursing through my veins kept me warm.

"Please tell me that my butt is not sitting on your face?" I asked suddenly, as mortification settled in.

"It's not," came a voice, and I detected a bit of humor in it.

Somehow, I didn't believe him. "So, so weird."

"This is great!" I heard Tinky say over the splashing of the waves.

As we approached the ship, House slowed down until we were floating just below its side. So far so good. House had kept his word. We'd made it here without being detected. That had been the easy part. The hard part would be getting our butts onto that massive ship.

"Now what?" whispered Tinky.

I stared up at the vessel. The sides of the ship were too smooth and tall for us to grasp on to. The ship creaked a soft moan as if it were in agony. Not a single light across the deck. Well, from what I could see from our vantage point.

"There's a rope ladder in a compartment under the seat," whispered House. "It's got a grappling hook. Grab it and see if you can toss it over the edge. There is a small porthole on the starboard side of the ship. It'll help you climb aboard."

Before I moved, Tinky had opened the compartment and grabbed the rope. She held the hook in her hand. "This makes me think of Captain Hook."

"And?"

"I hated the one-handed bastard." With a flash of golden fairy dust, Tinky flew up the ship's side with the end of the rope ladder. I heard a tiny scratch of metal sound, and then the rope ladder unfurled from above. Its hooked edges clamped into place.

I looked up, and she gave me a thumbs up.

"Quickly," said House.

I grabbed on to the rope ladder and did my best to climb. It was slow going, and more than once, I felt like I was going to plummet to my death into the black waters below, but eventually, I made it to the top. Trust me, rope ladders are nothing like metal ladders. They're soft, and climbing them takes longer than I'd anticipated, like trying to run through quicksand.

My heart pounded with anticipation. Finally, I reached the top, peered around the deck, and seeing no one, I hauled myself over the edge and plopped to the surface.

"Took you long enough," said the fairy with a smile.

"Careful," I panted, regretting all those late wine and cheese nights. "I might have a flyswatter with me."

Tinky giggled. "I'd like to see you try," she challenged as she fluttered her wings and hovered in the air next to me. "Though I wouldn't mind *him* swatting me."

I felt a low thud and turned to see House in his human-butler-ninja form again, crouching next to me.

Yup. The fairy was crushing hard on House. My world was a world of the bizarre.

I couched low, trying to stay out of sight. The ship was eerily quiet, which made me feel even more on edge.

I sent out my witchy senses, looking for wards or any magical traps that would alert our presence, but I felt nothing. That just meant I couldn't sense them, that my magic could only reach out so far. It didn't mean there weren't any magical traps.

The vessel's surface was packed with large containers and crates to transport goods, possibly even paranormals, though the thought made me shiver. The crates were stacked high around the ship's sides, a hundred feet up with no railings. If an unfortunate soul should fall, they'd plunge to their death.

The air stank of fish, sewage, and the decaying of metal. The silence made me uneasy, and I couldn't shake off the feeling that something was off. My instincts told me to tread carefully, and I didn't want to ignore them.

"House, do you sense any magical wards? Traps?" I whispered.

He shook his head. "No wards as such. But magic is here. On the lower decks. I can feel it."

Tinky's face scrunched up in confusion. "I don't feel anything, but I can hear voices."

"Voices?" My heart slammed in my chest.

"Yeah, just people talking. Men. I think they're somewhere on this deck."

"Probably just guards." I craned my neck, but I could barely see beyond the tall crates and metal containers.

"The ship is significant," said the butler. "Do you know where your aunts and friends are being held?"

"No idea. But my guess would be the lower decks where you sensed that magic." I knew in my gut that was where Benjamin was holding them. They were still bound by whatever magic he was using. He wouldn't risk taking it off of them, not until he brought them to whatever or whoever had made the highest bid.

I felt sick just thinking about it.

"You ready to fight?" asked Tinky, a determined look on her pretty face.

I stared down at my body, seeing it soft and curvy. I didn't have the body of a fighter. Hell, I didn't have the body of an athlete. And that's what was required here.

"Without my magic, all I've got is my wit and my clever one-liners. It won't help us here. I need strength. I need to be stronger."

"What do you have in mind?" asked the fairy, though she was staring at House.

And then it hit me. "Wait—if my magic won't do any good. I need physical strength. I need to *be* stronger physically."

"Yes. I agree," said the butler, "if you say this Benjamin has anti-magic weapons."

I blinked, my heart thrashing at what I was about to ask. "Can you transform me into something else? Can your magic do that?" It was a long shot. But I was a betting woman now.

The butler nodded. "Yes. My magical abilities will allow me to change your shape." He looked me over. "What will it be? A soldier? A two-hundred-pound MMA fighter?"

I grinned mischievously. "A gorilla. A big, beautiful, gorilla."

Tinky glanced at House. "No way. Can you do that?"

House was staring at me with a wide grin. "I most certainly can." He reached out and touched my shoulder.

The butler closed his eyes and began to chant in a language I didn't recognize. His voice grew louder, and the air around us started to crackle with magic. I felt a tingle run down my spine, and suddenly, I was engulfed in a bright light.

I felt a sudden warmth spread throughout my body, and I gasped as my bones began to shift and crack. Was this how Marcus felt? It might be similar, but he was born a wereape whereas I was shifting with House's magic.

My bones cracked and reformed, my skin ripping and reshaping as I felt my body grow larger, stronger, and *hairier*. Damn, that was a lot of hair. When the light faded, I looked down at my body in shock. Instead of my soft curves and delicate hands, I now had fur covering my body, massive arms with bulging muscles, hands the size of kitchen plates, and a fierce snarl on my lips.

I was a gorilla, just as I had asked for. It had worked!

When it was over, I stood on my knuckles, towering over the others, my massive chest heaving. I roared, feeling the power coursing through my veins. It was like nothing I had ever experienced, a primal surge of strength and fury.

Tinky whistled, impressed. "Damn, girl. You look badass."

House chuckled. "I must admit, you make a fine gorilla, Tessa. Very wise choice."

I grunted in response, testing my new body. It felt... strange but also exhilarating. I flexed my biceps, watching the muscles bulge under my fur. I knew I could take on anyone or anything now. I could crush Benjamin with one hand, rip him apart if I wanted to. And part of me did want to for what he had done to us, for the way he had treated us like objects.

I looked down at myself, marveling at the sheer size and power of my new form. My muscles bulged with incredible strength, my arms long and sinewy.

If only Marcus could see me now, I wondered what he would think.

For the first time in my life, I felt truly physically powerful. I'd never felt like this before. If this is how Marcus felt while in this shape, I envied him. Hell, I'd be a gorilla all the time if I were him.

"Leeetss gooo," I growled, my voice deep and guttural. Damn, that would take some getting used to.

I didn't need magical weapons. My hands *were* weapons. And I would tear Benjamin apart with these new babies.

Because *I*, Tessa Davenport, was a mother-fracken silverback gorilla.

CHAPTER

24

I charged forward, tripped on my new gorilla feet, and smashed my face into the nearest metal container.

Surprisingly, it didn't hurt. Thanks to my awesome gorilla body. Go me!

"You're like a drunk gorilla." Tinkerbell laughed. "Wish I had a phone so I could get you on video."

"Hhha. Haaa," I growled,

"Don't worry," said House, standing next to me. "You'll soon adjust to your new shape."

I hoped soon was in the next few seconds because I was making a lot of noise. Any minute now, Benjamin's goons would hear me.

I tried again. I rushed forward, my massive arms swinging at my sides. Running on all fours did take some getting used to. The ground shook with each step I took. Not the stealthy, creeping up on Benjamin that I was going for.

But *I* was a gorilla. Suck it.

House motioned for us to stop as we heard footsteps coming from the other side of the door. He peeked through a small hole and signaled that it was clear.

With House in the lead, we followed him as he reached a metal door.

"Guuun?" I told him and motioned to his jacket pocket.

House tapped his jacket. "Yes. Ruth's gun and bullets are safe with me."

I nodded. As a gorilla, it's not like I had pockets.

He yanked it open, and we rushed inside. The dimly lit room was filled with crates and boxes. My eyes quickly adjusted to the lack of light. It was like I had incorporated night vision goggles into my retinas, only way better.

I could hear the rumble of the ship's engine and the soft chatter of conversations. My gorilla senses were in overdrive. It was like I had a sixth sense on top of my heightened senses. It was exhilarating. It was freaking awesome.

We crept through the dark corridors. I was surprised at how agile I was despite my size. I could jump over crates and barrels with ease. It was like I was born to be a gorilla.

I was experiencing the world for the first time. Everything was so vivid and intense. I felt powerful, unchallenged, unbeatable. But then I caught a whiff of something else. Something that made my gorilla fur stand on end. It was the scent of fear, the faint smell of chemicals, blood, and human perspiration. My gorilla instincts kicked in. Something wasn't right here.

"We're not alone," came House's voice ahead of me. Damn, I'd almost forgotten that he wasn't human but a magical entity, or rather, a magical house.

"Ssstaaii klooss," I told the fairy, hoping she could understand my mashed-up words.

"I will." She nodded, flying next to my head.

My gorilla body tensed up, ready for whatever was coming next. I could hear House's low growl as he sensed the danger ahead.

We moved silently through the corridors, my massive form occupying most of the space.

Before I could investigate further, a group of armed men burst into the room. They were Benjamin's henchmen, and they were definitely not happy to see us.

"Hyyyiii," I said, giving them two gorilla thumbs up and grinning like a big ol' fool.

They didn't grin back.

"You're crazy," whispered Tinky.

She wasn't wrong. I felt crazy. I *was* crazy. Crazy mad that these asshats had taken my loved ones and were going to sell them like items on a Shopify site.

"How the fuck did they get here?" said one of the armed men. "One of them has swords."

"Ben's gonna want the monkey," said another taller man.

"Oorriiillla," I corrected, though it probably didn't sound right.

"Kill the guy with the sword," said a third man. "Get the monkey."

Idiots. I glanced over to House. He was grinning from ear to ear like he was about to receive a gift. This was so messed up on so many levels. I liked it.

We were a strange, ragtag bunch of misfits about to make Benjamin regret ever coming to Hollow Cove.

I was so, so ready for this.

I flashed the men a mouth full of teeth and flipped them the finger, flexing my gorilla muscles.

The men might not have understood my gorilla speech, but they understood my gesture.

The men responded by opening fire. I dodged the bullets easily, my wereape reflexes allowing me to move faster than they could track. Tinkerbell darted around me, her magic creating bursts of light that blinded our attackers.

I stole a peek at House. He had a strange smile as he moved in with his swords, cutting through their weapons and disarming them one by one. It was like watching a ballet of death, only with a butler in a suit and a bunch of military guys.

The man of the house wasn't here, but I'd settle for his goons for now.

So, what does a witch-gorilla do when she's about to fight a group of human thugs?

She shows off her new, powerful, fabulous, hairy body. That's what.

I roared, pounding my chest. I've always wanted to do that since I saw Marcus do it. A bit overkill, I'll admit that. But who cared?

I let out another ferocious howl as I charged towards the group of military men. Tinkerbell zipped around me, her tiny wings flapping furiously as she shot magic bolts toward our enemies.

House, our trusty butler, followed my lead and was a blur as he sliced through the air with his katana swords. He took down one soldier after another, his stoic expression never faltering. House's swords glinted dangerously in the dim light as he sliced through their armor like it was paper. More like their bodies were soft like paper as their limbs plopped to the floor, guns still attached to the severed hands.

Ew. I looked away. I couldn't get distracted by House's killer talents. I had to deal with my own thugs.

The men were armed with guns, but my friends were armed with magic. Tinkerbell's spells were wreaking havoc on their weapons, causing them to malfunction and explode in their hands.

"That's for Ruth!" she roared as she flew circles around their heads, taunting them with her high-pitched voice, though they couldn't see *her*, her. Maybe they saw a giant wasp?

As I reached the first man, I swung my massive fists and landed a solid punch on his jaw. He went down like a sack of bricks. I grinned, feeling the blood pumping through my veins. This was what I was born to do—fight for my friends and protect those I loved.

Movement caught my eye. Another man came at me. I recognized his gun. It was the same gun they used on me to launch that magical net.

I braced myself.

He fired. I blinked as the net hit, covering my entire gorilla body within a second.

At first panic surged—a wild, animalistic fear of being trapped. It ran deep into the core of my being, a type of fear I'd never felt before. It was primal, wild, and it spread through me.

I could have let the fear take over. But I didn't.

This was an anti-magical net—a trap for witches and other magical practitioners.

But I was a gorilla. I was strength.

As I struggled against the net, I felt a strange sensation coursing through my body. It was like a primal energy bursting forth from deep within me. And as I thrashed and writhed, the net began to tear apart, shredded by the sheer force of my rage.

With a final burst of strength, I broke free from the magical trap, my muscles rippling beneath my fur. Wild, animalistic instincts took over, and I let out another earth-shattering roar, my eyes blazing with fury.

"I believe your choice of shape is remarkable," said House as he beheaded one of the soldiers with his sword like he was chopping down wood.

"Annxx," I said.

The remaining men stood back, their faces pale with fear. But I didn't give them a chance to react. With a single bound, I launched myself at the nearest soldier, my massive jaws snapping shut around his neck.

The taste of blood filled my mouth, and I felt a wild thrill of satisfaction as I tossed the lifeless body aside. One by one, I took down the rest of the soldiers, my fists and teeth tearing through armor and flesh alike.

I had a "oh my god, what am I doing?" moment. That was the witch part inside me. But the gorilla part, my beast, took over. My beast didn't care about the way I killed these men. It only cared about saving my pack. My family. My husband.

And I set it free.

I swung my massive arm and crushed the skull of one of the military men. My gorilla form was perfect for combat, and I relished in the feeling of power pulsing through me.

I grabbed another man and hurled him across the room with ease. The others seemed hesitant to approach me, probably because of my massive size and intimidating presence.

The henchmen didn't stand a chance against my massive gorilla strength. I picked them up and threw them across the room like ragdolls. They crashed into crates and boxes, sending debris flying everywhere.

Pain flared. I looked down and saw a bullet hole in my side. It had gone straight through.

"Uuu ruuinnd mi ffuur," I growled.

But I ignored the pain. My beast was in control, and it had to protect my family.

In a blur of motion, I lashed out at the remaining soldiers. Each punch sent them flying back several feet, their lifeless bodies crashing into the wall.

We moved as a unit as House and Tinkerbell fought alongside me, taking down the remaining henchmen with ease. We were a force to be reckoned with.

I heard the sound of bones breaking, and soon enough, all of them were lying on the ground in pain.

With the racket we were making, Benjamin knew we were here. Maybe not us, us, but he knew someone was coming for him.

It didn't matter. I was ready for him.

But I didn't stop, couldn't stop. I was too far gone, my rage taking over. I kept moving, smashing and tearing through the henchmen one by one.

Finally, the last soldier fell, and the room grew silent. I looked around at the carnage, my chest heaving with exertion, and felt a sense of grim satisfaction.

Is this how Marcus felt after a fight? Yes, I bet it was.

"This way," said House, holding his swords up as he crossed the room.

As I stood there, panting and covered in blood, I felt a sense of triumph. These men had come for me, had tried to capture me and take away my freedom. But they had failed. I was still here, still standing, still alive.

But I had no time to celebrate. House was already moving.

Tinky and I followed House down another hallway, took a left and then another left, and then moved down a set of stairs to a platform as large as my cottage.

The butler-ninja stopped at another metal door. He put his hand on it and closed his eyes. When he opened them, he said, "In here. The magical pulses are strongest here."

I knew then that's where my loved ones were. It would also be where Benjamin would be waiting.

I gave House a nod, and he pulled open the door with ease before motioning for us to follow him inside. It was dark, but my gorilla eyes adjusted quickly.

I wasn't sure what I was expecting to see. Just not what my eyes revealed to me.

Rows upon rows of large, standing incubators. And each one held a person, a paranormal.

The biggest TV screen I'd ever seen was propped up on the wall across from us with the same timer listed above the live video feeds of the paranormals for sale.

The glass compartments were clear and covered in a thin layer of condensation. Most were in their human forms, but I saw some werewolves, and werecats, even an eagle shifter. The smell in the room was one of stale musk and fear.

My heart sank as I realized the true nature of this place. It was a paranormal trafficking ring, and my loved ones were somewhere in this room, held captive like the others. These people were being sold like commodities, their lives reduced to nothing more than a price tag.

Anger boiled inside me, my beast wanting to smash it all. I totally got Marcus's temper now. It seemed it came with the territory of being a gorilla.

I scanned the rows of glass compartments, my eyes searching for any sign of Marcus. A pang of fear shot through me as I considered the possibility of never finding him. As I looked closer at the incubators, I could see the exhaustion etched on each person's face. They were all so different, yet they shared the same fate—being held captive for someone else's profit.

But then, there he was. My heart leaped with joy as I locked eyes with him, and I could see the shock and fear in his own. Then the confusion as he took in my gorilla shape. I smiled at him, giving him a finger wave and hoping he recognized me. Okay, so I did a little dance. Then, the tightening of his anger around his eyes said he did. Yeah, he didn't look happy about my rescue. I'd deal with that later.

I scanned the other incubators, moving through the faces I didn't recognize until I saw them: Dolores, Beverly, Ruth, Iris, and Ronin. For the first time in my life, I was ecstatic to see Dolores's signature frown. Beverly and Iris's eyes were closed, so I didn't know if they were sleeping or dead. I shook those thoughts away. They were alive. Ben wouldn't sell dead paranormals. Or would he?

All that mattered to me at that moment was that they were alive. And I was going to get them out.

Suddenly, a figure stepped out from behind the rows of glass compartments.

"Well, well, well. Looks like I've got another wereape for my collection," said Benjamin.

It was game on.

CHAPTER

25

I felt my blood boil as I stared at Benjamin, the man who had imprisoned my loved ones and countless other paranormals. He stood there with a smug grin on his face, like he was untouchable.

"A well-dressed… butler, a gorilla, and a bug?" said Ben, with a laugh in his voice. "Are you the rescue team? If you are, I'll give you points for originality."

"I'm not a bug," hissed Tinky, but by Benjamin's obvious indifference, he couldn't hear her.

A growl reverberated in my throat.

"You think you scare me, wereape? I've dealt with your kind before," said the man. "I had no idea there was another wereape in Hollow Cove. This has been a very good trip. My wallet thanks you." He laughed.

I truly hated this guy. So I decided to use my expert sign language skills.

I gave him the finger.

That seemed to jar his memory. "Wait a second." Benjamin narrowed his eyes as he took me in. He looked across at Marcus and recognized the fear and desperation on his face. I saw the light come on in Benjamin's gaze as he turned back to me. "Tessa? Tessa, the witch? Is that you in there?"

"Inn de swwesshh." I bared my teeth and curtsied—an attempt to curtsey—as a gorilla, it came across as I was going to the bathroom with quite the effort.

A muffled growl escaped from Marcus as he struggled with his restraints inside the tank, the glass window fogging over with each straining breath.

Benjamin raised his eyebrows, seemingly impressed. "I had no idea your powers included shape-shifting." A smile spread across his face. "I can sell you for a lot more. A *hell* of a lot more. And I have just the client." He gestured his hand toward the screen. Only now did I notice tiny faces in blocks staring back at us like we were having a Zoom meeting.

I gave them the finger, too.

Then, there was the *snap* of Benjamin's fingers, and five of his men appeared from behind the glass compartment like they were hiding, waiting for the signal.

"You know," said Benjamin as he began to move around the upright incubators, standing next to Beverly, whose eyes were still closed. "I could say you shouldn't have come here. But then, I wouldn't have another incredible wereape to sell. The chief and his bitch."

I bared my teeth and let out a low growl. I lunged towards him, but House grabbed me by the shoulder, holding me back with surprising strength using only three fingers.

"Wait before you kick his miserable ass," said the butler in my ear.

I crouched low, readying my body. "Wyyee?" This was why we came here. Only Benjamin and his men stood in my way. And after what we did to the other men, I knew we could take on these thugs no problem.

"I sense a magical trap in this room."

Benjamin snorted. "You should listen to your butler. He *is* your butler. Isn't he?"

"House," the butler introduced himself, and I caught Dolores's confused frown. Yeah, that was another conversation I didn't want to have.

Benjamin just laughed, his eyes flickering between me and House. "You can't unlock the incubators without the magic word. If you try, they're rigged to release a toxic gas, and they will die. And I will never give it to you. Never. Face it. Your family is gone. You'll never see them again. We leave for the port of New York in ten minutes."

I felt a burning anger build up inside me, but House's words echoed in my mind—a magical trap. I needed to be careful. I stepped back and looked around the room, trying to figure out what Benjamin had done. My eyes landed on the glass tanks, and I realized each one had a small emblem etched onto its surface. I narrowed my eyes, studying the symbols more closely. Magical sigils.

I didn't know enough about magical sigils, wards, or any kind of written defense magic to attempt breaking open the cages. If he was telling the truth and a gas would kill them in my attempt to break them free, I was out of luck. Trapped, too, it seemed.

Damnit. I should have known he'd pull something like that. These were his prized possessions. He wouldn't make it easy for anyone to steal them or take them.

I needed to think of a way to get him to open the incubators. But how?

"Face it. You've lost, Tessa," said Benjamin, that smug smile returning to his features. "Surrender now, and you might live to see another day. Refuse, and I'll shoot you. Don't think I won't. I like money, but I like a kill even better."

I believed him.

I had no doubt he'd shoot me without a moment's hesitation. Benjamin was ruthless, and I knew better than to underestimate him. But I couldn't just give up. Not now. And I would make him talk. I would get him to give me that magic password.

"One way or another, you're never getting off this ship," continued Benjamin. "You signed your death warrant by stepping onto my ship."

His words rang true, but there was something he didn't account for.

My awesome gorilla self.

"You want us to kill them, or do you want to keep your new toys?" asked one of Benjamin's men. He was tall with a forgettable face.

Benjamin's face pinched as he thought it over. "She'll be too much trouble. Kill them. Kill them all."

Benjamin's goons launched into action. The forgettable-faced man was closest, so House lunged at him with a sharp elbow to the throat. The man stumbled backward, clutching his neck as he gasped for air. But it made no difference as House ran him through with one of his swords.

Could magical Houses, magical entities, enjoy killing? Looked like it.

Pop. Pop. Pop.

"Incoming!" shouted Tinky as she ducked behind one of the glass compartments.

314

Bullets flew over our heads, ricocheting around the walls of the room.

In a flash of black, the next thing I knew, a man rushed me with a long blade.

But I was ready.

I grabbed a nearby metal pipe, tore it from the ship's wall with my fearsome gorilla strength, and swung it at the motherfracker with all my might. The sound of metal colliding with flesh echoed through the room as the man crashed to the floor.

"Amm auussuum." I was awesome. Go me!

Bullets flew past my head as I dodged and weaved through the gunfire, making my way to the man in charge. The remaining men had formed a protective wall around their boss. I could hear Benjamin shouting orders to them, but I didn't let it distract me. I focused all my energy on the task at hand.

Which was getting Benjamin to give me that magic word. Or die trying.

I took a deep breath and made a split-second decision. With all my strength, I lunged into the wall of men, letting my gorilla instincts lead me.

My body slammed into the wall of men like a battering ram, sending them flying in all directions. I heard bones crunch and bodies hit the ground with sickening thuds. But I didn't stop there. I plowed through the chaos, my muscles bulging as I pushed myself harder and harder.

Benjamin was right there, just a few feet away from me. His eyes widened in surprise as I charged at him like a madwoman, mad-*gorilla*-woman. But he was quick, and he dodged out of the way just in time.

"Miinnne," I growled, sounding a lot like Marcus.

I pushed with my back legs and hurled toward Benjamin. But then something in his face gave me pause. He smirked as he saw me coming, his right hand hidden behind his back.

In a blur, he yanked out a long leather whip. I shit you not. It was like an Indiana Jones moment. But this was no ordinary whip. I could feel cold energies rippling from it and see the green magic sparkling along its length.

I skidded to a stop.

Too late.

The whip wrapped around my neck, cutting off my air supply. I let out a strangled cry as the leather burned my skin. Something was wrong. Very wrong. A strange coldness spread through my limbs, my entire body, rendering me weak. Benjamin tugged on the whip, tightening his grip around my neck. I gasped for air, choking on my breath. Panic coursed through me as I realized what was happening. The whip was spelled. It was draining my strength, feeding off my power. Weakening me.

I could see the green light of magic spreading from the whip and flowing into my body. My muscles spasmed, and my limbs shook as I struggled to break free.

But I couldn't. The more I fought, the colder and weaker I became. Benjamin tugged on the whip, pulling me closer to him. He smiled wickedly as he leaned in close to my ear. I gasped for air, my hands clutching at the leather binding me. Benjamin yanked on the whip, and I stumbled forward, my feet kicking up dust as I tripped. I felt my consciousness slipping away as the whip cut off my air supply. Panic set in as I struggled to free myself, but it was useless.

I clawed at the whip, trying to pry it off my neck. But it was too tight, too strong.

I was trapped. And there was nothing I could do. I'd failed.

Benjamin towered over me. I saw his face twisted in a cruel sneer.

"You shouldn't have come here, little monkey," he hissed. "You don't understand the power you're dealing with."

I gasped for breath as Benjamin yanked it tightly, pulling me towards him. His smirk turned into a sneer as he leaned close to my ear.

"Did you really think it would be that easy, my dear?" he whispered, his voice dripping with venom.

I stumbled backward as far as I could, clawing at the whip as it tightened around my throat. It must have been ten feet long.

Benjamin chuckled, his eyes gleaming with amusement. "Did you really think you could take me down so easily?" he taunted, tugging on the whip. "You're just a dumb animal, after all. Just like the others."

I growled, my vision hazy as I struggled to breathe.

I struggled against the whip, which only tightened its grip around my neck. I could feel my consciousness slipping away as the lack of oxygen began to take its toll.

"You'll never get the words," he spat, brandishing his blade. "You're going to die here, just like the rest of them."

"Tessa! Get down!"

I dropped to the floor. It was easy since I was just about to pass out.

Through my blurred vision, I saw House standing before Benjamin, a gun in his hand. A shotgun.

A shotgun in his hand? It was Ruth's.

Oh shit.

Before I could stop him, House fired the gun.

The bullet, Ruth's magical bullet infused with the memory charm, hit Benjamin square in the chest. A large cloud of bubblegum-pink gas followed, covering Benjamin. As the gas settled, Benjamin still stood, but he had the strangest look on his face. He glanced around the inside of the room like he'd never seen it before.

"Where am I?" he said, his voice soft and very unlike him. "Who are you?" Benjamin looked confused. "And why am I here?"

House lowered his gun slightly, eyeing Benjamin warily. "You don't remember anything?"

Benjamin shook his head. "No. The last thing I remember is...is..." He trailed off, looking genuinely perplexed. His eyes widened at the sight of me. "That's… that's a gorilla! We need to get out of here." He spun around, presumably looking for the exit.

Oh, hell. Now we were really screwed.

I blinked, and House was next to me, loosening the whip from around my neck. Then he tossed it.

"Are you okay?" For a magical house, he sounded and looked really concerned.

I rubbed my furry neck. Yes, I said furry. "Nooo. Witut de wurrd, kant uppen de tannkks."

"She's right," said Tinky as she settled on the ground next to me. "The dude's clueless. Look at him. How are we to get that magical word now?"

Benjamin looked like he was in hell as he stepped around the dead and unconscious bodies, a terrified look on his face. Such a change, a transformation from only moments before. He reminded me of Gilbert.

"I'll handle it." Before I could object, House moved over to Dolores's glass container and pressed his hand on it. As he did, the glass started to glow, and a soft hum filled the room. With a soft click the glass door from the incubator swung open.

Dolores stumbled out of it, gasping for air. She looked around the room, taking in the scene of chaos and destruction.

Her eyes met mine. "You've got a lot of explaining to do, Tessa. I know that's you under that monkey suit."

Yup. Good ol' Dolores was back.

The next thing I knew, House was standing next to me. He pressed his hand on my shoulder, and I felt a tingling from my head to my toes. A light grew, and my body shifted, shrank, fur disappeared, and then finally, I was me again.

Me, and buck naked.

"Here." House handed me a pair of jeans and a T-shirt.

I took them and quickly got dressed. "Did you just pull those out of your ass?"

House grinned. "Something like that."

Wait—hadn't I been shot? But when my eyes found a small scar on my side, I realized my gunshot wound had healed. Go wereapes!

"That's it?" I looked around. "That's all you had to do to open the containers? A touch?"

The ninja-butler's face pulled into a soft smile. "Yes. Not very complicated. Isn't that what you wanted?"

"It was very... anticlimactic." But I'd take it. I'd take it like a shot.

House's smile widened as he moved over to Marcus's container next. He did the same thing as with Dolores's container, and the next moment, the glass door to Marcus's container popped open. In a matter of seconds, they were all free. And very much alive.

"I feel like shit," said Ronin, running a hand through his hair. "And dirty."

"Can't say I feel much better," groaned Beverly. "It feels like I went under the knife for plastic surgery, but they forgot me on the table."

Iris wobbled forward like a newborn calf still figuring out her legs. "I had the darkest dreams. I felt like I'd never wake up."

My heart tugged at the anguish and despair I saw on my friends' faces. They'd been through something horrid. But it was over now.

"You were a gorilla, Tessa," said Ruth, a smile on her face. "Did you make that shifter potion yourself?"

I shook my head, my eyes on my beautiful wereape as he came close, wrapped an arm around my waist, and kissed my neck oh-so tenderly.

"You looked great as a gorilla," he whispered, sending tiny shrills down my spine.

I swallowed hard to tame that surge of hormones. "He did that," I said, pointing to House, who was now releasing the others from the incubator prisons.

"Who is that?" Dolores pointed at House. "And why does he feel familiar?"

Tinky snorted as she flew over to my shoulder. "This ought to be good."

"Everyone," I said. I cleared my throat. "Meet House."

Dolores frowned. "His name is House? What kind of idiot parents would name their child House?"

Ruth smiled. "I think it's great. I've always wanted to be called Shed."

I shared a look with Tinky. "I mean, yes, he goes by the name House. But he's *House*. The butler. You know. As in Davenport House?"

I waited for this information to sink in. And then…

"No way," said Ronin, eyeing House with some serious intrigue.

"Way."

"You mean to say…" Beverly walked over to House, rolling her eyes over him. "That this is our House. In the body of a sexy, handsome man?"

I laughed. "It is."

"Well." Beverly cocked her hip. "Would you look at him? He's fine."

I wanted to tell her that House wouldn't react to her flirtatious comments. He wouldn't even blink at her naked body. But she'd been through enough. I decided to let her have her fun.

"Interesting," said Dolores, watching House release the last paranormal captive from his glass cage. "I never knew the extent of capabilities of our home. How extraordinary."

"No kidding."

"And he transformed you into a gorilla?" asked Iris, seemingly looking more like her old self, the color returning to her face.

I grinned. "He did." And it was an incredible experience. Too bad I would probably never experience that again. The thought made me sad.

"I wish I could be a gorilla," said Ruth. "Or an orangutan!"

I laughed, feeling the stress of the past day's events ooze out of me at the sight of Ruth's cute face.

I spotted Iris sidling next to House, reaching out and picking lint or something off his jacket. No doubt she wanted to put some of his DNA in Dana for later.

"What are we going to do with all of this?" I asked, seeing Ruth talking to the five other paranormals. "The bodies. Those alive. Benjamin?"

"I'll take care of it." Marcus yanked out his phone and started to tap on the screen. "I'll have a clean-up crew here in a half hour."

"And Benjamin?" He'd left the room, so we'd have to search the ship to find him again.

"We can drop him off with the others at the nearest human hospital," said Dolores. "Let them take care of him."

"Good plan."

For a moment, I thought I'd lost them. Thought I'd failed. But my family was safe. Benjamin was… was not a problem anymore. We could finally move on with our lives.

"It's done." Marcus slipped his phone in his pocket. "We should head back."

"Yes. Let's go home," I said. "I know there are some wounded that need Ruth's help."

"Yeah, I could go for a beer," said Ronin, reaching out and grabbing his girlfriend's hand to tug her along with him.

"Agreed," said Dolores as she and her sisters made for the door. She was in the lead, of course.

My gaze found House. He was leaning on the wall, watching the scene unfold. He caught me staring and gave me a thumbs-up.

I smiled, grabbed Marcus's hand, and pulled him with me. The warmth of his skin had my heart squeeze.

But then it hit me. If House was here as a butler, did that mean my aunts had lost their house?

Whoops.

CHAPTER
26

The sky above me shone a deep blue, dotted with white clouds that glowed in the sun's bright yellow rays. The air was scented with roses and freshly cut grass, and the sweet fragrance of limelight hydrangeas permeated the atmosphere.

It was midday in Hollow Cove, and the town had come alive with the hustle and bustle of shifters, werewolves, hybrids, and witches of all ages running around, going from one event to the next.

Suspended overhead on Shifter Lane, spanning across two lampposts, hung an enormous banner: MISS HOLLOW COVE PAGEANT.

Yup. It was happening.

I crossed the street, hit the town square, and moved toward the large gazebo in the middle, surrounded by a small park with benches and a few fruit trees.

A platform had been erected for the pageant near the gazebo with a table of judges—two men, including Gilbert, and two women. Although this was somewhat disappointing for Beverly, the chairs around both sides of the catwalk were full.

I spotted my Aunt Beverly. She stood at the end of the catwalk, where it branched out into a T, wearing a gold satin bathrobe next to a group of ten other females. Her hair was up in a loose bun, delicate fringes framing her gorgeous face. Her makeup was perfect, not too heavy, and brought attention to her green eyes and full red lips. I suspected the touch of bronzer was one of Martha's instant-tan spells.

Her competitors were all wearing bathrobes in different colors with long hair colored the latest shades. High heels clamped around their perfect pedicures. I glanced at my feet and cringed at the disaster there. I was never good at keeping my toes from looking like I'd trekked through a forest barefoot. Nothing I could do about that now.

The women Beverly was surrounded by looked like runway models with perfect hair, skin, and bodies. Their smiles were wide, and their laughter loud. A quick glance at the women told me they were all younger than her, like at least twenty years younger. But looking at Beverly's face, her confidence, the way she stood with her head held high and her chest out, she didn't think of them as threats. More like obstacles. In her mid-fifties, she still had a rocking body, a face that was barely showing any signs of aging, and she oozed self-confidence. She stared at the other ladies as though she'd like nothing more than to push them off the catwalk.

I snorted. This ought to be fun.

Only a day had passed since our ordeal with Benjamin Morgan. The town was still picking up the pieces, mourning the dead. I visited every funeral for our community's deceased, even if I didn't know them. It was important for me to be present at each one.

I was surprised when Beverly woke me up this morning to make sure I didn't miss the pageant at noon.

"I thought Gilbert would have canceled it," I'd told her, rubbing the sleep from my eyes.

"Of course not, silly," she'd said, checking herself in my dresser mirror, a red bathrobe wrapped around her body. "It's good for the town's morale. Keep things operating as they should. We can't let that Ben and his idiots change that. Change us. We won't live in fear." She smiled at her reflection. "Besides, I'm too beautiful to let this opportunity pass. I'm giving back to the town."

"Giving what?"

"Giving a glimpse of my fabulous body to all those ugly men who never stood a chance." She giggled. "Don't be late," she said and sashayed her way out of my bedroom.

Okay then.

"Tessa! Over here!"

I looked up to find Iris waving me over. She and Ronin were sitting in the back seats. The half-vampire had his arm draped over his girl-friend's shoulders. They were so cute and per-fect for each other. A knot formed in my throat. I'd almost lost them. Strange how you realize how much people mean to you when you're about to lose them.

Moisture swept my vision, and I blinked quickly. I pushed my morbid thoughts away, walked over, and took the empty seat next to Iris. She leaned over and asked, "Where's Mar-cus? I thought he was coming to this."

"He's still talking to the other communities about putting out stronger detections for hu-man organizations and putting tabs on the ones they know. We don't want another Benjamin Morgan event."

"Hell, no," said Ronin, his sour expression marked that he was still upset about being cap-tured and auctioned. I didn't blame him.

"He'll come over when he's done."

"Can you believe Beverly is doing this?" asked Iris.

"Yeah. She loves this kind of attention." My eyes found Dolores and Ruth sitting in the front row. Hildo was curled up on the empty seat next to Ruth with Tinky sitting on its ledge, swinging her tiny legs. I could see a smile on Dolores's face. A smile? She looked like she was enjoying this, which was unusual for her. And when I saw the cards with numbers on them on Ruth's lap, it became clear that they were going to rate everyone who was competing.

"I don't." Iris's brown eyes rounded as she took in the contestants. "You missed the evening gowns. It's the swimwear now. I think I'd die if I had to strut on that catwalk in a bikini."

"You look awesome in a bikini," Ronin chimed in. "Even better without it."

"Stop." Iris hit Ronin on the shoulder, but I could see the spark in her eye, the large smile on her face. Nothing's better to boost your confidence than when your boyfriend says you look hot naked.

I laughed. "I'd probably scare away most of the people here. No one wants to see me in a bikini and in broad daylight. Maybe I should have entered. That way, Beverly would surely win."

We all laughed, Ronin the loudest, and I wasn't sure how I felt about that.

Our laughter was cut short as the announcer, Martha, stepped onto the catwalk.

"It's time for the swimwear competition," she said.

Ruth leaped to her feet, waving two tens in the air. "Go, Beverly!" she exclaimed and did a strange combination of movements that one might expect from a drunk cheerleader.

"Ruth has lost her mind," muttered Ronin.

"Nah." I smiled. "This is Ruth."

Martha glanced down at my aunt. "Uh, thank you, Ruth." She cleared her throat as Ruth settled back into her chair. "Now, let's bring out our first contestant for the swimwear competition, Charline!"

The crowd clapped as a tall blonde woman dropped her bathrobe and strutted down the catwalk in a blue bikini. Her long legs were seemingly endless as she effortlessly glided towards the judges. Her blonde hair cascaded down her back in golden waves.

"I didn't know legs could be that long," said Iris, staring at the woman who looked like she'd just stepped off the cover of a fashion magazine.

I made a face. "Me either. Makes her closer to the goddess."

Iris turned to the half-vampire. "What do you think, Ronin?"

"Too skinny. I like my females with some meat. I need to grab on to something when I'm mating."

I burst out laughing, and the contestant, Charline glared at me.

Oops.

Charline turned her attention from me and stared at the crowd. The woman flashed her final smile before stepping off the catwalk. The judges seemed impressed as they scribbled notes on their clipboards.

"Silvia, you're next," called Martha as she motioned to a shorter, though equally beautiful, dark-skinned woman.

The competition continued, and while each contestant was breathtaking in their own way, one stood out to me. Her name was Isabella, a curvy brunette with an infectious smile. She'd be my next choice after Beverly.

"Here." Ronin took Iris's hand, opened her palm, and dropped a set of keys.

Iris straightened in her chair. "What's this?"

The half-vampire smiled. "Keys to your palace, my queen."

"What?"

I stared at him. "Ronin?"

The half-vampire interlaced his fingers behind his head and stretched out his long legs. "You're looking at the proud new owners of the Crane Family manor."

"What?" I let out a laugh. "You bought it?"

"Yup. And we move in today." He looked at Iris. "That's if you want. You do want to live with me. Right?" That smug smile vanished from his face. "Did I get this wrong?"

Iris clasped his face with both hands and kissed him. "You did good, my vampire."

Ronin made a purring cat noise and kissed her back.

I laughed, feeling a soft spot for my friends. I was happy for them.

"Beverly! You're next," came Martha's voice.

Beverly slipped out of her robe to reveal that golden bikini I'd seen her show off back at Davenport House.

Ronin whistled and stood. "You go, girl! Work it, work it, come on now."

Beverly strutted out onto the catwalk, and her toned body was accentuated by the skimpy bikini she wore—skimpy used loosely. The audience let out a collective gasp when they saw her, and I couldn't blame them. She was stunning.

She twirled and blew kisses to the crowd, basking in the attention. I could hear Dolores and Ruth cheering loudly from the front row, their cards with the number ten held high.

God, I loved this town. These people. There was never a dull moment in Hollow Cove. Even if we'd nearly been hunted by a crazy-ass human, I wouldn't change a thing.

Lips brushed the back of my neck, and I jumped. I whirled around, seeing fine gray eyes staring at me.

"It's time," said Marcus, standing up and extending his hand.

I pressed my hand in his and let him pull me up. "See you later, guys."

"What about the pageant?" said Iris. "Don't you want to wait and see who's going to win?"

I shook my head. "Beverly's going to win."

"Yeah, she totally is," agreed Ronin as he sat back down.

I let Marcus drag me with him away from the pageant. The cheers continued as I suspected Beverly took longer on that catwalk than the other contestants.

But as we hit the corner of Stardust Drive, the voices and cheers soon died out, leaving me to hear only the distant rumbles and the chirping of birds.

A massive farmhouse came into view with a black metal roof, white wood siding, and a glorious wraparound porch supported by thick, round columns. It was flanked by rose bushes and Annabelle hydrangeas with red geraniums and purple petunias draping from the flower boxes that hung over the porch's rail.

Yes, after dropping off a clueless Benjamin to the human hospital in Cape Elizabeth, House, my ninja-butler companion and friend had transformed back into his usual shape, much to my regret. Although my aunts were thrilled to have their farmhouse and their family home back, I was left feeling a little sore.

"Will I ever see you again? I mean, this you?" I'd asked House two nights ago, waving my hands around his humanoid body.

He'd smiled at me. "You know what to do."

That's all he'd said, and then the next thing I knew, he'd walked up the stone path and stood where the farmhouse had vanished. Then, with a blinding flash of white light, the butler was gone, and a massive white farmhouse stood in his place.

But we weren't going there now.

Marcus led me to the smaller version of Davenport House. Davenport Cottage.

Once we stepped into the cottage, Marcus let go of my hand. "You ready?"

I grinned like a fool. "Ready."

My heart pounded as we both struggled out of our clothes until we stood in our naked glories.

A slight grin crossed over his lips. "You look great."

I let out a feral growl in response. My heart raced, and warmth spread from my abdomen down to my lower limbs. Damn hormones. To make matters worse, my nipples were rock-hard. Down nipples! Down!

I took a breath and said, "House, if you please."

The thing is, yes, House the ninja-butler was gone. But that didn't mean he was *gone*, gone.

A warmth ran through me, and I gasped as my bones began to twist. My skin stretched into fur, my arms bulged in size, and my hands grew larger than dinner plates. Then, it all stopped. I stared down at what used to be my soft body and delicate hands but was now a gorilla body with muscles that rippled under fur and a fierce snarl on my lips.

My furry awesome self was back.

I glanced at Marcus and saw the massive silverback gorilla staring back at me.

"Rready?" said the wereape, his words much more coherent now.

"Weeny." Me? Not so much.

We were both grinning like gorilla fools as the back door opened on its own—no, House opened it for us—and together, we ran out.

The wind rushed past us as we ran, our feet pounding against the ground. It felt exhilarating to be running wild and free with nothing but the trees and the sky around us.

Ley lines were also thrilling, but this was different. I could feel it in my hands, my feet. It was my own power, not borrowed from the ley lines.

As we ran, I couldn't help but notice the way Marcus moved. He was at once powerful and graceful, his muscles rippling under his silver and black fur. I found myself drawn to him, my body responding to his in ways I never knew were possible.

The air rushed over my fur, and I felt a burst of energy that I'd only felt once before—primal, raw, and free. I ran faster and faster, my massive arms pumping and my heart pounding in my chest.

Marcus kept pace with me, his own silver-back form moving with incredible speed and dexterity. We were wild beasts, untamed and unbridled, and we reveled in the freedom of our forms.

We ran through the woods, past trees and streams, our bodies moving in perfect unison as we leaped over boulders and dodged through the underbrush.

The world looked completely different from the perspective of a gorilla, and every sense was heightened.

What would sex be like in this shape? Don't lie. You were all thinking it too.

As we ran, I couldn't help but feel a rush of excitement and desire. My body was charged with a primal energy, and I knew Marcus felt it, too. We were both animals, driven by instinct and freedom. Nothing else mattered.

A wave of happiness and excitement over-whelmed me. I grinned as the warm wind brushed against my face. I felt fulfilled and content. I was blessed with a great job, family, friends, and the most incredible life partner ever.

Look at me go.

I was going to have me some gorilla-witch babies. Hell, yeah.

Life could not be better.

Accepting my new gig could be my doom...

After fifteen years of marriage, I catch my husband cheating on me. What do I do? I laugh, which probably wasn't the reaction he expected.

And then I laughed some more.

So, when a job comes my way from The Twilight Hotel—a paranormal hotel in midtown Manhattan that serves as a sanctuary and residence—I take it.

Cue in tattooed, sexy as sin, grumpy restaurant owner Valen, who can't do drama or high-maintenance women. The problem? He's cruel and dangerous. And he's hiding something.

Rumors arise of a dark spell that would mean the hotel's closure, and I don't know who I can trust. Do I have what it takes to fight this new evil? We'll see.

Brace yourselves. It's going to be a bumpy ride.

ABOUT THE AUTHOR

Kim Richardson is a USA Today bestselling and award-winning author of urban fantasy, fantasy, and young adult books. She lives in the eastern part of Canada with her husband, two dogs and a very old cat. Kim's books are available in print editions, and translations are available in over 7 languages.

To learn more about the author, please visit:

www.kimrichardsonbooks.com

Printed in Great Britain
by Amazon

28394508R10196